PAGE

OF

SWORDS

TALES FROM THE TAROT

CHRISTINE CAZALY

For Louis

CONTENTS

Page of Swords

Verily, the Page of Swords, a herald of intellect and youth, doth emerge from the realm of air, brandishing a blade of keen perception. Like a novice scholar, he seeks knowledge with a curious heart and an inquisitive mind, unafraid of challenges.

Yet, in his youthful fervour, caution befits him, for the sword can cut both ways. He is a messenger of ideas and swift change. A harbinger of intellectual growth and the quest for truth, but his rashness may lead to unintended consequences.

CHAPTER ONE
Epera, Castle of Air, 1605

High on the slopes of the northern mountains, the Castle of Air sheltered its sleeping inhabitants in a fortress of ancient stone. Early morning mist kissed the hard edges of the towers and turrets, lapping insistently at windows and battlements. Weary gate guards hunched their shoulders against the dew and longed for their rough pallets. Torches hanging on iron brackets sputtered and died as the sun crested the eastern hills to greet the morning.

The harsh, triumphant cry of a lusty cockerel echoed around the castle mews, and startled young Sir Dominic Skinner, Master of Falcons, from his stupor. Clutching his head, he levered himself upright. Nausea nagged his stomach as he plucked straw from his face. He squinted lopsidedly into the grey light, trying to work out where he was. An empty wineskin lay at his side. Stiff with dried mud, his breeches scratched his thighs. A dull ache throbbed on his cheekbone, beating in time with his pounding head. His left eye, sticky with sleep, refused to open. He winced as he probed it, tracing the outline of a decent bruise. The familiar essence of horse and dung and the proximity of the cockerel decided his whereabouts for him. The stables. A longtime place of refuge. Somewhere, an impatient hoof stamped, and the cockerel greeted the morning once more from atop the nearby dung heap. Swallowing heavily against his gorge, mouth stale, Dominic rolled to his knees and creaked upright. His second-best woollen cloak laid tangled at his feet. Barely even recognisable as a hat, his favourite cap languished, crushed and dirty beside it.

Guildford. It was slowly coming back to him. Yestereve, he'd played Primero. Gambled against Guildford of Wessendean, the King's bastard. Guildford was two years his junior, twice as broad, and probably two hand-spans taller. The young noble hadn't enjoyed losing to a former commoner, and his fists were brutal, as were those of his friends. Patting his sore ribs, Dominic grimaced at the flaccid pouch that had held his winnings.

"Bastards," he mouthed under his breath.

Limping to the door, he creaked it open and blinked at the stable yard. Somewhere nearby, the hounds barked, whining for exercise. More horses joined the stamping chorus. A group of grubby stable hands erupted like a colony of dung beetles from their quarters across the courtyard, rubbing sleep from their eyes. The cock crowed again, loud enough to wake the dead. The rising sun made his eyes water.

Dominic shrunk into the shadows with another groan and did his best to straighten his clothing. He was due in the mews. Work did not wait, and there was a hawking expedition to prepare for. Tomorrow, there would be a jousting tournament in celebration of Prince Ranulf's third birthday, followed by a lavish feast. There were people to instruct, hunting birds in need of his care, and lessons to attend later in the day. He almost envied the menial tasks of the stable lads in their dusty britches and soiled shirts. Three years ago, at the tender age of twelve, he'd been one of them. Ragged, starving, tired, and overworked. But at least he'd fitted in. He'd known who he was, and so did everyone else.

A grimace of discomfort shadowed his face as he straightened his back. Things were different these days. He was a member of the nobility, knighted by Queen Petronella herself. Gritting his teeth against the pain in his ribs, he bent to the straw-strewn floor to retrieve his battered cap. He took a moment to smooth the jaunty falcon feather that decorated it before replacing it on his head. Raising his chin with an effort, his gaze clashed with the dark brown stare of a lad he'd never seen before. He wore the uniform of the stable yard and balanced a pitchfork over his sturdy shoulder. Contempt hardened in his eyes as he took in Dominic's battered headgear, and his face twisted into a mocking smile when he noticed the swollen eye.

"Who does he think he is? Jumped up little weakling. Thinks he's better'n us. Deserves every beating he gets."

Dominic's face blazed scarlet as he caught the edge of the boy's thought. His Blessed gift of telepathy had developed slowly over the last three years. Petronella had woken it during her incarceration in the castle dungeon. Once the novelty wore off, he hated it. It was unreliable and uncontrollable. There were days when he could swear the whole of Epera gathered to shout at him and drive him mad. At other times and, usually, when it would have come in handy, the gift remained stubbornly mute, taunting him with its silence. His uncle, Terrence Skinner, said the gift would settle for him on his sixteenth birthday. Dominic cast his one good eye at the rose-pink sky and counted the days. Two to go.

Shoulders slumped, he trudged to the kitchen courtyard well, where he dunked his sore head in a bucket of moss-tainted water. Hunger joined his other maladies, and his heart sank. He would have to brave the cook and beg for some food.

Hoping to avoid attention, he slid into the kitchen via the battered courtyard door. Harassed kitchen servants glanced at him from the edges of their eyes, as ever uncertain what to do with him. Shouting voices and the bustle of early morning energy echoed off the low ceiling and clanged from the edges of huge iron pans. The air was already thick with the smell of small beer and bread. A reek of hanging meat drifted underneath it from the butcher's quarters. Perspiration bloomed on his forehead in the heat from the massive fireplaces, already stoked for the day. He reddened at the wrinkled nose of a nearby scullery maid as she caught the stench of the stable that hung around him.

"I suppose you'll be needing some ale?" Dominic shrunk under the one-eyed gaze of Marjorie Ashburn, the castle cook, as she loomed before him. She wiped rough red hands on a cloth hooked over her belt and poured off a tankard from a nearby barrel. "Here. Rough night, was it?"

He took the drink with a shrug of his narrow shoulders, dreading the inquisition to come. It was the price he paid for her bounty. "I've had worse."

"From what I hear, you bring it on yourself, lad. Can't keep your mouth shut when you've taken too much wine."

Dominic scowled and winced when the action reminded him of his black eye. "Who said that?"

"Never you mind."

"I want to know."

"Well, I'm not tellin' you. If you don't want to be the subject of servants' gossip and easy pickings for young Guildford, lay off the wine and stick to beer." She gave him another hard look. The twisted skin around her empty left eye wrinkled. "Or learn how to fight better."

"Easy for you to say," he mumbled, swiping a hand across his mouth. The ale stung a cut on his lip that he'd not noticed.

Marjorie shrugged, her bosom jiggling. "Easy for you to learn if you just put your mind to it. A bit of training with Sir Dunforde, and you could joust and wrestle and sword-fight with the best of them."

"Huh, the size of me compared to the rest of them? I don't think so."

He finished the drink and handed the empty tankard back to her.

"My thanks, Mistress," he said. Pulling his cap firmly over his ears, wishing it was as concealing as his old tunic hood, he turned to leave. Marjorie clamped an iron hand on his shoulder.

"You'd better eat something. Wait here."

She marched across the kitchen, retrieved a ladle, and used it to knock a dawdling scullery maid into action.

"Get you going, wench, fetch more water."

Rubbing her head, the girl scurried past Dominic to the courtyard, rolling her eyes at him as she passed.

Dominic shrugged. Marjorie ruled the kitchen. If she took to you, she'd feed and bully you. If not, a knock on the head with a ladle was as much as you might expect in the way of affection.

Saliva flooded his mouth as the cook returned with a small loaf of rye bread and a hunk of Argentian cheese.

"Break your fast with this, lad. You need feeding up."

He took the food with a nod of gratitude, his thoughts already running ahead to the many duties waiting for him in the mews.

"You'll think about what I said," the cook warned as he headed for the door. "Strong wine is no good for a lad like thee."

Dominic's eyes narrowed, and he turned around, squaring his shoulders. "When you are a courtier, strong wine is hard to avoid," he said pointedly.

The woman bristled, setting her jaw. "Oho! Quite the gamecock this morning! Gentleman, are you? Master of Falcons, are you? Then what are you doing beaten up, sleeping in the stables, and looking for comfort in my kitchen, young man?"

Squashing the bread in his fist, Dominic turned on his heel for the sanctuary of the mews. Marjorie's voice and the titters of the kitchen scullions dinned in his ears as he retreated, face scarlet, ears burning.

"What are you goin' to make of yourself, Dominic Skinner?" she bellowed after him. "Servant or noble, it's up to you."

CHAPTER TWO

F ace flushed with impotent rage, Dominic strode the length of the stable yard to the tall wood building that housed the castle's hunting birds. The echoing courtyard bustled with mews staff scurrying about their daily duties. A group of workers carrying out repairs to a nearby roof muscled a heavy ladder across the cobbles. Dominic winced at the sight of it. Heart racing with trepidation, he stopped with his hands screwed into fists as a young stonemason bounded up the narrow treads and shinned onto the relative safety of the roof. Swallowing heavily, his attention turned to a knot of falconers gathered in front of the high gable wall. Thurgil, the oldest of them, held his hand to his brow, squinting against the sunlight. Dominic frowned. Something was wrong. Spirit sinking, he followed their collective gaze upwards. Guildford's half-trained tiercel perched on the apex of the roof, jesses dangling from his leg.

"Well, what are you going to do about it?" Thurgil demanded over his shoulder to young Trinian, his apprentice. "You're the one who let it go."

The boy, a skinny ten years of age, trembled in his shoes and sucked blood from a gash on his thumb.

"'Tweren't my fault. It bit me."

"What about your glove? What did I tell you yestereve? The bird don't know you yet, and it's only half-trained. You don't go handling them without yer glove."

"I forgot. We could borrow that ladder?" the boy suggested.

"No ladders!" Dominic's voice coming from behind jerked Thurgil's lined face towards him. Trinian blanched under his habitual grime. "T'weren't my fault, Sir Skinner," he gabbled.

"Don't be daft, lad. The bird'll fly if we come at it like that," Thurgil said, scratching his head. "It's touch and go now. Tetchy it is."

"Was it fed?" Dominic squinted up at the falcon. His brain felt like a stone in his skull as he tipped his head back. "Some of them are already in moult."

Thurgil shook his head. "Not yet. Master Guildford wants to train with it. We've not fed it today."

"Fetch a lure and his hood, then."

Thurgil clapped his apprentice on the shoulder, a hefty shove that caused him to stumble to the door. "Make haste, lad. Afore the bird remembers he's wild and we never get him back."

Above their heads, Guildford's falcon observed the activity in the courtyard. His head turned skywards to the swooping castle starlings who circled the battlements, preparing to fly, his wings lifted. Dominic drew a breath and let it out slowly into the sound of a pigeon and its gentle coo. The falcon's head lowered, searching for the source of the sound.

Trinian scurried back, lure in hand. Dominic took the looped cord from him and retreated into the courtyard, where he had more space. He swung the lure in a figure of eight. Guildford's bird followed the passage of the bait, and the busy courtyard stilled to watch the entertainment as he soared from the gable. Dominic turned with the lure. The bird swooped, missed, and circled once more, gaining altitude and speed. Another pass. Dominic turned again, the bird following. Another five passes, and then he let the bird snatch the bait and take it to the ground. A murmur of appreciation rumbled around the watching servants. Armed with the hood, young Trinian lurched forward. Dominic held out a hand to stop him.

"Steady. Let him eat; he's earned it." He took the blind and approached the hungry bird calmly, crouching in front of him as the falcon snatched at the dead chick it had won. Intent on his meal, the falcon didn't flinch as Dominic waited patiently for it to finish. He offered his wrist to the bird, who stepped forward willingly and submitted to the hood.

"That was well done," Thurgil said as Dominic preceded him into the mews and returned the falcon to his perch.

Dominic grinned, wincing through the pain in his ribs swinging the lure had awakened. "You taught me well, Thurgil," he said, "none better."

Thurgil returned the smile, although his eyes creased with concern at the bruises adorning Dominic's face. Jaw set, he returned to his duties, trailed by Trinian, who followed in his footsteps like a faithful hound.

Avian eyes followed Dominic with interest from their tethered perches as he made a circuit of the aviary. Strolling along the row of cages, rubbing his bruises, Dominic found a measure of peace as he noted their condition. Satisfied that most were sound and content, he conferred with Thurgil, who issued a series of instructions to the men and women of the falcon mews. United in their mission to care for the precious birds, his fellow falconers spread to their daily tasks with quiet competence.

In a thoughtful mood, he exchanged his velvet cap for an old tunic and hood. He offered his fist to the Grayling and attached the jess to his falconer's glove. The Queen's bird would not be required on the forest hunt planned later in the day. For that, they'd be hunting with goshawks, which were better suited to ground prey. But the Grayling was about to moult and needed to fly. It was just the excuse he needed to remove himself for a space.

Bidding a good day to Thurgil, he left the confines of the castle. A little-used path to the high moorland that skirted the foothills beckoned. The chill of the morning dew soaked his feet. Calf muscles burning with effort, his breath rasped in his lungs as he panted his way further up the gorse-wrapped slope. Attached to his wrist, the falcon swayed with the rhythm of his stride, its wings raised for balance whenever Dominic slid on the damp grass. They stopped at the top of the steep hill, and Dominic turned to survey the view, catching his breath.

Stretched in stony magnificence below him, the Castle of Air could almost be a toy fort set up for his pleasure. Queen Petronella's blue and grey standard billowed from its mottled turrets in the breeze that swept the mountain pass. More pennants and banners surrounded a narrow area freshly set up on the flat ground just in front of the draw-bridge. Servants began a steady procession from the castle, manhandling benches between them. Easily identified by their more colourful clothing, a group of squires followed the servants. They were setting up for the celebratory joust in honour of young Prince Ranulf's third birthday on the morrow. Watching the activity, Dominic sank on his haunches and pulled his hood up. An old habit from the days when he'd scurried about his duties at the behest of Old Harold, the stable master. The thick cloth muffled clouts across the back of his head and could be mistaken for a sack in dull light. Chewing his sore lip, he shrugged his bag from his shoulder. Marjorie's offering and a flagon of small beer lay inside. He unpacked his breakfast one-handed. The Grayling put his head on one side, watching his progress with interest.

"Your turn, my friend?" Dominic said.

Free from constraint, the falcon soared from his fist. Catching a rising swell, he ascended into the fresh blue air. Dominic broke bread, ate cheese and drank as the bird hunted and the castle prepared. Above him, the Grayling circled, watching for movement. Dominic scrambled to his feet, shading his eyes from the sun to follow his swooping progress over the wild hillside as he sighted his quarry. When the falcon brought down a fat partridge, Dominic raised his flagon in salute and took another swig of ale.

Guilt stabbed at him. By rights, he should still be down at the castle in the mews, supervising matters in the falconry, ensuring every available bird was ready for the hunting party later in the afternoon. He was a courtier now, with a well-paid position. Old Harold, still the stable master, had no authority over him anymore. Dominic Skinner, stable boy, was now Sir Dominic Skinner, Master of Falcons. He sighed and took another swallow. It was a good thing, of course. His mother had chirped her pleasure a hundred times the evening he received the honour. His father had regarded him with his wise, steady gaze and wished him good fortune. A pang of pure loss pierced his chest at the memory, and he scrubbed at the tears that threatened, forcing them down with the heels of his hands. Ellen and Tobias Skinner lay in the crypt in the castle temple. Swept away in the tide of sickness that overcame the population in the first grim year following Petronella's ascension to the throne. The Starving, they called it. Grain had flowed back to Epera in the weeks that followed the Queen's victory over the Dark Army, but feeding the desperate population took time. Weakened and still hungry, few had the resources to fight the new sickness. Ellen and Tobias had succumbed within days of each other.

The Grayling swept low over his head, and Dominic's good eye turned to the right. In the distance, the city of Blade dominated the valley, smoke already wafting from its many chimneys as the citizens there started another day. The Temple of the Mage once again dominated its skyline as the stone masons sweated to rebuild it to the queen's command. The snaking path of the rushing Cryfell tumbled from the western mountains. It sparkled clear and pure at this altitude. But Dominic was the son of a tanner and of Blade. Those pristine waters would soon foul with the detritus of a city recovering from the dark days of its recent past.

Struggling with a sudden, overwhelming tiredness, he pressed his lips together and forced his attention to the future. The dark days were over. He'd be sixteen soon. A man. He was Master of Falcons and the owner of a thriving tannery inherited from his father. Perhaps everything would become clearer, and his memories of blood and terror would fade. He shook his head free of the dark mood as he packed up his belongings and scoured the sky for the Queen's precious familiar. A shrill whistle brought the Grayling back to him. Dominic stroked his plumage. The Grayling observed him, head cocked. Comforting somehow. A clutch of bloody feathers stuck to his beak, and he waited patiently as Dominic plucked them away.

"Well, lad, it's just you and me now. Are you fed and flown?"

Talons tightened on the thick leather glove Dominic wore, and the bird stretched his magnificent wings to their fullest extent. His freckled breast glowed in the sunlight, and Dominic took a moment to admire him. The Grayling lowered his savage beak and grasped Dominic's finger. He shook his head, a light tug, and released. Dominic allowed himself a wry smile. "Besides me, you are the only person the Grayling does not try to murder," Petronella had said. And then she'd elevated him to the nobility and made him Master of Falcons, and his parents glowed with pride.

The Queen had meant his position as a reward for his service. But three years on, Dominic still struggled to believe he was worthy of her faith in him.

CHAPTER THREE

T he edges of a headache clung to the inside of his skull as he returned to the bustle of the mews with the midday sun high overhead. Grateful for the shade after the brightness of the morning, he ushered the Grayling into his cage and turned for the door, eager for dinner. He clapped Thurgil on the shoulder as he passed. The tall falconer was leaning on a cage, scratching his thick black beard.

"Ready to eat, Thurgil?"

"Noticed anything about Lady Wessendean's merlin?" Thurgil asked in return.

Dominic looked at the bird, perched asleep, with her head under her wing. His face creased in a frown. "I could see she was sleepy this morning. Lady Wessendean has not hunted with her for a couple of days. Has she eaten?"

"Nay. That's the thing."

The two falconers left the mews for the Great Hall. Dominic's stomach rumbled as the familiar smell of roast boar and freshly baked bread rose to greet them. As tradition dictated, they bowed towards the royal dais as they entered. Heavily pregnant with her second child, Queen Petronella sat in state at the top table. Her husband, Joran to her right. Domita Lombard, her First Lady to her left. The rowdy courtiers crowded the narrow tables set at right angles to her, and the chat and gossip dinged his ears. Receiving a nod and a smile from the queen, the two men took their seats at the board. Greeting their fellow diners, they helped themselves from the laden platters lining the centre of the table.

"She'll be coming into moult," Dominic said.

"Aye, but so's the Grayling and some others. They don't want to sleep the day away. Seems strange she's so low." Thurgil picked up a flagon of ale and filled their tankards.

"She's maybe sickening. Should I mention it to Lady Wessendean?" Dominic wiped his face with his sleeve, smearing fat across his cheeks.

"Should do, I suppose." Thurgil scratched his beard, dark eyes thoughtful. "Lady Felicia can't hunt with her today, that's certain."

"I'll tell her this afternoon in the library."

Ever hungry, Dominic filled his stomach with roast boar, his gaze drifting to Felicia of Wessendean. Neatly robed in sky blue, the maid nibbled daintily at the contents of her platter several seats away from her usual place alongside Guildford. She seemed engrossed in her food, her shoulder subtly turned from her twin. Dominic frowned. Normally, the Wessendean twins formed an impregnable duo at mealtimes, surrounded by the sons and daughters of other noble Citizens. Seated in his usual place, Guildford had filled his pewter plate with enough food for three people. His square jaw chomped through it with relentless efficiency. Under cover of his own meal, Dominic noted how many times the lad's eyes turned to his sister. Searching for what? Recognition? Approval? He nudged Thurgil with his elbow.

"Guildford and Felicia have had a row. Look at that."

Thurgil turned his gaze to the pair and grinned, showing a row of crooked teeth. "Aye, seems to be so."

Ignoring the surrounding conversation as much as her brother, Felicia turned the page of a small book, and Dominic cursed.

"God's take it. My books are still in my chamber."

Even as he watched, Felicia pushed away her tankard and left the board, sketching a bare curtsey to the queen as she left the room for lessons. Guildford followed her without even a token acknowledgement of the pregnant monarch. Nodding at his nearest neighbours, Dominic tore another strip of meat from the dripping joint. Swinging his legs over the bench, he received a tired smile from the queen as he bowed. Hurrying as much as he could, given the sorry state of his bruised body, he headed for his remote tower chamber at the end of the western wing.

"What happened to you? You're late. I've told you before about keeping the others waiting." Terrence Skinner, his saturnine, dark-eyed uncle, peered impatiently over his glasses.

"My apologies." Breathless after his run across the massive castle, Dominic slumped into a hard wooden chair and tried to compose his mind to study. The Great Library dwarfed him on every side. Tall oak shelves crammed with books and scrolls loomed above his head. Lamplit, the surrounding air smelled of dust and parchment. Other alcoves contained various groups of scholars, with a selection of tutors in attendance. Terrence's desk commanded a space near the vast central fireplace. As Chief Librarian, he ensured the smooth running of the largest collection of knowledge in Altius Mysterium. Besides his normal teaching, his duties also included the transfer of magical knowledge and ability to the Blessed population. Whether or not they wanted it. Dominic had been studying there for only three years. A mere sliver of time compared to that of his younger classmates, Guildford and Felicia of Wessendean. He'd barely been able to read at first. Had endured hours with the youngest students, shoulders clenched with mortification as he rubbed mistakes from his slate. His skill at forming letters was still rudimentary, his embellishments shaky, his spelling atrocious. But mathematics was alright. He could manage that. Just.

Struggling to ignore Guildford's smug expression, he pulled parchment and quills from his bag. The boy sat directly opposite Dominic and was busy sharpening a quill with a wicked-looking blade. After one quick, gloating glance that took in Dominic's battered visage, he kept his face down, concentrating on the task at hand. Dominic's swollen eye narrowed painfully at the satisfied twitch of Guildford's lips, half hidden under the dip of his stylish hat. Flanking him, his twin, Felicia, massaged her forehead, and shot him an impatient glare. Her pale hair dulled beside her brother's gold magnificence, but the siblings shared the same grey eyes and scattering of freckles across their narrow noses. Guildford's face glowed with sunlight, evidence of long hours in the saddle. His meaty forearms threatened to split his sleeves. Felicia's skin shone paler than the moon, her expression habitually remote. A dowdy hen beside her brother's brash cockerel.

The Wessendean twins. Illegitimate son and daughter of the late King Arion. Grinding his jaw, Dominic forced his attention to arranging scrolls, quills, and ink. The old table rocked a little as his uncle took his own seat.

"So," Terrence said, "The Art of Enchantment: A Journey into the World of Mathematics for Young Apprentices".

"Oh, no." Guildford's groan of dismay ended sharply with an elbow in the ribs from his sister. He ignored her and dropped his quill to the knife-pocked desk. "What about those of us who are Citizens, Master Skinner?" he demanded. "What can studying that," he flicked a disdainful finger at the leather-bound tome in front of his tutor, "have to do with us?"

"Plenty, if you would only apply your brain," Terrence said. "Not being able to use magic should not prevent you from a basic understanding of trigonometry."

Guildford rolled his eyes. Terrence ignored him.

"Now, Felicia," he said. "Perhaps you can explain the first theory?"

Obedient as ever, Felicia replied, her soft voice hushed as a falcon's wing, haunting in its melody. Dominic kept his eyes down with an effort. The lads in the mews called Felicia plain. He could never understand it.

At the end of her reply, Felicia sat straight, upright as a pine tree against the hard back of her chair, hands neatly folded. He blushed as her direct stare clashed with his. The tiniest smile curved around her rosebud mouth.

"Dominic?"

Terrence's voice. He started.

"Sorry?"

"If I could have one ounce of your undivided attention, perhaps you could explain the second theory?"

Felicia stifled a giggle under her hand. Guildford sat back in his chair, hands behind his head, legs sprawled wide, and smirked at him.

Dominic stumbled through the previous day's lesson while Guildford stifled an ostentatious yawn. He floundered as the younger boy cracked his knuckles and gazed at the ceiling, tipping his heavy chair on its back legs.

"Forever waiting for the peasant to catch up," Guildford mused, seemingly at the sky. His chair tipped further and then suddenly lurched backwards with a crash that took Guildford's ink and parchment with it. Felicia slid sideways with a cry of dismay, but failed to avoid the pool of ink that flooded the heavy table. Opposite them, Dominic clutched the edge of the desk as though he were drowning. His breath came in sharp pants, hatred clutching his chest like the Grayling's talons. His hands tingled with energy. The pressure in his head clanged like a temple bell.

Terrence observed the chaos with a quizzical expression and tipped back in his own chair, finding the balance point with a skill born of much experience.

"The art and science of balance," he declared. "Clearly a lesson for another day."

A quick gesture of his hands righted the fallen inkstand and collected the scattered parchment.

"I suggest you find a cloth and clear up the mess. Felicia, go with him. The ink will stain your gown," he said.

Face crimson with temper and embarrassment, Guildford extricated himself from the chair. A chorus of jeers erupted from students clustered in the vicinity as he clambered to his feet. Dominic winced as the young noble barged past, elbowing him in the shoulder as he went.

"I know you did that. I'll get you later. Just you wait," he hissed.

"You can try." His headache easing slightly, Dominic stifled his own smirk and stared down at his hands. He flexed his fingers, marvelling at the energy fizzing under his skin.

"Feels good, doesn't it?"

His uncle's voice, as mild and unassuming as if they were discussing the weather, made him jump.

"I didn't...It wasn't..."

Terrence quirked a cynical eyebrow. "Yes, interesting, but perhaps not surprising. Your telepathic gift we know about. Now, we can add telekinesis to the mix. The Mage has surely Blessed you. Just like your grandfather."

"I didn't mean it, not really," Dominic stuttered.

Terrence rolled his eyes, dark against his pale face and snow-white hair.

"Oh, I think you did, young man. Intention is everything. I should know."

He raised a finger and rotated it in Dominic's direction. Dominic yelped as his clutching fingers left the table, and the heavy chair spun like a dancer beneath him. He grabbed the seat and stifled nausea. His uncle's face was a study in nonchalant concentration, seen in spare glimpses on every giddy rotation. The mocking laughter of older students studying at nearby tables drummed in his ears.

"You can stop whenever you like," Dominic gasped, his belly roiling. "I'm going to be sick."

Terrence folded his hands in his lap, and the chair shuddered to a halt, facing the wrong way. Dominic staggered to his feet to haul it back to the desk.

"Are you going to show me how to do that?" he demanded.

"In good time. Come, let us walk." his uncle replied. He removed his spectacles and polished them on the sleeve of his gown as he preceded Dominic away from the central fireplace. Clambering to his feet, Dominic followed his uncle further into the stacks, trying to match his long-legged stride. Away from the cluster of desks, the air grew chill, the shadows watchful.

"It is interesting to find latent telekinetic power within you. Powerful as well, to move the entire chair with our young would-be king sitting in it and no training at all." Terrence continued, once they were out of earshot of the other students.

"Then I'm glad I have it," Dominic said, rubbing his sore face. "I'm sick of him and his friends using me as a punch bag and stealing my money every chance they get."

"Ah, so that black eye is the outcome of your little game of chance last night?"

Dominic stared at the stone floor under his shuffling feet. He shrugged.

"Tell me, did, perchance, your telepathic ability have anything to do with the fact that you won every game? Don't think that went unnoticed."

His toes curled in their worn boots. Another shrug.

"So, you, a member of the Blessed, used your ability to gain an advantage over a Citizen?" Terrence's voice was as quiet and relentless as sea ice.

"Could have done. He deserved it. Always laughing at me and calling me a peasant." Dominic mumbled the words past his bruised jaw.

They stopped in the history section. Carved in the Mage's pattern, a small, unassuming dark oak door in the far wall snared his attention. Dominic glanced around with a frown.

"What? Why are we here?"

Terrence leaned against a shelf and waved a hand at the immediate vicinity. "Do you notice anything about this section?"

Convinced something hidden behind the ancient door was watching him, Dominic barely heard him.

"What's in there, behind that door?" he asked.

"Nothing that need concern you. I asked you a question."

Dominic shrugged. "Too easy. The wood is paler, not so intricately carved. These shelves are not as old as the others."

"Correct. You need to listen to me carefully now, Dominic."

Dominic dragged his attention from the mysterious door and met his uncle's serious gaze.

"I'm listening."

"When I was a lad in this very library, studying architecture, I used my gift to bring down the original shelving in this section on top of a Citizen. He was a member of the King's Guard. I injured him badly. They arrested me for it and sent me to the mines."

Dominic's eyes widened. "I knew they took you. I never knew why."

Terrence nodded, his face as shuttered and remote as a statue. His long fingers trembled as he fingered the neck of his robe. Dominic frowned at the ridged and rippled knot of scar tissue that encircled his uncle's throat. He'd never noticed it before.

"Lord Falconridge had sent the King's Guard after me. I was trying to protect the Restricted section." Terrence paused, his gaze resting momentarily on the door that so captured Dominic's attention. "That room contained Epera's magical knowledge. If the soldiers had found it, the Gods know where we would be now. As it was, I trusted the law. I knew I had hurt a Citizen, and I went with the soldiers. They hanged my father when he threatened the King to save me. Used him as an example of what would happen to the Blessed if they attempted to use their magical abilities against the new regime. I was the first ever sent to the mines. Lord Falconridge used the Skinner family to prove a point."

Open-mouthed, Dominic stared at the door, marvelling. His head twisted, looking at the heavy shelves laden with literature. Terrence's fingers still fidgeted at his neck, tugging against a chain that now existed only in his memory. Dominic blanched in realisation, and he took an involuntary step back. His uncle saw it. His mouth thinned, and suddenly he seemed old. Stooped with years and bitter with injustice. Unnerved by the chill in the atmosphere and the fact that his tutor's eyes had turned entirely black, Dominic whimpered as Terrence raised a hand. Heels sliding across the flags, Dominic heaved a breath against the sudden constriction in his chest as his Uncle's Blessed ability forced him hard against the nearest shelf.

Locked in the past, Terrence remained on the spot, cheeks ashen, clenching, and unclenching his free fist. Terrified, Dominic's eyes darted away, all his instincts telling him to run. Skewered in place like a butterfly by the power of his uncle's will, his legs refused to obey. He swallowed as Terrence's remote gaze snapped towards him.

"Yes, nephew. I was part of that darkness once. Trying to protect what I believed was right. I paid a bitter and terrible price. In the silence of the mines, the hatred and injustice in my heart made me easy prey for the Shadow Mage. I am the founding member of what became the Dark Army. A subject of Lord Falconridge's early experiments as he sought to harness its power and turn us into weapons for his own purposes. The Shadow Mage still has my soul in his claws. I battle him to stay in the light every day of my life."

Open-mouthed with horror, Dominic swallowed, his skin crawling. "You were part of the Dark Army?" His mind reeled, remembering the devastation at the battle of Sunira and then later, in the castle throne room. The Queen had almost died facing the power of the Dark Army with only the power of her newfound magic to help her. Dominic had tried to come to her aid and received a broken jaw from the fist of Lord Falconridge, her father, for his trouble,

Terrence clenched his fists, his whole body shaking as he fought to remain in control. His eyes regained their usual dark brown, although terrible memories churned within his gaze. The horror inflicted on the peaceful inhabitants of Sunira. The merciless, unescapable command of the Shadow Mage. Dominic gasped as the pressure against his chest lifted, and he stumbled away from the shelf, rubbing life back to his limbs. His uncle cleared his throat and his eyes softened. He held out a hand, half in comfort, half in supplication. Dominic stared at it. The power it wielded at his uncle's mental command. He shuddered, and Terrence lowered his arm stiffly to his side. His voice was sad when he spoke. Burdened by years of self-reproach.

"That's all in the past, lad. And it is my burden to bear, not yours. For now, you need to understand this, above all other things. A member of the Blessed should not use their abilities to injure or kill a Citizen who cannot retaliate in kind. We are powerful. Gifted with skills beyond their understanding. The Mage considers it unjust. It is not a fair fight."

Dominic's face creased into horrified pity. "But you still have your gifts," he pointed out, his throat dry.

Terrence swallowed, massaging his scarred throat. "That was the Queen's choice. She had the right to judge all of us for our crimes. She understood we were under the control of the Shadow Mage. We had no choice. She could have ended us where we stood. Instead, she spared us," his voice dropped, almost as if he was talking to himself.

"Perhaps that was the worst punishment. Letting us live in full knowledge of our deeds."

Dominic nodded. Unbidden, his voice narrowed to a whisper. "What would happen to me if I used my ability against a Citizen? Would the Shadow Mage come for me?"

Terrence chewed his lip and shrugged his broad shoulders. "The Queen banished the Shadow Mage. I doubt he would come for you. His influence remains within those who once wielded his power, however. We were bound to him, you see. But times have changed. I see no reason you should ever have to use your powers in that manner."

"But if I did?"

His uncle raised a chalky eyebrow. "Persistent and so full of questions, are you not? Old King Francis is the best example of that. He lost his powers and became a Citizen when he used them to murder his own wife. It was that terrible act of injustice that paved the way for an entire nation to plunge into darkness. So be warned."

"How do I get even with Guildford, then? What can I do?"

Terrence leaned in, pushing his spectacles further up his nose. His eyes glittered, huge and predatory, behind the glass. "You shouldn't use your magic, lad. Not if you want to keep those gifts. The Mage gives them to those he deems worthy. Those who can wield them with honour and discretion. He can also take them away."

"But Guildford's stronger than me. He beat me up and stole my money."

Terrence smiled, a rare expression on his habitually sad face.

"You got that money by trickery. So, really, all he did was punish you and take it back. There are better ways to vanquish your enemies. Learn the lesson, my boy. Learn it from me."

He whirled abruptly, the edge of his robe swirling on the flagstones.

"Come. Back to your studies."

Brain churning, his respect for his last remaining relative mixed with a healthy dose of pure fear, Dominic obeyed. But his head kept turning, glancing behind at the low door. There was someone behind it. Watching him. He could feel it.

CHAPTER FOUR

B y the time the sun reached its zenith the next day, the clashes of arms at the birthday joust had already sent two knights to the infirmary. The air was thick with dust, the blare of trumpets, and the stamp and thunder of horses' hooves. The heralds announcing the next events strove to raise their voices over the clamouring, sweating throng. Dressed in her favourite midnight blue, Queen Petronella sat with Prince Ranulf on a raised seat beside her. Diamond light flashed from her famous ring as she fanned her face. A page waited at her shoulder with a tray of sweetmeats and a jug of small beer. The ladies of her household surrounded them on the dais, shaded from the blistering sun by silken cloth. Crowded at the lists, the population of the castle rubbed shoulders with merchants and peasants alike. The squires had spent the previous day pitching a series of tents. Each flew banners that distinguished the noble houses that competed for the company's entertainment. Here, the silver adder of the Wessendeans. There, the bear and beaver of the Buttledons. The largest flew the pennant of the Eagles, quartered with the waves of Oceanis. Joran's own device in shades of blue and green.

Dominic braced himself at the side of the lists and lifted his tankard. The best tourney of the day was yet to come. Joran, as the Queen's husband and champion, had never claimed his true title as King of Epera. His destrier, a magnificent grey with the strength of two normal horses, waited, tossing his noble head and stamping his impatience on the hard ground. Joran's opponent, Henry, Earl of Wessendean, held a vast estate to the east of Epera, near the town of Farthing. The family had long associations with Petronella's court. Three years ago, Wessendean's sister, Arabella, former mistress of the late king, had been a member of Queen Petronella's household. She'd tried to take the throne herself until Petronella put a stop to her ambitions and banished her from court in disgrace.

"What's going on? Have I missed it?"

A burly man, the size and shape of a black bear and greasy with drink, elbowed his way next to Dominic and leaned over the flimsy boards. Overwhelmed at the stench of stale alcohol and sweat, Dominic moved to allow him more room.

"There is one joust to go before the prince's tourney," Dominic replied, glancing up at his neighbour.

The enormous man rubbed his fists together and grunted his satisfaction. "A grudge match, to be sure."

"You think so, Sir?" he asked, raising his tankard. He gulped the drink, regarding the man cautiously over the edge of the cup.

His neighbour scoffed at his ignorance. "Everyone knows the Wessendeans are the Queen's mortal enemies. Where have you been, lad? Surely you know that?"

Dominic smiled into his beer. He'd seen a fair bit of the Queen's battle to claim her throne right up to the point when her father, Lord Falconridge, had knocked him out. And there had been plenty of people after the fact who had talked of nothing else. Lady Domita Lombard, his special friend, included.

"I believe the Queen is more than capable of fighting her own battles, sir," he returned mildly. "She does not require her husband to fight them for her, at the joust, or anywhere else."

The man spat over the boards onto the lists, and Dominic's eyes narrowed at the insult. "Faugh," he said. "The Blessed and their Magic. Still think themselves better than us, they do. Like in the old days.

Queen can't change that. She doesn't want to. Why would she? Look at her. Sitting up there on her pedestal, living on our taxes, while everyone else slaves for their bread."

Dominic's free hand crept to his knife. "I'd be careful what you say," he ground out, swallowing his temper with an effort.

"Oh, really?" The man looked down his nose at Dominic, still dressed in his old tunic and hood. "And who are you, supporting them? Aren't you from Blade, then? A Citizen?"

"I'm from Blade," Dominic admitted, his fingers coiling around the worn hilt of his plain old dagger. The one he polished to razor sharpness every night, as his father had taught him.

His heart rate increased, and the din of the crowd receded to a dull blur. The tickle of telekinesis pricked his fingertips, and the pressure behind his eyes increased, demanding release. Slowing his breath, he forced the magic down and withdrew his knife instead. The point gleamed evilly inside his fist as he pressed it against the taller man's stomach. "I'm Dominic Skinner of Blade, son of a tanner and Master of Falcons at the Castle of Air. I am a member of the Blessed. Because of all those things, I can assure you that you are in danger of losing your life if you do not close your mouth. You do not insult our Queen in my presence."

His opponent surveyed him with insulting indifference, ignoring the prick of the knife at his midriff.

"A bantam like you, lad, stinking of the stable, couldn't harm a soul."

He moved as he spoke, and Dominic hissed as the man drove an arm like a lump hammer hard against his narrow wrist, forcing his hand down. His dagger dropped from his numbed fingers, but he had no time to look for it. The stranger twisted a meaty fist in the rough cloth of his tunic and jerked him off his feet, holding him easily off the ground with one hand. Up close, his features were even less appealing. Greasy, pockmarked skin. The telltale strawberry nose of a heavy drinker. Yellow tinged the white of his eyes. His breath was fetid with stale beer and onions.

Dominic's stomach pitched, and he choked against the stricture at his neck. His magical gift blazed to life, and he gritted his teeth, fingers itching to release mayhem. Only the memory of yesterday's library lecture and his uncle's bleak face stopped him from violence. Furious with impotent rage, Dominic barely had time to draw breath before it whooshed out of him. The giant shook him, a mastiff with a mouse, and then dropped him onto the narrow fence that ran the length of the lists. Winded, he flapped uselessly like a rag on a clothesline as the older man thrust his grimy face into his vision.

"Word to the wise, lad. You've neither the weight nor the size to take on a man like me. Next time. Less talk, more action."

Scarlet with embarrassment, Dominic slid boneless to the close-packed dirt on the wrong side of the lists. The chuckle of laughter from the spectators closest to him did nothing to ease his mortification.

Someone held out an arm. "Here, lad, let me help you. The Herald has called the next bout. The horses will trample you to death."

Eyes streaming, Dominic looked up into the face of Joran of the Eagles. Around him, the crowd muttered, and many of them knelt. Joran stood easily amongst them, his armour yet to be fixed to his broad shoulders. His strange aquamarine eyes were alight with amusement and a tinge of empathy. The murmur of interest from the spectators at this royal attention sent a flush from Dominic's chest to his ears. Gritting his teeth, he took the prince's arm and struggled to his feet, scanning the crowd. His assailant strode away through the sea of people.

"Are you well, Dominic?" Joran's voice pitched low, meant for his ears only, and Dominic managed a jerky nod. "He insulted the Queen. I couldn't just let him, could I?"

The prince clapped him on the shoulder, nearly sending him to his knees again. "Then 'twas well done. I will tell her of your support."

Dominic stood on his toes to search the crowd for the drunk, but the man had vanished, perhaps in search of more beer.

"He spoke against the Queen, your highness," he muttered.

Joran smiled easily.

"There are many who still yearn for the days when magic was banished. If we persecute them, all we will do is prove them right in their assumptions."

"So I am to ignore it when they speak ill of her in front of me?" He stood his ground, narrow shoulders thrown back. At the head of the lists, the marshal waited. A mounted knight turned his destrier in another impatient circle. The crowd buzzed. Heads craned in their direction, wondering at the delay.

"'Tis not for you to worry about. Come lad, hop to. We are in the way."

Joran's voice held a note of command, and Dominic's challenge crumpled beneath it. He dodged back under the fencing and bowed his thanks.

Nodding pleasantly to the onlookers, the prince strode back to his tent, and Dominic forced his way through the crowd. The ground trembled under the rumble of the destrier's hooves as they made their first pass. The pounding echoed the pressure in his head of building magic. His assailant was long gone, and Dominic had lost the desire to find him.

At the furthest edge of the throng, he turned, peering over their heads to the distant royal dais, where the Queen sat in state. Petronella shifted in her seat, and just for a moment, he heard her voice, a gentle brush of concern across his tumbled thoughts.

"Be at peace, my friend. All is well."

Biting his lip, he turned away for the quiet and solitude of the mews. He didn't think all was well. Not at all.

CHAPTER FIVE

A lone in the mews, the relative peace calmed his battered ego. The birds rested on their perches. A faint smell of offal and droppings lingered at his nose. He took his time amongst the avian army, checking the occupants slowly for signs of distress or illness. Felicia's merlin had perked up. Alert as she hadn't been the day before, she tore into a meal of dead mice. Dominic's mouth crooked into a wry grin as he watched. Felicia had merely scowled when he relayed the news and continued to scrub at the ink stain marring her gown. So much for her care for her birds. Shrugging at the memory, he continued his inspection. The Grayling was starting his moult. Just as well, the Queen was about to give birth. She'd not be needing him for the hunt for a few months now. Grabbing a broom, he swept the stone flags, soothed by the repetitive action. Around him, the usually busy courtyards lazed in the afternoon sunlight. Everyone was enjoying the birthday celebrations, a day away from toiling. A dull roar from the festival grounds told him Joran's joust was underway. He kept sweeping. No need to wonder at the outcome. Joran was Epera's greatest warrior, his skill at arms famed throughout the continent. His mouth tightened as he relived their conversation.

"Alright for you," he muttered under his breath. "You give an order, and everyone obeys. Me, they pick on or ignore."

He glanced up as the Grayling chirruped and then stopped dead as a stranger's mental voice trickled into his consciousness. His broom stilled, and he tilted his head, listening. Who was that? Whoever it was, they were in turmoil. He had a sense of confusion and urgency, along with the thought itself. Was it female?

"What do I do? I can't let them know."

He heard that. Loud and clear, a sob of pure fear and then nothing. The mysterious voice drifted into silence as if it had never been.

Scrubbing his dusty cheeks, he frowned as he stepped to a barrel and drew a cup of small beer. He sipped it casually, glancing across the aviary. Sunlight filtered through the motes of dust he'd disturbed with his sweeping. The silence of the mews was almost soporific in its heaviness. He did not need to look around to know that the immediate vicinity was clear of people. The building lay peaceful and undisturbed. Whoever owned the voice was further away, in the castle itself, but he'd never heard it before.

Grateful for the distraction, he swigged his drink, dried his mouth on his sleeve, and abandoned the broom.

A search of the outhouses and cellars revealed nothing untoward. He disturbed more rats than people. He tiptoed past couples who had sneaked away from the riotous festivities to indulge in more amorous pastimes in shadowed corners. Dominic continued his search, noiseless on his softly shod feet. The kitchens contained a skeleton staff. Marjorie turned her one eye to him as he poked his head around the door. "You can wait to be fed," she rapped out.

Rolling his eyes, he let the door close with a bang. No point looking in there. As far as he knew, there were no telepaths amongst the kitchen staff, trained or otherwise.

Entering the castle through the cellars, he did a quick circuit of the ground floor. Joran's tourney over, the Master Chamberlain, Lord Colman, had herded the servants back to work. Preparations for the evening's feast were underway.

Dominic strained his senses, but his opportunity to find the owner of the voice was diminishing amid the bustle of day-to-day activity.

He gave up. The person could be anywhere in the myriad rooms and apartments of the upper floors. She could be a guest at the castle or a newly arrived servant girl. But she'd sounded distressed. He'd have to listen for her again.

"By the Gods, Dominic Skinner, are you ever going to dress as a noble?"

He jerked round as Domita Lombard, Petronella's first lady, bounded up beside him. Dust stained her freckled face, in marked contrast to her gleaming bracken-red curls.

"Did you see it? Joran won, of course. Henry of Wessendean is bested, although his destrier this year is much improved. I believe the new bit is making a difference," she continued, not waiting for an answer. Her hot brown eyes turned thoughtful.

"Domita?"

"Hmm?"

"Is there someone new at the castle? Another telepath?"

She glanced at him. "Not that I know of. The Queen would have told me by now, why?"

"I don't know. Thought I heard someone earlier on. They sounded upset, but I couldn't say who it was." He tapped his head, knowing she would understand. "T'was a fresh voice."

"Someone just coming into their powers? A child?" Domita suggested.

"Whoever it was, they don't want it known. They sounded scared."

"And you think they need help?"

Dominic shrugged. "Maybe."

"You realise this trait of yours always leads you into terrible trouble, don't you?" She regarded him with her hands on her hips, curly head on one side.

His mouth stretched into a grin, some of his brooding melancholy evaporating in the cheerful warmth of Domita's presence. He managed another shrug, accompanied by a wince. "Can't help it," he said.

Forever sharp-eyed, Domita threw him a concerned glance. "You're hurting, and you look dreadful," she remarked. "Who hit you? Was it Guildford again?"

"Him and his friends."

"It's your own fault. You shouldn't annoy him."

"I can't help that, either! He wanted to wager. It's not my fault if he loses."

Domita raised her eyebrows. "No one can lose at Primero all the time, Dominic. It's a game of chance."

"Well, he did. He can't bluff. I'm not even sure if he can add up. I did him a favour, really." He avoided her quizzing stare and looked down at the flagstones. The ancient sigil of the Mage, worn smooth with the passage of time, mocked him.

"That's not quite true, is it?"

He bit his lip, conscious of his ready flush, and Domita laughed.

"He's not the only bad bluffer. You're redder than a robin in winter. And you're a clever lad. You don't need to cheat."

He shuffled his feet as she leaned over and placed her hands on his shoulders. Steady warmth from her fire-wielding palms radiated through the thick cloth of his grubby tunic, easing some of the aches in his abused muscles.

She cuffed him gently as she took her hands away. Dominic's head swam, and she chuckled as she steadied him.

"Hie you to your chamber and rest, Sir Skinner. I'll order water and warm it for you. I presume you have a change of clothing for the feast?"

"Aye."

"Do you have a tub and soap?"

"I've a copper. I'll get it down off the wall. I thank thee."

"And do you promise not to annoy Guildford and use your abilities to take his coin?"

He paused, taken by surprise, and favoured her with his best scowl. Domita regarded him with amusement.

"I won't heat the water unless you agree," she prompted.

His shoulders slumped. "I suppose so. You drive a hard bargain."

Domita flashed him a quick grin. "'Tis true. I do. Mind my words. No gambling tonight." She turned on her heel and marched down the corridor in search of a servant to do her bidding. Dominic headed for his chamber, already calculating the coin remaining in his coffer.

The feast lived up to its promise. Banners printed with the infant prince's name festooned the hammer beam rafters. An imported group of musicians from Oceanis performed the latest airs and lays for the assembled company. After supper, servants pushed the heavy oak boards against the walls to make room for the revels. Jugglers, contortionists and fire-breathing athletes from Battonia formed human pyramids. A small dog with a ruff around its throat and a shrill, excited bark turned somersaults on command. The Great Hall resounded with the stamp of feet, the clash of tankards and shouting voices. Sweet wine blended with foreign scents from across the continent. That night, the castle rang with merriment.

One hand on her aching back, the Queen had long since retired, her husband with her, leaving her court to dance and drink themselves insensible. Feet smarting after one reel with Domita, who danced with the enthusiasm of at least ten normal people, Dominic retired from the floor, face flushed from exertion and drink. Across the smoky hall, Guildford sat in his habitual place, cards already in play. Spotting his interest, Jared Buttledon beckoned to him, a sly grin curving the edge of his wide, pock-marked mouth. Fired with revenge, Dominic sauntered across.

"Ready to lose, Skinner?"

Dominic shrugged, careful not to catch Domita's eye as he took a seat and squared his shoulders. "Are you?"

Two hours later, guttering candles sent smoke to the shrouded rafters and shed light on the table where Dominic still sat. Surrounded by empty goblets, he squinted through a haze of good cheer at the cards he held and pushed a couple of nobles towards the centre.

"Raise you two," he said.

Opposite him, Guildford narrowed his eyes and glared at the wall of coins piled in drunken columns in front of Dominic's chest.

"You're cheating. You must be." He took a swig of the tankard in his right hand and slammed it back on the table when he realised it was empty.

"That's a very serious accusation, my lord." Dominic placed his cards facedown on the board and rested his chin on his fists. "You can try to prove it if you like. But I am not cheating. Just winning."

A muscle ticked under Guildford's eye. "I can't work out how you are doing it." His voice was rough, laced with fatigue. Shadows crept into the hollows of his cheekbones. Up close, his grey eyes appeared red-rimmed and sore. The fingers clutching his hand trembled just slightly. Enough for Dominic to know that the boy opposite him held the losing hand.

"You could fold," Dominic pointed out.

Guildford straightened his shoulders at the suggestion and renewed his glower. "I'll raise you and see you," he said from between gritted teeth.

Seated beside him, Felicia flinched as if someone had hit her. "Guildford," she hissed. "Do not do it. That's all your money."

Guildford ignored her. He slid two more beautiful silver nobles across the rough table.

"Go on then, Skinner, show us what you've got."

First out of the game but still watching with owlish interest, Jared Buttledon tittered at the sally. Dominic glanced up at him and then away before he turned his cards over, one at a time. Guildford's ruddy face paled under its outdoor tan.

"You bastard." He slammed his own cards to the board and stood up, almost knocking the table over in his haste to depart. Felicia shot her brother a despairing glance and turned her head to glare at Dominic. He met her feral gaze with one eyebrow raised in a mocking smile, already scooping his winnings into his purse. The weight felt good. Strong wine swirled through his veins, mixing with the pipes and drums of the players and the pine scent of the nearby fireplace. Felicia leaned across the sticky table. Her grey eyes held a sparkle of gold in their icy depths, barely there. Warmth flickering under the icy surface. He sat back against the tapestried wall, suddenly dizzy.

"What are you about, Dominic Skinner? He'll finish you. You know he will." Her breath was warm with Oceanis wine. Her lips were pink, albeit stretched thin with anger. He didn't think. He leaned forward and pressed a gentle kiss on her flushed cheek. Shocked, she reeled away, eyes sparking with tears.

"He's a fool if he doesn't listen to you," Dominic said. He stood up, his knees wobbling beneath him, and executed a shaky bow.

"I'm for bed. Your servant, mistress." He paused, even in his drunken state, noting the girl's distress. "Your brother could have folded at any point this evening," he said more gently. "I did myself, many times. He has to learn when to stand down. Otherwise, his own nature will kill him in the end."

A small, determined soldier, Felicia folded her arms across her stomach. The sadness in her expression found a crack in his own heart, and he blinked, startled by an unfamiliar urge to protect her.

"You'll be the end of each other if you don't stop, Dominic," she whispered. Nodding to him once more, she whirled in a rustle of grey satin, like mist after rain, and was gone.

CHAPTER SIX

T he strident trumpet call of the gods-forsaken cockerel far beneath his window blasted Dominic awake the next morning. Cursing, he rolled upright and waited until his head stopped reeling. A bleary glance around his small chamber revealed a drunken entry the previous night. His door stood ajar. An empty flagon of wine dripped remnants of prime Oceanis like blue tears into the grimy bath water. Outside, a blushing sky stained the distant snow-topped mountains pink. Rubbing his right hip, where a new bruise had developed as he slept, a satisfied smile curved the edges of his lips. He patted his pocket. The satisfying clink of coinage rewarded his exploring fingers and accounted for the bruise.

Light-hearted, the effects of alcohol still brushing his skull with good cheer, he hefted the purse and pawed through its contents. Success! And not a jot of magic used as per his promise. The grin that spread across his face was full-fledged this time. His comment to Domita about Guildford's skill with cards had contained more truth than he'd thought. He was right. Guildford really stank at playing Primero, and his friends were little better.

Reclining on his bed with one arm hooked lazily under his head, he flipped a shilling into the air. Narrowing his eyes, he let a tingle of power into his fingertips and spiralled them underneath it as it fell. The coin danced under his command, rotating languidly in the fresh sunlight. Encouraged, Dominic fumbled another coin from his hoard and sent it skyward. Then another. Within a few moments, the contents of his purse flocked around him. A grin split his mouth. This was easy, really. Why had he never thought so before?

Removing his attention, the coins rained silver and gold, and he scooped them together, sifting through the pile. He had nobles. Crowns. More money than he had ever seen in one place. A momentary frown flickered across his brow as snatches of the previous evening flashed across his mind's eye. A chink of coins and the heartening fool making wine. The venomous gazes from Jared and Guildford across the narrow boards as Dominic raised the stakes and their purses dwindled. The fluid dance of his mind as he calculated cards laid and yet to play. Biting his lip, he ran his fingers through the pile, cursing the power of alcohol to overtake his caution. He must have taken Guildford and his friends for everything they had. Felicia's last warning drifted across his mind. He'd have to be wary, else they'd be after him to get it back.

"No," he said, out loud, to the ever-present invisible jury in his head. "I didn't cheat this time. They lost."

Casting a hasty glance at his partly open door, he pushed his head out into the narrow corridor. His was the only room at the very top of the tower, cold in the winter, blisteringly hot in the brief summer. It contained little save a narrow, cord-strung bed, a mostly empty coffer, and his copper tub, a hopeful gift from his mother. The winding stair corkscrewed into the gloom below him, empty of footfall at this hour in the morning. He locked the door, just in case, and secreted his newfound wealth beneath a loose flag under his narrow bed. Jubilation returned. Perhaps he could use his winnings to purchase a new hat and maybe a sword. He was a nobleman, wasn't he? Shouldn't he look like one?

Tugging on a semi-fresh tunic and hood for work, he was about to leave when his reluctant gaze marked the tub full of grimy water still standing at the foot of his bed. Two huge wooden pails stood beside it.

A weary servant had hauled them up the twisting stairs to his remote roost yestereve, and dumped them, steaming, at his door. By rights, Dominic should empty the tub and take them back, but he'd lost time this morn, playing with his newfound wealth. Aware of the trickle of power still fizzing in his hands, he glanced at the tub and then the window set halfway up the stone wall. Was it possible?

A jerk of his fingers swung the narrow window open, and a fresh breeze skidded around the room. Dominic set his gaze on the soap scum floating atop the grimy water and lifted his hands, palms up. The old tub shifted uneasily in his mental grip. Ignoring a faint, interior warning that what he was doing might not be the best idea, Dominic bit his lips and increased his effort.

Full of water, the bath lay like a lead weight on his mind. Shifting position, pushing his feet into the cold floor for purchase, Dominic tried again. Perspiration dripped from his matted hair into his eyes. The front edge raised, sloshing water over the rim. Moving one of his hands, he struggled to level the load. Lifting it was hard enough, but he had to steer it to the window as well. Grinding his teeth, he took a pace forward, driving the tub like an old cow too stubborn to go to market. The window beckoned. If he could just...get it...higher. Grunting with effort, he ignored the water sluicing towards him, concentrating fiercely on his intention to tip the contents of his bath through the window. His heart raced. An insistent pulse pounded in his temples. A trickle of blood from his nose tasted metallic on the tongue clenched firmly between his teeth. Nearly there! He hissed a breath, straining to balance the load when all he wanted to do was drop it.

"Agh!" The edge of the tub caught on the ancient stone windowsill and twisted in his mental grip. Powerless to control the outcome, he stood, resigned in his clean clothes, and gasped with shock as a wave of cold, dirty water drenched him from head to foot. The empty tub hit the stone floor with a flat clang, like a dented temple bell.

"By the Gods." A cascade of water swept over his feet and pooled at the doorway. Dripping wet, he shoved strands of hair out of his face and surveyed the damage. His few clothes lay unwearable on the floor. Cursing his own laziness at not hanging them up, he kicked tunics, hoses, and hoods into a soggy heap. The fine, embroidered outfit he wore to feasts hung undamaged from its hook on the wall. Going hawking in it was not an option. Guildford's sneer and the disdainful, puzzled looks of the courtiers would be unbearable. No. Wet he was, and wet, he'd have to stay. A trip to the castle laundry would have to take place. Resigned to his fate, Dominic crouched to his stash of coin, and thumbed a few coppers into his pouch. Heaving a sigh, he dumped the sodden cloth into a bucket, collected the key to the falconry from the table, and squelched miserably downstairs.

The mistress of the laundry received the load with ill-humour. Piles of freshly folded linen lined the wooden shelves of her domain. Steam wafted through the archway behind her, the air thick with the smell of lye and the heavy slap and pound of cloth against the washing boards. Wiry of build and wary of expression, she guarded the door from behind a rough wooden counter. Impatience snapped from a pair of deep brown eyes as he dumped the sodden contents of the bucket in front of her.

She put her hands on her skinny hips. "Well?"

A dour smile tugged at her mouth at the coppers Dominic slid into her roughened hand.

"Please, Mistress," he begged. "I have nothing left to wear. Do you have anything?" He plucked at the soaked linen of his tunic. Rolling her eyes to heaven, the woman turned to her shelves.

"Think yourself lucky, lad," she said gruffly, as she handed him a clean shirt. "'Tis rare we have second-hand clothes to spare."

Dominic shrugged out of his damp tunic and added it to the pile of clothes to be washed. He pulled the newly washed offering over his head and tried not to be dismayed at the number of repairs it held.

"And?" the woman prompted, holding out her hand.

"What? I've just paid you," Dominic pointed out, "and this is more or less a rag."

"Not for the extra." The woman sniffed, drawing herself up and looking so much like the cook. Dominic caved.

"Here." He slapped his last copper into her palm and turned to go. "I want it all back by this evening," he said over his shoulder.

"You'll have it when the Gods will," she said, "it's not as if we have nothing else to do."

Dominic thanked her from between gritted teeth and set off for the kitchen, hungry as a horse.

He jigged around Marjorie, avoiding her heavy-handed swipe at his head, and snatched a loaf still hot from the ovens.

"Why are you so wet?" she said, watching him with her hands on her hips as he dodged away, juggling the hot loaf from hand to hand.

Dominic swept her an ironic bow and ignored the question. "My thanks to thee, Mistress," he said in his best imitation of a noble accent.

Marjorie shook her head and chased him to the door to the titters of the serving maids. Seeing the fire in her one good eye as she snatched up her ladle, he bolted.

Dominic hastened to the falcon mews as he munched on his bread, spraying crumbs with each mouthful.

CHAPTER SEVEN

T he tension in the aviary trickled into his subconscious mind even as he turned the key in the lock. Obeying an instinct he didn't know he possessed, he shoved the door open and rushed in. A wash of fear raised gooseflesh across his shoulders, much like the ruffled feathers of the nearest inhabitants. A chorus of alarm calls greeted his shrinking ears and sent shock waves of panic through his blood. Heart pounding, Dominic stared round at the usually peaceful scene. Joran's great Gerfalcon bated at the end of his tether, wings stretched, his harsh, urgent cry dominating all the rest. Lesser hawks and falcons stood high on their perches, blind under their hoods, adding their voices to the din. The floor was a littered mess of feathers and scattered with panicked droppings. In a daze, he moved forward, down the length of the building. At the end of the row, his head falconer, sturdy Thurgil, lay slumped in a pool of blood. His own club lay beside him. And The Grayling's cage, Gods help him, The Grayling's cage was empty.

Dominic swallowed and fell to his knees at the falconer's side. His fingers trembled as he reached for the man's arm and shook it. Thurgil responded with a groan but did not move. Calmed by Dominic's presence, the birds gradually settled on their perches. Every hooded head turned towards him. Dominic tried not to cringe under their blind, accusing stares. He shook his friend's arm again.

"Thurgil, can you hear me? Thurgil, wake up!"

Nothing. Dominic clamped his hand over his mouth to hold back a whimper of panic. A man down, badly injured, and there was no point looking for the Grayling here. Someone had him. The whimper escaped him as the implications shot through his befuddled brain. His bowel churned with dread.

The Grayling was gone. The Queen's pet. Her priceless, irreplaceable, legendary falcon. The bird who had carried the Queen's soul and battled the Dark Army to save the kingdom was gone. And he, Dominic, was to blame.

Thurgil muttered something, his voice indistinct around his thick black beard. By the Gods, how long had his friend been lying there? Dark crimson, his blood congealed on the freshly swept floor, his cheeks ashen white. Heart pounding, bowel churning with dread, Dominic ripped his second-hand shirt off and used strips of it to wind around the older man's head.

"Uncle, help me!" He begged through the ether.

Silence. Dominic cursed under his breath. Of course, his uncle could not hear him. His blessing was telekinesis, not telepathy.

Glancing once more at Thurgil and then at the empty cage, Dominic looked at the door. Beyond it lay freedom. He could leave. Cloak his mental signal and tunnel like a rat into the harsh underworld of Blade. They'd think he stole the bird for money. The Queen would curse his name. She'd send her soldiers after him. Regret her decision to appoint him master of her falconry. But if he ran, he would never have to see the fear and disappointment in her navy eyes when he told her what he'd done. Never have to risk the light of her Blessed power turning its mighty light on him. He swallowed. What did it feel like? The judgement of the Gods?

Heart racing, a leaden weight in his chest, he levered himself to his feet. The birds in the falconry had quieted. Their cages stretched like prison bars on either side of the passageway. Dominic shuddered, feeling the rows of sharp, accusing eyes from under their leather hoods.

The morning sunlight edging around the door beckoned. Snatching his sturdy falconer's tunic from a hook, he shrugged the garment over his head. He took a step towards the door, then another, his fertile, panicked brain hatching scheme after scheme. He could retrieve his money and then leave. Head for the coast. Take a boat far away. Argentia would take in a hard-working lad. They surely had need of stable hands there. Or perhaps further south, to Domita Lombard's sun-scorched land of Battonia, where they bred and sold the fleetest horses. Petronella had been wrong, giving him this responsibility. He'd let her down. Failed her. Just like his brother.

The door loomed in front of him, polished smooth with the touch of many hands. Someone long ago had carved the symbol of the Mage across the oak panel. It taunted Dominic as he pushed it open and took a last step.

"Don't you dare!" Dripping with censure, the light, feminine voice slashed through his traitorous thoughts and echoed like a bell inside his mind. *"You are better than this, Dominic Skinner."*

He stopped and braced his hands on the edge of the door, every nerve end trembling as he searched the courtyard for any sign of the girl who could own the mystery voice. The stable hands glanced at him, questions in their eyes, and Dominic dashed hot tears away from his cheeks, scalded by his own miserable guilt. Heaving a shuddering breath, his gut still trembling in fear, he gestured wildly at the nearest person.

"Get help! Thurgil is hurt!"

Dominic lingered in the courtyard long enough to see Thurgil into the care of the castle physicians. "He needs the best of attention," he said, swallowing against the dryness in his throat as two stable lads grunted the stretcher to their shoulders. "The finest medicines. I will pay."

"We will see to him." The most senior of the castle healers, a gentle Argentian robed in dark green linen, laid a plump brown hand on Dominic's narrow shoulder. "Do you require aid, lad?"

Ducking his head under the doctor's wise, penetrating stare, Dominic twisted away. "No, Master Mortlake, I must go to the Queen. There is something I have to tell her."

Mortlake chuckled. "Not today, Sir," he said. "The Queen is in labour."

Dominic's eyes jerked upwards. "Truly?" he breathed, hardly able to believe his ears.

"Indeed. Her pains started late last night. Mistress De Winter is with her now. Whatever you must tell her will wait, I'm sure."

Bowing slightly, the little man bustled away in the stretcher's wake.

Dominic stared at his retreating figure and then lifted his eyes to the skies. Above him, the castle starlings wheeled around the towers and battlements. No perching peregrine falcon lingered amongst the narrow windows and turrets. No. The Grayling had not freed himself. Blessing all the Gods for the reprieve, fired with a new sense of purpose, he hurried back to the castle.

Word of the Queen's confinement followed him from the depths of the sweaty kitchens to the lofty expanse of the Great Hall. Morning sunlight dappled the wooden floor in the long gallery. The huge tapestries decorating the wall glowed with hunting scenes. Crowded around the unlit fireplace, a group of Guildford's spotty friends were already up. They played a leisurely game of dice while they waited for instructions from their masters. He hunched his shoulders and lengthened his stride as he drew level with them.

"What Ho, Sir Skinner, I want my money back," Jared Buttledon shouted as he passed. "I'll lay you a wager. A crown on the child being a boy. What say you?"

Jaw set, Dominic whirled on his heels. "I say you should spend your time praying for her safe delivery, no matter the sex of her child."

The group of pimpled squires exchanged glances and erupted in derisive laughter.

"Dominic's got it bad for the Queen!" Jared said, nudging his neighbour in the ribs. He thrust his narrow hips forward. "You wouldn't say no, would you, Dom?"

Dominic didn't stop to think. Fists swinging, he advanced. Taken by surprise at the force of the attack, Jared rocked back and stumbled into his friends. Dice scattered amid shouts of outrage. Propelled by rage, heart pumping, Dominic followed up with a powerful kick to the lad's chest with all the force of his work-hardened leg behind it.

Jared crashed to the floor, and his companions gaped at Dominic.

"Yea, so brave when Guildford's not around," Jared sneered, massaging his ribs.

"You don't insult the Queen in front of me," Dominic ground out. His head ached with the strain of keeping his magic in check, and he clenched his fists, forcing it back.

"What is this?"

Terrence Skinner's deep voice cut across them like the blade of an axe. His eyes flashed behind his spectacles as he took in the scene.

"It is forbidden to fight in the castle," he said. "Dominic, you will go to your chamber and cool down."

"Rescued by your uncle, Skinner? That won't be enough to save you. I want my money back. Next time. I'll have your hide and your purse." Aided by his friends, Jared lurched to his feet, white with anger. Dominic surveyed the growing bruise on the lad's jaw with grim satisfaction. At least one of his tormentors knew the force of his rage.

"Think yourself lucky I didn't use magic," he said. His uncle stiffened at his side and clapped a powerful hand on his shoulder.

"Enough, lad. You've had your say," he said. "On your way."

Dominic stumbled a few steps forward as Terrence gave him a shove, aided by a blast of mental energy that had him sliding down the room.

Glancing back as he gained the broad staircase that climbed the upper regions, he caught his uncle's dour gaze. The man stood like a sentinel between him and Guildford's cronies, lean and weathered like a lightning-blasted tree. His expression unreadable. Respecting the shiver of warning that tickled the hair at the base of his skull, Dominic returned to his mission, sucking his sore knuckles.

As his uncle bade, he returned to his chamber, but only for long enough to tip his stash of coin into a purse and tie it around his neck. He grabbed the army-issue bag he'd stolen from a fallen soldier three years before and stomped back downstairs.

Another quick foray to the castle kitchen gained two pilfered loaves and a hunk of cheese. The same serving wench who had suffered under Marjorie's ladle a couple of days previously fetched up a hunk of bacon and four rosy apples on the promise of a kiss. Blushing, Dominic stuffed the haul into his bag, trying to ignore the guffaws of the other servants who witnessed the exchange. Their laughter turned to trepidation when the cook appeared, arms akimbo. She grabbed Dominic by the back of his hood as he attempted to scuttle past her and yanked him around, throttling him with the neck of his own tunic.

"Where are you off to, boy?"

Never appetising, the cook's face up close was not a sight Dominic wanted to endure. Ire sparked in her one good eye. A crisscross of spider veins mottled her florid cheeks, leading the way to the brutal twist of flesh that covered the other empty socket. He twisted in her iron grip like a rat.

"Let me go, Mistress," he said, forcing the words out around his crushed windpipe.

"Stealing from me is stealing from the Queen. She'll have your hands," Marjorie said. "I'll see to it." She shook him again. "Come on, give it over."

Struggling to breathe, Dominic glanced around the gloomy kitchen. The massive fireplace and the steaming pans hanging over the flames drew his attention. Casting a plea to the Mage for forgiveness in a good cause, he bit his lips and reached into his power.

A shout came from the fireplace, and the entire staff turned to gape as the contents of the nearest pot upended to dump its load into the blaze. Smoke billowed, followed by a chorus of coughing, and Marjorie dropped him to the floor. She glared at him in the general panic as hot coals scattered into the soiled, fat-coated rushes on the kitchen floor. Flames leapt upwards, and the kitchen staff rushed to stamp out the blaze before it could take hold. Marjorie gave him one last, vicious cuff that made him see stars and then turned her back on him as she barked orders.

Forgotten in the melee, Dominic fled, coughing, eyes smarting. His purloined food banged against his hip as he ran for the stables, leaving the shouts of the beleaguered kitchen workers behind him.

Saddling his horse, a lively mare named Kismet, was the work of a moment. His fingers flew, tightening girth and chin straps. He used the old mounting block to boost himself up. The horse, a bay with a shining black mane and a star dotting her mahogany forehead, whinnied as he tightened his thighs, ears pricked, happy to exercise. The gatehouse loomed in front of him, promising freedom. Clattering towards it, Dominic had a sudden vision of himself as a carefree youngster approaching the same drawbridge. It had been night then. He'd been ragged and starving, driving the knackers cart carrying a dead horse with a fugitive Queen and a poisoned princess hidden alongside it.

Saluting Tim, the tall, cadaverous Gate Guard who had let him through that long ago, fateful night, he grinned as he spurred the horse. He'd been carrying stolen food then, too.

Chapter Eight

More rutted cart track than road, the way to Blade wound steeply downhill. Dominic swayed with his mount's stride, his bruised face touched with warmth from the sun rising over the mountains. Ancient trees rising on either side provided dappled shade. The air was crisp and sharp as wine, sweeping the smoke from his lungs. He greeted the carters, who drove sweating oxen up the road from the town, carrying daily supplies to the castle. A brace of hunters armed with bows passed him with a nod of recognition and turned left into the deep forest.

Free of daily care, questions crowded his mind. Someone wanted the Grayling badly enough to attack Thurgil. And that was no mean feat. But why? Worrying his split lip as he rode, the only reason that Dominic could see was for money. A man could fatten his purse easily with the sale of a bird like that on Blade's black market. But again, why? Why the Grayling in particular? There were other peregrine falcons in the mews. Joran's great white Gerfalcon was worth more, but the thief had not taken him. He sat up straighter in his saddle, bowels clenching with self-disgust as one other horrible thought crossed his mind. His open chamber door. The key to the falconry lying on the table. The thief had taken it from him last night as he lay drunk and senseless in his own bed. Let himself into the mews. And used Thurgil's own club to knock the man senseless as he guarded the precious birds. He groaned aloud, Kismet's ears pricking at the noise, as once again his own failure flooded his body with shame.

Mind racing but unable to stop it, Dominic twisted in the saddle, scanning the shadows amongst the trees as a flock of birds screeched their alarm and took flight. Another uncomfortable thought struck him. If not the more valuable Gerfalcon, then this could be more personal. Aimed straight at the Queen. Designed to cause her as much distress as possible when she was vulnerable. He slowed Kismet to a walk, looking back at the castle. Did he have this wrong? Was the bird still hidden in a remote room back there? The Gods knew there were enough of them. His captor could have left the bird shut up alone. He could starve. Icy sweat trickled down his spine. By the Gods, was the Queen herself in mortal danger? What if that thug at the joust was still at large in the castle? What if Joran was mistaken? Too sure of the Queen and her enormous power? What if that man was the thief? By his own admission, he hated the Queen. Was he a killer as well?

Confused by his sudden indecision, Kismet slowed her pace and twisted her head to look at him, one ear back. She turned in an uncertain circle as Dominic braced his fists on his knees and looked first at Blade, and then at the castle. Where was the Grayling? Which direction should he take?

Cursing himself, he slammed a fist into his thigh, wincing at the immediate pain. Kismet jinked underneath him, darting sideways, and the act of soothing her before she dumped him into the ditch brought him back from the edge of panic. He circled her, more deliberately the second time, and closed his eyes. Strove for the calm Terrence Skinner always insisted upon, despising his own vacillation.

"Where are you?"

Nothing, Darkness.

Swiping perspiration from his forehead as it dripped into his eyes, he tried again, picturing the Grayling flying free against a deep blue sky. The texture of his wings, the wild yellow intelligence in his gaze.

"Where are you? Show me!"

Nothing. Darkness. At the furthest edge of Dominic's magical perception, a tiny chirrup of distress. His heart clenched. The bird was wearing a hood. He couldn't see.

"Town or Castle?" He strained to picture the scene as the Grayling might see it from above. The castle with its turrets, flags, and battlements, the town with its smoking furnaces, noise, and activity.

This time, the image was unmistakable. *Loud, loud, loud.*

Unsure whether he could trust his mental vision, Dominic tried to project a sense of himself and the horse riding to Blade to the Grayling. *"I'm coming."*

Clapping his knees close to his mount's mahogany flanks, he urged her to a canter along the stony path. Kismet tossed her head, mane flowing, and stretched out.

They were ten miles out of Blade when Kismet stumbled and cast a shoe. Cursing his luck, Dominic pulled her up and dismounted. The mare trembled, mahogany coat twitching as Dominic ran an expert hand down her flank to her near fore. He squinted back down the rough road, thanking all the Gods her hoof was undamaged. The shoe lay several feet back. He picked it up with a frown. He'd seen Kismet re-shod not four weeks ago. She shouldn't have thrown a shoe.

Glancing up at the light, he grimaced at the sun. It was just before noon, but he'd have to complete the journey on foot. There was no question of riding Kismet on the hard, rutted road.

"Well, my lady," he said, loosening the girth of her saddle, "We'll have to limp along together."

Kismet nudged his arm and flared her soft nostrils. Dominic walked round to his saddle packs and retrieved some food. He palmed an apple and offered it to his horse. She munched, throwing back her head, and Dominic leaned against her in the quiet sunshine for the time it took to wolf down some bread and cheese.

Looping her reins over his fist, he picked up his pace, and Kismet paced placidly alongside him, her oaty breath huffing softly in his right ear. She gave him a nudge from time to time as if in apology for her lameness. Dominic patted her.

"Not your fault, girl. I'll get you to the blacksmith soon as we get to Blade," he promised.

The sun climbed higher as they descended, swarmed about with flies and midges. The horse flicked her tail. Dominic perspired under his tunic. The stout stone wall of Blade loomed in the far distance, the sky hazy with smoke around it. Traffic grew heavier, drawing people to the city from the outlying farms and hamlets dotted amongst the low hills.

Dominic moved to the side of the road to make way for a farmer and his cart. The man took in his sweating face and jerked a thumb at the flatbed behind the driver's seat, loaded with sacks of peas.

"Want a lift, lad? You can hitch yon horse to the back."

Dominic shook his head. "My thanks, Sirrah. I'll be stopping to water her soon."

"As you like, young sir." The farmer settled his cap more firmly, and the cart creaked off, raising a cloud of dust. Choking in the aftermath, Dominic steered Kismet with him into the cool, dappled shade of the trees.

The path was softer than the road under his hot feet. Grateful for the respite from the blistering sun, he followed it off the main track downhill. The trees rang with bird calls, their branches old and moss-covered, twisting like voluptuous limbs over his head. The air was warm and close with the smell of damp loam. Squirrels darted across their path. Faintly, in the distance, his ears caught the rush of a stream, and he quickened his pace, eager to refill his water skin from the fresh spring nearby.

Only a few feet away, the mare shied, nostrils flaring, ears flat in alarm.

"Woah, there. Steady, my lady." Dominic took a couple of steps with the mare as she backed and felt for his blade. The worn handle fitted comfortably into his palm. He glanced around. They were away from the road, and this spring was a well-known spot for travellers to stop. Easy pickings for bandits and thieves. The mare calmed, ears pricked forward, eyes curious. Dominic stared around at the under-growth but could see nothing. He advanced, clutching his dagger. Around him, the birds had stopped calling. Apart from the insistent, gentle call of the spring, the forest seemed to have fallen silent. A chill crept up his spine.

There. In the shade cast by an ancient oak, a pale blue cloak, edged with a delicate embroidery of flowers, lay like a tangle of sky across the dark earth. A muffled sob drifted to his ears as he drew closer, and he looked about him. This could easily be a trap. But Kismet's manner was calm, even eager. The mare did not scent immediate danger. He sighed, glancing back to the path that led to the road, and then once more around the sunlit forest. But there was no-one else in sight, and this girl was alone. He was honour bound to lend aid. Resigned to carrying out his knightly duty, Dominic wound Kismet's reins about the trunk of a slender birch and dropped to his knees in the dust-dry leaves.

"Mistress?" he said, reaching a tentative hand to the hunched shoulder.

"Go away, leave me alone." The girl buried her head further into the folds of the cloak. Her accent was noble, with an air of command. Skin prickling with goosebumps, Dominic shook her.

"I cannot leave you alone and untended, Mistress. Please, sit up. I mean no harm," he reassured.

"I said, leave me."

Dominic sat back on his heels and scrubbed a grubby hand through his hair. Recognition bloomed, and mistrust crinkled his brow. No mistaking that petulant tone or the familiar ash-blond braid that escaped the confines of her cloak to curl across the forest floor.

"Felicia, it's me, Dominic Skinner. What ails you? Where is your mount? Your escort?"

He glanced up at the sky, conscious that the sun had reached its zenith.

"Come on, sit up." Aware he was probably breaking all the chivalric rules of propriety, he picked up the rope of hair and tugged.

"Hey!"

Dominic wound the thick plait in his fist and continued to pull as if he were leading a horse to the farrier.

"Well, move then."

Red-faced from the confines of her cloak, Felicia glared at him as she emerged and jerked her hair from his fingers. His smirk died when he saw the tear stains on her freckled face and the bruise on her narrow jaw.

Alarm sparked in his chest. "Who did this? What happened?"

Her face clenched like a fist, and she raised her swelling chin. "None of your business," she snapped.

"Where is your mount? Surely you did not walk here?"

Felicia glowered at him. "Of course not. My horse spooked at something when I stopped to drink, and before I could stop him, he was gone." She waved a slender hand at the dense greenery. "You can look if you wish. He's probably back in the stable yard by now. Stupid beast."

"But your face…" He reached out to touch her cheek and then drew his arm back, suddenly aware of her rank. "If someone has hurt you…"

She sniffed and wiped her nose on a fold of her cloak. "And if someone has hurt me? What can you do about it, Dominic Skinner? Barely able to read and write; a puny stable boy. A would-be nobleman, one of the Blessed, favourite of her majesty, the Queen." Acid laced her voice, grey eyes narrow with spite.

He stared at her for a second and then got to his feet, throat clenching around the words he longed to throw. Turning his back, he unwound Kismet's reins and loosened the bridle. He led her to the stream and watched as the mare drank, swallowing down his own anger at Felicia's mocking tone. He closed his eyes and listened to the soft chatter of the brook, to the sound of birdsong alive in the trees above him. Behind him, dry leaves rustled as the girl stood up. She approached the bank and crouched on its edge, soaking her kerchief. He stood at Kismet's side, one hand automatically smoothing her mane. Bubbling resentment clogged his throat.

He froze at the light touch on his arm.

"I am sorry, Dominic," she said, her voice low.

"No, you're not." He opened his eyes, momentarily blinded by the sunlight bouncing off the water, and turned to face her with a scowl on his face. "You are not sorry. You are ten miles away from the city. Another ten back to the castle. You are on your own, stupidly unarmed, and you want me to help you."

Surprised, her eyes widened at his words. For a second, she almost looked like the vulnerable fourteen-year-old she truly was. Water dripped from the cloth dangling from her fingers. Dominic gave her no pause. "You might as well admit what you want, would-be Princess. Daughter of a traitor."

She gasped, face smeared with a blush of anger, and Dominic's left cheek stung with the force of the wet rag as it whipped across his face. Kismet tossed her head and took a couple of steps away, nostrils flaring.

"How dare you!" Felicia's face twisted, her grey eyes cold as stone.

"I dare because it's true." He left the shelter of Kismet's warm flank and leaned across the narrow gap between them. "You were not there the day the Queen reclaimed her throne. I was. Your mother spied on the Queen for years, poisoned her youngest maid, and did whatever she could to take her throne."

Felicia put her hands on her hips. "Petronella was barren. My mother gave the King his children. Guildford and me. She should have been the Queen."

"You're a Citizen. You don't understand. The Queen and Joran are the rightful rulers, bonded to the land. Arion should never have ascended the throne. He was the second-born son and could never take the Ring of Justice while his brother was still alive. Joran was always the true King. Petronella was always the true Queen. That is the way our magic works. It's the source of our nation's strength and health. The kingdom is doomed without it. Starving and in the dark."

Felicia ignored him. Her lips tightened. "She used magic to kill my father. In cold blood. She's evil. Magic is wrong."

Dominic rolled his eyes. "Is that what you believe? Truly?"

"My mother would not lie to me." The girl's voice rose to a shout that started the birds from the treetops.

Anger still riding him, Dominic drew breath to argue and stumbled as Kismet nudged him in the back, soaking his tunic with her drenched muzzle. Jolted, headache returning to throb between his eyebrows, he looked at the girl in front of him more closely. Her eyes glittered, her face pale as chalk beneath the hectic spots of red on her cheeks. He saw her tension, the light, shallow breathing, the tremor of her shoulders and the fear she was so desperately trying to hide behind her aristocratic mask. *Fourteen*, he reminded himself. *She's barely fourteen.* The Queen banished her mother from court. Her father is dead. She's housed and educated at the Queen's behest, looked after by servants. Her brother is an arrogant, stupid brute. None of this is her fault.

He sighed, forcing himself to calm down. "Pax," he said quietly.

"What?"

"Peace, my lady of Wessendean. You must want to travel to Blade. Is that so?"

She nodded, wariness and hope warring within her expression like clashing blades.

"Come then," he held out his elbow and nodded to the path. "The day is wasting. I will escort you, but you will have to walk. Kismet is lame."

CHAPTER NINE

T he would-be Princess did not take well to the requirement to use her own legs. Dominic regretted his impulse to help her before they even regained the main road.

"Why can't I ride? You can walk."

Her pale face shone faintly green in the light under the trees. The girl strode like a noble. Back straight, head erect on her shoulders. She complained like one, too.

"You know you can't ride a horse that has lost a shoe, Felicia."

"I don't see why not. I hardly weigh anything."

"By the Gods. I grew up around horses. I know these things. Are those the best shoes you could find for riding in? And what are you doing all the way out here, anyway?"

That shut her up. She tramped alongside him, cursing occasionally as she stumbled on the rough ground. Dominic glanced across at her as they continued. Sunlight had already ripened the pale pink of her cheeks to rose. The breeze lifted tendrils of dark blonde hair from her hastily tied braid. Almost, she could almost be mistaken for a country girl were it not for the grim expression on her face and her expensive clothes.

Forehead wrinkling in a frown as he marked the fresh bruise darkening her jaw, he tried again.

"What has happened, Felicia? You are not wearing riding clothes. No hat, supplies, or escort."

The girl put her nose in the air and ignored him.

Dominic ground his teeth. "I could help you, you know," he muttered. "If you were not so bloody stuck up."

Her eyes narrowed. "I told you before, it's none of your business."

"I still want to know who hit you."

She tossed her head. "You can want all you like. I'll still not tell you."

Dominic kicked at a stone and turned his face to Blade.

"As you wish, my lady."

They proceeded in awkward, stiff-necked silence as the sun began its slow, late summer descent to the Western hills. Dominic's thoughts raced ahead. He'd have the horse shod, drop into the Sign of the Falcon, and get news of anything unusual happening. He shot a heated glance at the girl as she stalked along. Damn her and her high-necked ways. He'd drop her somewhere, and she could do whatever she wanted.

Five miles further, perspiring in the heat, Dominic handed his waterskin to the girl. She took it with a grunt of thanks and sank her teeth into the apple he tossed to her. Dominic whistled an off-key ditty between his teeth and wiped sweat from his grubby brow. The afternoon turned humid. Heat blanketed the hillside. Blade shimmered before them like a mirage.

"Ho! Want a lift!"

They turned at the shout. A fresh-faced young woman in workday clothing hailed them from her heavily laden cart. Two stout horses strained in their harness to heave the vehicle around the worst part of the steep junction that led to the tiny hamlet of Offindon.

"By the Gods, it's hot! Tie your horse to the cart. Make haste, or we won't make the gate before curfew!"

Felicia didn't wait to look at Dominic. She placed her foot on the high cart step and did her best to clamber onto the tall driver's seat. Dominic watched, amused, as she struggled. The driver cast him a look that plainly chided him for his manners and held out a helpful hand. Felicia took it to hitch herself up and glared at him from her roost.

Dominic grinned and hitched Kismet to the back of the cart. He hoisted himself easily into the cart bed and settled himself amidst the grain sacks, grateful to be off his feet.

"Well-a-day, I'm Miranda. What brings you two to Blade?" Their rescuer started the horses with a slap of the reins and a joyous "Up there!" Less enthusiastic, the team lowered their heads and plodded onward.

Face turned to the town walls, Felicia held her tongue, bracing herself against the seat as the cart lurched on the rough track.

"We're not together," Dominic said pointedly. "She's on some mission of her own she doesn't want to talk about. Me, I'm going to Blade on the Queen's business. My horse threw a shoe way back there."

"Ah. I wouldn't normally be going to Blade with the grain, but our mill is being repaired, and the baker won't wait for his flour. Hope we get there before the weather breaks. 'Tis threatening to storm."

Grateful for someone less prickly to talk to, Dominic ignored Felicia to chat with the miller's wife. He offered his food, and Miranda stooped to the footwell to retrieve her own basket. She dumped it onto Felicia's lap.

"Here you are, lass. There's bread and ale in there, plus some salt beef and cheese. Help yourself."

Felicia looked at the basket as if she did not quite know what to do with it.

Miranda laughed. "Not much used to eating on the move, are you? Here."

She dipped an exploratory hand into the depths and came up holding a sealed flagon of ale. "Have some of that, lass," she advised. "And hand it over here when you've finished. I'm parched as a priest."

Felicia muttered something that may have been thanks and fumbled with the seal. Dominic watched her from his position at the rear. Her slender hands shook as she raised the flagon to her lips. A fleeting frown crossed his face. Mouth full of bread and salty bacon, he wondered once more just what this gently bred girl wanted so badly in Blade that she'd set off on her own to get it.

Laden with grain, the cart clattered and jolted ever closer to the lichen-stained walls surrounding Blade. Afternoon shadows lengthened across the busy road as they approached the long line of carts waiting for entry at the Northern Gate.

The cart jolted to a halt. Dominic roused from a half-dream in which he was struggling mightily to catch a dozen stray birds and rolled across the sacks, stifling a yawn. Miranda's horses put their heads down and wheezed.

Felicia looked round with faint disdain at the length of the line and managed a tight smile at their rescuer. "My thanks, Mistress. I must away."

She stumbled from the driver's seat and marched off before Dominic could stop her, rubbing her narrow rear, head still in the air.

He manoeuvred himself to take her place next to Miranda, who shook her head as Felicia marched to the head of the queue, ignoring the mutters from those she passed.

"She's a rare 'un," the woman observed, slapping the reins as the line moved forward.

Dominic scratched his chin. "Aye," he acknowledged as the slim figure in sky blue tossed a coin to the saluting gateman and wound her way under the moss-covered archway leading to the town.

He caught his neighbour's eye and nodded at her worried expression. "You're going to say you hope she knows what she's doing, aren't you?"

The woman paled slightly under her weather-worn tan. "That's exactly what I was thinking. How did you know? Are you one of them? The Blessed?"

Dominic nodded. "I'm a mind talker. Your thoughts are easy to read."

She clapped a hand to her mouth as if that would somehow prevent him from hearing her.

"There's nobbut a few of you these days," she said from beneath it. "Not since King Arion still ruled. He got rid of so many." Her voice lowered. "There's still Citizens about who are angry about magic coming back."

"Yes, I know." Dominic stood in the seat, straining his eyes for Felicia's retreating figure, but she'd vanished in the crowd.

Miranda shuddered. "Creepy, it is," she declared, although her eyes appeared more curious than scared.

Dominic fumbled in his pouch and pressed a shilling into her work-hardened palm. "There, Mistress, to thank you for your trouble," he said, preparing to leap off the cart.

She stared at the money, shaking her head. "'Twas nothing, young Sir. That's too much."

Dominic grinned, noting her change of title now she realised his magical status. He shook his head. "You don't have to be polite to me, Mistress," he said. He unhitched Kismet from the back of the cart and came back to the front.

"Well, but..." she said, still fingering the silver. It glinted in the afternoon sun.

"You don't need to because you are also one of the Blessed," he said. He winked at her as she gaped at him.

"Nay, not me. I'm a Citizen. That's all I want to be."

"If you couldn't project your thoughts, I could not hear them," he pointed out helpfully. He gave her tired horses a pat.

"Ask at the Castle for my uncle, Terrence Skinner. He will help you develop further if you wish it."

Leading Kismet, limping beside him, he left the dumbfounded woman and her cart and prepared another coin for his entry into Blade.

CHAPTER TEN

Pushing his way through the usual tangled throng around the narrow northern gate, Dominic grinned as he entered his home town. He stood on his toes, searching for Felicia. A wasted effort. The young noblewoman had vanished, swallowed up in the tide of jostling, perspiring humanity.

Stretching in a rough circle, bisected by the rushing Cryfell, Blade throbbed with energy. A tang of soot and scorched metal soured the air. Tall, narrow houses flanked the cobbled streets. Many of them contained shops at ground level and living accommodations above. After the relative quiet of the mountain descent from the Castle of Air, the noise and bustle delighted his city-bred senses. Everywhere he looked, someone was busy doing something. Barrow boys sweated in the sun with their carts. Children, untended by their parents, darted amongst the traffic, carrying messages or bundles from the market. Servants from the more well-to-do houses strolled baskets over their arms. Apprentices shouted their wares from doorways. The narrow streets rang with the iron-clad wheels of carts and carriages and the hearty clop of horses' hooves. A contingent of the Queen's guard paced slowly amidst the crowd. Armed with swords, they were a less dangerous breed than their predecessors. Still, Dominic shrank from them, hugging the walls as best he could as he led Kismet to the nearest farrier.

The rhythmic clang of hammer on iron greeted his ears as he poked his head around the door of Wat Smith's dimly lit establishment.

"Ho, Wat," he yelled through the steam as the smith plunged the horseshoe he was making into a wooden bucket of water.

Eyes on his work, the farrier grunted an off-hand greeting. Dominic looped Kismet's reins around a hitching post and leaned against the narrow door frame, tapping his foot and scanning the crowd for Felicia as he waited.

Minutes passed as the farrier measured the shoe against the ebony mare. Wat huffed a sigh as he finished and tossed his hammer onto his cluttered workbench. He gave the horse a pat and led her backwards before he recognised Dominic, silhouetted against the afternoon sun.

"By the Gods! Dominic Skinner!" He removed his cap and pushed sweat-soaked yellow hair from his ruddy forehead. "What're you doing down here? Come to check on the tannery?"

"Something like that." Dominic staggered as the farrier's huge forearm surrounded his shoulders. He had to cock his head back to meet Wat's blue eyes, narrowed from peering through steam and flame. The smith waved a hand at Kismet. "That one lame?"

"She cast a shoe on the way down. Can you check the others, too? She was only shod a sennight ago."

"Aye. Can." Turning to the wall, where a pile of half-made shoes waited for fitting, he selected one and measured it against Kismet's hoof.

"Can you give the bellows a pump, lad?" he said over his shoulder, returning to the forge. "I sent the 'prentice off to get more water."

Dominic led Kismet into the cluttered heat and bent his back to the bellows. Above him, Wat grabbed his tongs and thrust the half-made shoe into the fire. Sparks danced up the small stone chimney, and Dominic wiped sweat from his brow.

"That'll do, lad."

Brushing spent embers from his hose, Dominic straightened and went to stand next to his horse. She nuzzled against him, and he patted her neck.

"Nice mare, that," Wat said. He withdrew the shoe, glowing red, and placed it carefully on his anvil. The small workshop rang with the regular blows of his hammer as he banged it into shape. "Battonian, is she?"

"From the Lombard estate in Battonia, aye. Domita Lombard made me buy her."

Wat chuckled, peering up at him over Kismet's near fore, checking the shoe against her. "I've heard of Lady Lombard. Knows a lot about horses, she does."

"Her family owns some of the finest stock in Altius Mysterium."

He waited, wafting his hand to clear steam, as Wat plunged the shoe into a nearby wooden pail. The smith filled his mouth with nails and bent over Kismet's hoof, jumping slightly as she goosed him.

"Alright, madam, that'll do," Dominic said, pulling her face around. He dug into his pouch and found the last apple. Kismet took it with a toss of her mane and crunched the treat, dripping juice, as Wat hammered her shoe into place.

"There. That's done. Let me check these others while I'm here."

He bent to each hoof, checking carefully for missing nails or damage. Straightening, he gave the horse a slap and shrugged at Dominic's querying gaze. "All look fine to me. Don't know how she cast the other if it was as good as these. Who did 'em? Was it Andersson, up there in the castle?"

"Aye."

"Then I don't know, lad, just bad luck. That'll be four pence,"

He held out a broad hand marked with the scars of a thousand sparks. Thanking the Gods he'd brought most of his hoard with him, Dominic handed over the money. Aware of the creeping fingers of

Blade's pickpockets, he strung his purse around his neck and stowed it beneath his heavy tunic.

The smith grunted his approval. "Aye, best so," he said. "That's one thing that's still the same since the Queen took the throne. Light-fingered little beggars everywhere you look. Where you off to now?"

"The Sign of the Falcon on South Street. Sommerton's tavern."

"Well-a-day, then. Take care, lad, and thank thee."

Wat waited until Dominic had tightened the girth of Kismet's saddle and flung him to her back like a sack of meal. Blinking in the golden light of the afternoon, Dominic saluted and trotted away through the busy streets.

His route took him across town, every cluttered corner offering a memory of his childhood. Here a saddler, owned by Master Alder, a regular customer of his father's tannery. There a chandler, owned by Mistress Goodbody, who always dressed in black. As a child, he'd hated the dank interior of her shop. Her gimlet-eyed gaze watched him like a spider over her bubbling cauldron, filled with liquid, rancid tallow.

Wooden scaffolds and a tangle of ladders surrounded the weed-covered walls of Blade's greatest temple complex. Dominic had grown up in its faded shadow, the golden years of its glory long forgotten, but his father had told him tales of it. People from across Epera had once worshipped there. The area was home to the Temple of the Mage and also offered religious facilities for other races. Wells and fountains had once offered Blessed water. A lively market, filled with incense, flowers and artefacts as offerings to the four Gods traded night and day. It was a place to go for fortune-telling, healing, and to consult the Gods. During the dark days of the recent past, the buildings had been left to ruin, closed up and shuttered. Weeds grew unhindered in the gaps between the ancient flags. The Temple of the Mage had suffered following a lightning strike, its roof badly damaged. Years of incessant rain had wrecked the interior. Since then, at Queen Petronella's behest, the entire area swarmed with workmen. Dominic averted his face from the crews toiling to lift heavy stone slabs into place, balancing on ladders and platforms so narrow it made his head spin. He wiped suddenly sweaty palms on his tunic and rode on with a shudder of his shoulders.

The tavern of the Black Eagle still attracted the city's soldiers. Sprawled on the busy corner at the entrance to Blade Market, its freshly painted signs tilted gently in the breeze. A waft of hop-soaked air escaped every time someone creaked open one of its tall, narrow doors. The blare of drums and fiddles crept, muffled, through its many diamond-paned windows.

Dominic's habit had always been to pass this tavern at a run, shoulders squeezed up to his ears beneath the comfort of his hood. After the death of his brother, he'd always felt that the soldiers were looking for him. That one day, he'd feel the press of an iron hand on his elbow, the sound of a drawn blade as it left a scabbard. The narrow square behind the market contained the city's gibbets. In King Arion's day, these were often full. The broken corpses left to dangle barely had time to stiffen before the next unlucky miscreant felt the deadly scratch of the noose around his neck. Risking a glance sideways as Kismet trotted on, he relaxed a little when he saw the hanging station was empty. The ropes lay in tidy coils at the edge of the platform. People bustled past, ignoring the scaffold, even as the lowering sun threw the long shadow of the gibbet across the cobbles. Dominic shuddered and only relaxed when he pulled Kismet to a stop at the entrance to the huge market.

Business was slowing with the passing of the day as he led the horse to the nearest livery. A couple of pence bought her feed and lodging. Dominic splashed his dusty face with water from a nearby well and entered the market, intent on finding out anything he could. He browsed the stalls with an expert eye, taking in the improvements that had taken place since Petronella gained the throne. There were two wells, and the stalls were plentifully stocked. He watched, with a half smile on his face, as the owner of a fish stall used her magical ability to chill her stock. She caught his gaze and winked at him as he stood there, hands on her ample hips.

"Buying, are ye?" she called across the way. He'd taken a couple of steps in her direction before his brain caught up with his feet. Doffing his cap, he bowed to hide the flush in his cheeks. He'd forgotten the lure of the Oceanians. Their powers with water and the effortless seduction of their smiles. Last time he'd felt it was the evening in his parent's house, when Princess Alice had smiled at him, and he'd lost his boyish heart. The fishmonger's knowing chuckle followed him as he moved on. Master Dingle's knife stall had never lacked for trade, and it didn't disappoint. The harsh grate of the knife sharpener's wheel snagged him, and he stopped to eye the array of utensils and weaponry laid out in neat rows on the broad table.

"Knives, daggers, and blades," the apprentice sang, his youthful voice rough with shouting above the noise. He caught Dominic's eye and waved expansively at the display. "Want something, good sir?"

"Master Dingle about?" Dominic moved closer and trailed covetous fingers across burnished hilts, lost in admiration for the engraved blades. It crossed his mind that an additional dagger might serve him well.

"Aye, I'll get 'im. Pa!" he yelled, some 'un wants thee."

The grinding stopped, and the canvas at the back of the stall folded back to reveal a tall, cadaverously thin man with a patchy brown beard and a worn expression. His eyes brightened momentarily when he spied Dominic, and he jerked his head at his son. "Get goin' lad, there's another dozen to do before sundown."

The boy darted like a sparrow behind the curtain, and the grinder started up again.

"Greetings, young Skinner." Master Dingle loomed over him.

"Greetings, Master," Dominic said.

"Need a blade, son?"

Dominic nodded and waved a hand at the selection of daggers.

"I need information," he said in his head.

Master Dingle jerked in surprise, his tired blue eyes flashing with alarm.

"This one, Sir?"

Dominic held out his hand and waited for the knife man's instinctive fear to settle. He could understand the older man's trepidation. Despite Petronella's dismissal of the previous regime, the Blessed found it hard to display their gifts in public. The borders between the four nations stood open now, as they had not during the hard days of his childhood. He'd passed Battonians in the crowd, horse traders and warriors to a man, many of them blessed Fire Wielders, as was Domita Lombard. The Oceanians loved their siren songs. Their establishments offered everything from love potions to fortune-telling. The Argentians' skill lay in their solid business sense, and their Blessed enjoyed the gifts of the earth and healing. None of them had suffered in the way the Eperans had. At the mercy of their own Citizens, forbidden the use of their magic, their temples sacked, their families decimated, enslaved or murdered. Old habits died hard.

"What do you seek?"

The mental voice was slow and rusty. Little used. Dominic turned the blade in his hand and sighted down it.

"The Queen's falcon is missing. Have you heard anything?"

He couldn't miss the shock in his companion's gaze or the tremor of his wrinkled, liver-spotted hands.

"When?"

"Just last night. Stolen from the mews."

Master Tingle blanched. *"Does she know?"*

Dominic shook his head and then remembered he was supposed to be discussing the purchase of a knife. "Not this one, Master, have you another? Longer than this?" he asked out loud. *"I must find him,"* he added mentally.

"Here, try this." Another dagger. It felt easy in his hand. His palm tingled. Intrigued, Dominic turned it over to find the maker's initials carved into the pommel.

"I like this," he said.

"You should. Made by Mistress Tinterdorn. She specialises in blades and magic, the Gods know how. That knife's made for mentomantists. Guess that's you, as well as mind talk?"

"Aye." Mesmerised, he turned the knife over, squinting at the delicate patterns chased along the blade itself. It took him a moment to identify their shape as ancient runes. Blue fire chased each line, sparking in the bright sunlight.

"This is truly beautiful. What does it do?"

The old man shrugged. *"For me, nothing out of the ordinary. For you..."* he paused. *"I don't know. Anything you want it to, I should imagine."*

Dominic's eyes glinted with possibilities. He forced his mind back to the matter at hand. *"So, about the Grayling. Have you heard anything? Seen anything in the market today?"*

"Nay lad, but if the bird's to be sold, quiet-like, it won't be at the market. You want the back door of Goodshank's on Silver Bridge, or try The Sign Of The Falcon. Jacklyn Sommerton knows everything that goes on in the black market. Always did. You'll be careful displaying your magic around here. There's many a Citizen still unhappy with Petronella on the throne. Stirred up by that snake, Dupliss. She should have killed him when she had the chance, that's what I think."

Dominic's gaze flicked to the old man's. *"Dupliss? Lord Falcon-ridge's old friend? Are you sure?"*

The old man's lips thinned. *"Oh, aye. Makes no secret of it. Won't patronise the Blessed at all. Not that he's much to spend now the Queen took his estate. Drinks with the soldiers at the Black Swan."*

"I'll take this. How much?"

Relieved to end the mental conversation and make a good sale so late in the day, Master Tingle named a price. Dominic's cheeks paled.

"It's an enchanted blade," the trader insisted in a hoarse whisper. "Meant for the likes of you. I've only the one. I'd take it."

Dominic swallowed. Thanks to his recent win, he had the money, much though it went against his instinct to spend so much. But still. A magic blade! His soul thrilled.

The exchange made, he took his leave. Master Tingle threw in an elaborate tooled scabbard for the dagger, and Dominic strapped it securely around his waist. A newfound swagger in his stride, he pushed through the crowd towards Silver Bridge, considering what he'd learnt.

Near the end of the market, at the last stall, his eye snagged on a familiar sky-blue cloak. It hung at the back of a herbalist, a bright flash of colour amid the drab greens and greys of the bundled herbs dangling from its tented roof. The stall holder was busy packing up her wares, humming a light air as she layered her goods in folds of muslin and laid them carefully within her saddle bags. A mule tethered to the stall snatched idly at a pile of hay as the woman loaded her stock on his dusty back.

Dominic's gaze flitted around the immediate vicinity, but there was no sign of Felicia. He chewed his lip and glanced towards the river. Trading hours were almost over. Goodshank's would close soon. The stall holder took the cloak from its hook and smoothed the costly velvet. A satisfied smile curved her full lips. She glanced up, alarmed, when Dominic marched up to her.

"Where's the girl who gave you that cloak?" he demanded before he could stop himself.

She pressed the cloth to her capacious bosom and regarded him over its embroidered edge, thick eyebrows drawn in a scowl.

"And who's asking?"

Dominic scowled back. A jerk of his fingers and the cloak flew from her unwitting grasp. He caught it before it hit the ground.

"Here, that's mine!"

"I'm in a hurry. Tell me what I need to know, and you can have it back."

"She gave it to me in exchange for some herbs. She had no money."

He rolled his eyes. Felicia had really prepared well for her trip.

"Which way did she go?"

Bemused by his urgent tone, the woman gestured at the river and drew herself up to her full height. "Can I have that back now?"

On the verge of handing it to her, Dominic paused. The stall holder snatched at the cloak. He put it behind his back.

"What did she buy?"

The woman shrugged. "Nothing much, just some Heartease and Valerian."

Bewildered, Dominic frowned. "Heartease? Are you sure?"

"Do ye take me for a fool? Of course I'm sure. Cloak?"

He tossed it to her and took off at a run, mind whirling. What did a Citizen like Felicia want with a magic-altering drug like Heartease?

CHAPTER ELEVEN

S hadows were lengthening on his left as he jogged towards Silver Bridge, the sweeping multi-arched thoroughfare that crossed the river. The magnificent expanse of the Cryfell had receded over the last few years as the weather improved. A stern reminder of the savagery of the river in flood, the bridge spread its graceful arches further than it needed to. Muddy banks swarmed with water fowl, pecking for food in the fertile soil. A cool, rain-scented breeze ruffled Dominic's hair, and he glanced up stream to the distant mountains. The battlements of the Castle of Air could be made out for those with sharp eyes, but his gaze was drawn above it to the darkening sky. Storm clouds gathered over the northern range. Over his head, sea gulls soared on the current, driven inland. His mouth narrowed. The weather was about to change. His mind drifted to Felicia, with no money for shelter and no robust clothing. He shook his head. No point looking for her. She'd have to shift for herself. Pulling up his hood, he squared his shoulders and prepared to test his luck on the most expensive street in Blade.

An entirely different class of people browsed the establishments of Silver Bridge. Haughty women strode by, noses buried in oranges stuffed with cloves against the stench of manure wafting from the dung spattered cobbles. Their servants trailed behind, weighted with bags and surly expressions. The dandies of Blade promenaded their fashions in a riot of puffed sleeves and variously coloured silk hose. Sunlight reflected from earrings and hatpins and cloaks embroidered with silver thread. There were taverns aplenty on Silver Street, but very few serving drinks that Dominic could afford. He stepped aside to make way for a bevy of courtesans, leaving one of the famous brothels. The smallest of them thanked him with a slight nod of her head, green eyes dancing in her pale olive face under a mass of golden curls.

"There's a likely lad," she said, running a gentle finger across his downy chin. "He'll make a fine man one day."

Cursing his blush, and the automatic quickening in his loins, Dominic cast his eyes down. The girl's laughter drifted behind her along with the scent of carnations as she followed her companions to ply her trade at the nearest tavern.

"Bloody Oceanians," he murmured under his breath. Shaking his head, determined not to be distracted, he tramped doggedly onward. Jewellers and tailors abounded. Unimpressed, he marched on. Harder to ignore, the narrow window of Tressel's bakers demanded his attention. The famed pastry chef, native of Argentia, displayed his creations on stacked trays. Sweetmeats, comfits, and pastries vied for his attention. A complex aroma of fruit and spices drifting from its open doorway made his mouth water and his stomach growled like a beast as he passed. Pressing his hand against his empty midriff, Dominic gritted his teeth and hastened past the shop.

Goodshank's Mews proclaimed its excellence in proud gilt embellishments around its windows and doorway. Peering in through the rippled glass, Dominic squinted at the range of equipment available to buy. One shelf contained thick, finely tooled gloves. Jesses and lures hung from hooks pressed into the rough plaster walls. Leaning on the polished counter, a plump merchant counted out coins. His purchase, a pretty merlin obviously destined for his wife or daughter, perched uneasily in its cage, wings beating in agitation. One glance at her, and his guts churned with unease.

Even from behind glass, he didn't like the look of the proprietor. Stiff backed and long nosed, like his charges, the man eyed the coins and scooped them into his pouch with a swift, practiced sweep of his hand. He bid his customer good day and stood back, arms crossed. A satisfied smirk grew on his narrow face as the merchant picked up the cage and started for the door. Taking a breath, Dominic stopped the man with a hand on his elbow before he'd gone more than a couple of steps.

"Your pardon, Sir."

Shrewd, watery eyes deep-set in a bulbous, wine-flushed face took Dominic in at a glance. Temporarily blinded by her soft leather hood, the merlin cocked her head, "Aye, lad? And what do you want?" The man's tone was brusque, but not unkind. His breath drifted, sweet with Argentian wine.

"Your bird, Sir. I beg you, see you feed her as soon as you can."

The merchant frowned. "Feed her? What, you mean she's hungry?"

He raised the cage and peered at his purchase more closely. Dominic glanced sideways and encountered Master Goodshank's ferocious scowl on the far side of the glass.

"She's too thin," he explained, conscious that the proprietor was approaching the door. The back of his neck prickled, already scenting danger.

"Well, by the Gods," the merchant exclaimed. "She did not look so when first I saw her, only this morn."

"If I may, Sir." Dominic gabbled, taking confidence in the man's concern. "I'm a falconer, and I believe your merlin is starving. Look at her feathers."

"What about 'em? I know nothing about birds. Tis my wife that likes them."

"Her feathers should be smooth. Not fluffed up on a hot day like this. Are you sure this is the same bird they showed you this morning?"

"Are you saying he's swindled me? Is he trying to pass off his dying stock on me? I'll have him up before the guild!"

The man turned on his heel and shoved the door open, almost into Goodshank's face. It closed with a bang that rattled the panes in the window, followed by the outraged bellow of a merchant deprived unwisely of his wealth.

Biting his lip, Dominic beat a hasty retreat to the narrow alleyway that divided Goodshank's establishment from its neighbour. Gods help the man if the Grayling was here and injured or sick. He'd have more than the Guild to worry about.

The Goodshank's mews, guarded by a tall fence, squeezed narrowly between the shop and the balustrade of Silver Bridge. Below him, busy with boatmen, the river meandered onward to the south. The view towards God's Peak shimmered like a mirage in the far distance, the tip of its majestic spire topped with snow. Shrugging his hood over his head, Dominic sauntered to the ornate iron gate leading into the mews yard, and gave it an experimental push. Bolted from the inside. He pressed his face against it. Distant shouting still resounded from the main shop, but the yard was quiet. A bell rang somewhere in the city. Curfew was close. Perhaps Goodshank had sent his apprentices for supper already.

Moving a bolt from inside the door should have been a straightforward task for a mentomantist. As the sun began its late afternoon slide behind the western mountains, Dominic swore under his breath as his control slipped, and slipped again. He could hear the bolt rattling, but that was about all his power could do. Frustrated, he swiped perspiration from his forehead and massaged the back of his neck. What had happened to his telekinesis? Could someone like Mistress Tinterdorn have spelled the lock? Was that possible?

Leaning against the wall, he thumbed a copper from his pouch and flipped it into the air. A quick spiral of his fingers should be more than enough to stop its downward flight. He bit his lip, utterly dismayed, as the coin ignored his mental command and dropped uselessly to the greasy cobbles.

"By the Gods. What is happening?" He stooped to pick the copper up, his gut cramping with dread. Was this it? It was the eve of his birthday. Had the Mage decided he was undeserving of his Blessing after all? He shivered as the first set of storm clouds raced in from the north, hair rising in the fresh wind. A low rumble of thunder dragged his attention to the skies, and he looked up to see the ominous yellowing that presaged a thorough drenching. Voices from the direction of the shop prompted him to move away from the iron gate. He pressed himself against the sturdy wall, out of sight, listening.

"'Twas not my fault, Master Goodshank. I gave him the bird ye told me to!"

The shrill tones of the Goodshank apprentice ended with a thump of a fist on flesh and a sharp yelp. Dominic winced in sympathy and pulled his hood up more securely around his neck as the first pecks of rain pocked the dusty street.

"Not that one, you imbecile," the Master snarled. His tone was vicious. "You can forget about payment this month, lad. And your supper. You just lost me a fine sale."

"But..."

"Get rid of it."

"But..."

"Kill it and throw it in the river. Do it, or you'll feel the rod, and you won't eat for a week."

The Master's tone was final as he marched away.

Silence in the yard. Dominic's sharp ears caught the luckless apprentice's sniff. He jumped when the bolt rattled, and the boy appeared, cradling the doomed merlin in his hands. Olive skinned, as malnourished as the hawk he carried, the lad's chocolate brown eyes streamed with tears, a picture of misery.

"I don't want to do it," he said to the bird. "But he'll half kill me if I don't." His thin fingers closed gently around the fragile bird's neck. She stirred, feeble in his grip.

Dominic shuddered. "Nay, don't!"

The boy jumped with fright.

"Master, you scared me!"

"Let me see that bird."

"She's sick. Master Goodshank... He wants me to...to kill her, but I don't want to. I can't." The apprentice squared his jaw, but his thin lips trembled. He glanced behind him into the yard, shoulders hunched in his ragged tunic.

"She's sick because she's hungry, that's all. Give her to me."

Grateful for someone with more authority to take control, the boy gave her over.

"Good at catching beetles?"

"If I have to."

Dominic nodded at the dampening ground. "Get looking. Beetles, worms, mice. Quick as you like." He stroked the merlin, conscious of the rapid heartbeat beneath her concave chest.

Startled, the boy sprinted into action. He disappeared into the ginnel that ran between the two shops and returned in minutes with a handful of grubs, two worms, and a warm, freshly stomped mouse.

"Will these do?"

"Perfect. Let's see if we can get her to eat."

Squatting against the fence, the apprentice watched, breathless, as Dominic offered her the food.

"Here you go, beauty." He lowered the merlin carefully into the gap between his crossed legs and put the meal in front of her. She eyed it with laconic interest but made no move to eat it.

"What's your name?" Dominic asked, watching the bird.

"Aldric."

"Does your master have more birds like this one?"

The boy squirmed. "He's not the best falconer, sir. We had Cuthbert Wideacre for a while. He was the headman here, but then he fell out with Master Goodshank and left. The birds have no-one but me. And I don't know anything much."

"Well then, I'd find Cuthbert Wideacre and get him to tell you what you need to know. How long will you be 'prenticed to Goodshank?"

The boy's face fell. "Four more years. I'd have run a long time ago, but..."

"You love the birds?"

Aldric shrugged. "I do. Also, me pa would tan me hide and send me back if I broke me contract."

He stroked the merlin's fine feathers with a grimy finger. "Love it when they fly, I do," he said dreamily. "So fierce and proud."

"Well then, here's something to give you hope. Find Wideacre, and learn all you can if he'll tell you. Your master may not like it, but at least the birds will get better care. And when you're done, come to me at the castle."

Both boys smiled as the merlin finally launched into her meal. Worms finished, she tore into the mouse.

"At the castle? Who are you?"

"Dominic Skinner. Master of Falcons."

"You're Dominic Skinner?" Aldric's dark eyes were wide with wonder. "Heard of you, I have. They say you can whistle birds down out of the sky. The Grayling obeys you."

Dominic's heart clenched like a fist. "I'm not so great," he said. "What do you want to do with her now she's eating?"

"I could keep her and make her better."

"And what do you need?"

The lad recited the meal, his eyes shining.

"Merlins will eat most things," Dominic said, "and when birds are in captivity, we must feed them. Don't hope that they will sell quickly. Keep their surroundings as clean as you can. You need a supply of fresh meat. Fresh rainwater. If a bird looks sick, separate it from the others. Here."

He transferred the merlin back to the lad's possession. Aldric cupped it gently between his grubby hands, eyes soft. "'Tis even worth the beating," he murmured under his breath.

Dominic bit his lip, struggling to harden his heart at the boy's plight. He remembered it so well from his days as a stable boy under Arion's reign. "I've got a secret to tell you. Can you keep it?"

"Aye, for the help you gave, I can." His companion's huge brown eyes were serious.

"Someone has stolen the Grayling." Dominic whispered it, shame flushing his cheeks. "I am looking for him, I'm...afraid for him and the Queen."

Aldric's face paled. "Is that why you're here? You think Goodshank has him?"

"The bird is somewhere here, in Blade. I must get him back."

"He's not in our mews," Aldric said. "We've had no new birds this week..." His voice tailed off, thinking.

"But?" Dominic prompted.

The lad sighed. "I overheard Master Goodshank talking to someone yestereve. Something about meeting a woman who used to live at the castle who had the bird they'd been waiting for."

Rain spat more fiercely from the sullen sky as Dominic leaned closer.

"Did he say her name?" he asked, all his senses clamouring danger.

"Aye. Arabella of Wessendean, it were. Never heard of her."

"By the Gods," Dominic swallowed, and the blood drained from his cheeks.

"You know her?"

Dominic nodded, his face grim. Pieces were dropping into place.

"I do," he said.

He placed his hand on the boy's arm, skinny as a twig beneath his grip. "Tell no-one what I've told you," he whispered. "The Queen's life could depend on it."

CHAPTER TWELVE

B row creased with worry, Dominic hunched his shoulders against the rain and scurried to the end of Silver Bridge. The river churned uneasily below. Ferrymen made for the banks as a grumble of thunder drifted to him on the chill breeze. People hastened past, heading for the place they called home, hoods up for shelter in the gloomy light. Racing clouds completely obscured the setting sun. The comfort of candlelight beckoned from Blade's grimy windows.

By the time Dominic reached the Sign of the Falcon, the rain had increased to a downpour. Shivering like a stray dog, he blundered into the timbered taproom and headed for the fireplace. Water dripped from his woollen hood to the well-swept flags. The low, stone-walled room was a fog of tobacco smoke and ale. A fiddler scraped a plaintive air to the rowdy displeasure of his audience, who were roaring at him for something livelier. Lost in his tune, the fiddler turned his shoulder and continued his melody, unconcerned. The place was thick with conversation, and Dominic's mouth watered as he smelled the stew on offer for the night's meal.

"How now, Master? What will ye have?"

He jerked round and conjured a grin for Rose Sommerton, Jacklyn's comfortable-looking wife. The woman stood in front of him with her hands on her hips. Her ruddy cheeks glowed in the warmth from the fire, her fine blonde hair bound beneath a neat cap.

"Well, Dominic, 'tis right good to see thee!" she said. "Food?"

"For Jacklyn's stew, yes," Dominic said, salivating at the thought.

She smiled. "Sit you down then. I'll be back."

He sank to the nearest trestle and shoved his damp shoes toward the blaze, watching with interest as steam curled from the leather. His thoughts churned like the storm clouds he could just make out through the opposite window as the sun slipped further in the sky. Rain rattled like pebbles against the glass.

Rose returned bearing stew, bread, and a huge tankard of ale. Dominic thanked her and tore into it, rolling his eyes in pleasure.

"No-one makes stew like Jacklyn," he said between mouthfuls. "No-one."

Rose laughed, her eyes twinkling. "Aye, although it wasn't always so. I used to give his stew to the pigs. It was all it was good for."

"Is he about?"

"He will be. I'll tell him you're here. Is all well with you? 'Tis rare we see you these days."

Dominic wiped his mouth on his sleeve and shrugged. "It could be better," he admitted, his voice low.

The landlady's eyebrows raised, but she said nothing as she turned for the door.

Savouring rich gravy, a hunk of bread halfway to his mouth, a rumble of angry voices rose across the drone of conversation. Dominic's attention lifted from his supper, and he slid backwards in his seat, clutching his bowl, as two burly men jerked to their feet to square off in the middle of the room. The fiddler stopped playing, and the conversation died. All eyes turned to the erupting argument. Dominic shrunk into the shadows as he recognised one as the towering man who had bested him at the joust. Like many of his fellow customers, he flinched as the fellow slammed his tankard onto the rough planks and grabbed a handful of the slighter man's tunic.

"Queen's right? Queen's right, you say? What right does she have to rob us blind with taxes and bleed us dry? It's time we stopped her!"

His detractor shook his head, eyes bulging from the pressure at his neck as the bigger man levered him one armed from the floor. His feet strained, and he tugged at the hand that gripped him. Dominic glanced round the tavern. A frown crossed his brow at the number of nods. The fiddler slipped by him, clutching his instrument as he disappeared to the rear corridor.

"Aye, Carl. You're right," someone said. "Dupliss has the way of it. We should demand our rights."

"Aye. Aye."

Dominic stared around the room. Anyone on the side of the queen had buried their gaze deep into their bowls or tankards. "Get up! Say something!" his own mind jeered at him, mocking the cowardice that kept his backside firmly in his seat. Swallowing, he put down his bowl, hands trembling, fingers clutching for his dagger. He cleared his throat. Heads turned.

About to stand, he'd never been more thankful for the heavy hand at his shoulder, squashing him down. His grateful glance flashed to the dark brown stare of Jacklyn Sommerton, as the tavern keeper advanced into the room.

"How now? What's to do? You know I don't allow fighting in my tavern," he said, spearing Carl with his gaze. His square fingered hand drifted from his gravy smeared apron to linger at the worn hilt of a sturdy, army issue sword, but his tone was mild. The voice of a man who knew how to take charge. His fiddler lingered at his heels, still fingering the neck of his violin.

Carl glared, his mouth tight over his broken teeth. "I'm just saying what everyone says. Dupliss is right. We've had enough of the Blessed. Haven't we paid enough? First the Starving, and now the blasted taxes?" He gave his opponent a shake, but opened his fist as Jacklyn took another step forward. His victim slid to the worn planks, coughing, hands at his bruised throat.

Jacklyn raised one eyebrow. "I've told you before about fighting in my tavern. Any disagreements you have, you can take outside." He paused, his glance raking the room. "And that goes for anyone else who wants to cause trouble here. You're welcome to leave and pay extra for the watered wine and slop they serve at the Black Eagle."

He waited. Dominic watched, open-mouthed, as Carl cast another glare around. "We all know whose side you're on, Sommerton," he said.

Jacklyn shook his grizzled head. "I make no secret of it. Never have. But this is my place. My tavern, my rules. Take a walk." He nodded at the door, black ice in his stare. "Off you go now. Give Dupliss my regards. Good to know he's as deluded as ever."

Silence. The rattle of rain against the glass, and the gentle crackle from the hearth, underpinned the tension in the room. Carl glared at Jacklyn for a few seconds longer and then turned on his heel for the door.

"You're making a mistake, Sommerton," he hissed, as he opened it. Chill wind wound its way inside, sending smoke around the room. Dominic buried a cough in his sleeve, dumbfounded at Jacklyn's easy assurance.

Jacklyn just shrugged. "I think not. Don't come back," he added, eyes narrowed. "No-one will serve thee." He cast a frown around the room. "Anyone else?" he asked. "Don't let me keep you if you'd rather be elsewhere."

His customers looked at each other and then at the rain driving down outside. Dull murmurs started up as they returned to their meals. Someone climbed to his feet and closed the door.

A wry smile on his face, Jacklyn reached behind him and jerked his reluctant musician forward towards the fireplace. "Get playing, lad," he said. "Make it lively." His gaze clashed with Dominic's as he turned and he nodded to the corridor.

Dominic left the price of his meal on the table and scrambled in his limping wake down the rear passage. His shadow stalked before him. Larger now than it had appeared in the days of his childhood when he'd run messages to Jacklyn Sommerton from his father at the tannery. Timbers in the low ceiling still showed scorch marks from the fire the King's Guard started during their pursuit of the fugitive Queen four years ago. A half smile crept across his face as he remembered the people who had escaped the city from this tavern, back in the dark days of the last king's doomed rule.

Jacklyn stood to one side to usher him into his counting room. Old ledgers crowded a row of shelves behind his sturdy desk. Slightly stooped and silvered with age, the man followed him in and sat behind it. Humour sparked his dark eyes as their gazes clashed. A set of scales wobbled as he took his place. Light from a pair of pewter candlesticks flickered across a heavy piece of parchment crammed with text awaiting his attention.

"Well met, lad." Jacklyn gestured to a thick decanter. "Have a seat and help yourself. It's Argentian."

Dominic took the solid chair in front of Jacklyn's desk and sat on his hands to prevent himself from reaching for the wine. "How can you do that?" he demanded. "Most of those people were on Carl's side. I could tell."

The older man shrugged. "I've got a lot on many of them. I know their little secrets. Who is secretly swiving another's wife. Who owes what to whom. They know it." He tapped his head with one blunt finger. "Information, lad. That's what keeps the world running." He gestured at the wine. "Not drinking?"

"I need a clear head, Master Sommerton. There's trouble brewing."

Jacklyn threw his eyes to the low ceiling and huffed a laugh. "I am aware, as you saw. What's to do this time?"

He reached for his pipe and puffed in silence as Dominic related his tale. Fragrant smoke wreathed around them as it curled to the white-washed ceiling.

"I spoke to the 'prentice at Goodshank's. He says no new birds have arrived this week," Dominic finished. He scrubbed grubby hands through his hair and squinted at the older man through the soft blue haze.

"I don't know what to do, Jacklyn. I think the Grayling is in Blade. Now I've heard Arabella mentioned, I'm sure the Wessendean twins are involved somehow." He jumped from his seat and paced the room, "It's all my fault. If he's hurt or dead. The Queen will never forgive me. I must find him. I must!"

"Slow down there. Let's not panic."

Dominic's shoulders relaxed at the innkeeper's words, but agitation still twisted his guts. "There's another thing," he said. "I've lost my telekinesis. I should be able to move stuff around." He nodded at the pouch of tobacco in front of his host and placed his intention on it. The flap that closed it flapped feebly like the wing of a dying bird, but eluded all his attempts to open it.

"Stop, lad. You'll do yourself an injury." Jacklyn's hand raised in consternation. Dominic crushed his hands to his face against the sudden pounding headache. They came away bloody.

"Nay. Stop trying so hard." Jacklyn's rough voice was soft with concern. "Ye have not reached your sixteenth birthday. Of course, your powers have yet to settle. Don't force them."

"But what if the Mage takes them away?" Dominic blotted his dripping nose on his sleeve.

"A good lad like thee? He won't."

"But he could. I used it against Guildford. Took all his money. He and his friends beat me up and stole it back, but I took it all from him again at cards the next night. Only that time I didn't use magic."

"We know about Wessendean around here," Jacklyn said, his tone dry as bone. "Young thug. Too big for his age and his boots. Everyone treats him like a man full grown. He thinks he's one, too, but he ain't. Got himself in some terrible trouble with Tremble, I heard. They're after him for his gambling debts. Big as he is, with his fancy sword, I still don't fancy his chances if he don't pay up."

Wide-eyed, Dominic stared at him. "That makes sense. He's stolen the Grayling. Thinks he can swap it in payment for what he owes." He frowned. "But then Arabella's expecting a special bird."

Jacklyn chuckled. "Welladay. Cheating comes natural to him, doesn't it? Disobeying his sainted mother as well? Tut tut!"

"But what does Arabella want with the Grayling? She can't want to sell him."

The laughter fell from Jacklyn's face. "Aye, lad. You're right," he said. "That's a lot more serious. Hates the Queen, she does. Always has."

"Guildford doesn't even bow to her when he should anymore," Dominic said, remembering.

Jacklyn shook his head and smoothed his greying beard. "Petronella banished Arabella from court. Took her land, separated her from her children. I can understand why she did it, but she was too soft. There were always going to be consequences with that woman alive. Too much bad blood between them. Those twins are spies in the camp, no matter that the Queen sees to their welfare."

"So Arabella's here, in Blade?"

"She used to have a townhouse here, in the rich end, hard by Guild Square. 'Tis all closed up now. The Queen forbade Arabella the city." He shrugged. "Doesn't mean she's not here, though, curled up in some dark corner. Snakes, the Wessendeans. Like the adders on their standard."

Anger coiled in Dominic's chest. His fists clenched. "If she hurts the Grayling, I'll kill her."

Jacklyn's eyebrows lifted, and his eyes moved from Dominic's determined, battered face to the tips of his wet shoes. He stood and limped to the wall, where a clutter of discarded cloaks and hoods hung from wooden hooks.

"You're in no fit state to kill anyone right now," he said over his shoulder. "But you need better coverage if you're intending on heading out in the storm." Selecting a couple of thick cloaks, he held them out to Dominic.

"Never ceases to amaze me what the rich folk leave behind when they're drunk," he said, mouth twitching in a half smile behind his beard. "Take yer pick."

Dominic stared at him, brow quirking. "I can't believe you're not trying to stop me," he said.

The older man shrugged. "I'm an old soldier, lad, and I've seen it all. Right from the start. Mistress Eglion swore me to the Mage's service when I was just a little older than you."

He nodded with approval as Dominic's fingers tested the fabric, closing on a dark wool that would shield him from the worst of the weather.

"Aye, that's right. Practical, like. Bit big for you." He stifled a grin as Dominic put it on, the ends trailing on the floor.

"Doesn't matter." Dominic removed the cloak and attacked the length with his old dagger. "Hemmed," he said, shrugging it over his shoulders.

Jacklyn smiled as he stooped to pick up the remains of the fabric, folding it tidily on his desk.

"Don't waste time, do you?" he remarked. "I was going to offer thee a bed for the night. You look all done in."

Dominic gritted his teeth. "I can't sleep. Not until I have the Grayling. My thanks for your help." He turned for the door.

"Welladay, then. Gods go with thee, Dominic Skinner. Happy hunting. Just one thing…"

"Yes?"

Jacklyn's face closed, remote and severe in the flicker of candlelight. "Tis not yet my fight. But if you find out Arabella of Wessendean is behind all this, by all means, kill her." He paused, his brown eyes glowing like coals. "Just don't use magic."

CHAPTER THIRTEEN

Hard by the north bank of the Cryfell, hidden amid a jumble of alleys and back streets, Tremble's Gaming Hell did nothing to advertise its presence. Huddled against the ramshackle boards of a disused stable, Dominic shivered as rain washed rubbish down the filthy back street. Thunder rumbled in the distance, a long, low tone, like the breath of a sleeping giant. Water dripped from the low portico that sheltered him. He tugged the overlarge cloak higher around his neck and glanced up at the sky. A brisk wind showed a weak moon in snatches between the tumbling clouds. He'd passed few people on his way from the tavern. The sudden storm kept the townsfolk indoors, safe against its edge. Dominic's sharp ears caught the sound of merriment drifting from behind the misted windows of Tremble's domain. A rough shout of laughter, a snatch of song, the blare of a sackbutt, and the reedy tones of a recorder. Stray dogs nosed through the gutters, their narrow flanks slick with water, eyes watchful. A rat scurried across his foot and darted across the narrow street. Dominic jumped as a huge mastiff, iron-studded collar clamped around its sturdy neck, bounded out of the shadows by Tremble's door. It lunged for the hapless rodent. Pounced. One shake, and it was dead. Dominic shuddered with distaste as the dog threw back its head and swallowed the rat whole. It stood solidly in the street before him, bullish head on one side, tongue dangling from its mouth, before returning to his post by the battered door. It lowered its haunches to the dirt floor, a black shadow against the mud-spattered wall.

Dominic heaved a sigh and felt for the daggers at his waist, the purse at his neck, his battered knapsack. All were secure. If only he could rely on his powers to aid him. Tremble's. His bowel quivered at the thought of entering. A disreputable place during the day. Purely dangerous at night. But if Guildford had obeyed his instinct for survival, then that's where the boy would go. The Grayling with him. Either that, or risk a beating from which he might never recover, or worse. His lips thinned to a blade's width. Felicia must have known about this. Only the safety of her precious brother would propel her willy-nilly from the shelter of the castle.

Swallowing down his trepidation, he patted his daggers once more. About to step away from the comforting planks of rotten wood that supported his weight, he froze as the door opposite slammed open. A giant stood in the doorway. His shoulders all but filled the frame, blocking the lantern light shining at his back. A wave of strong liquor and stagnant perfume wafted from behind him. Tiny eyes, banked in fat, like specks of obsidian, flickered up the stinking alleyway in both directions. Satisfied there was no immediate threat, he reached behind him and hauled a man into the street with a single, well-timed thrust. Dominic stifled a gasp under his hand. The unlucky client, slim but well-muscled, was all but naked, clothed only in his cross garters and loin cloth. He glared at the doorman, his finely drawn face a mask of outrage.

"Master Tremble thanks you for your custom, as does Aramida," the giant intoned. "You owe him ten nobles. Pay up by this time next week, or we'll take your thumbs, as well as your clothes and weapons."

"How dare you! The Queen's Guard will hear about this!"

On the verge of closing the door, the giant paused, raking the angry aristocrat with his mocking little eyes. "We own the Queen's Guard, my lord," he said, satisfaction in every syllable.

The door slammed shut. Eyes wide with admiration at his bravery, Dominic watched as the debtor rolled his shoulders and stalked back to the door, raising his fist to demand entry. Disregarded in the shadows, the mastiff leapt to his feet, hackles raised, teeth bared, eyes feral, and the man backed away. Slowly, one foot after the other. The hound followed. Menacing, the warning rumble from its barrel chest mirrored by the thunder returning to play amongst Blade's many chimneys. The two paused. Eyes, pale in the dim light, flashed alarm as the stranger looked for shelter. The dog bided his time. A drool of saliva dropped from its tongue to join the slime of the streets. A brief flash of lightning showed every welt, dip and hollow between the animal's ribs. He started forward again. The stranger yelped with sudden fear, and Dominic reached for his haversack and precious stash of salted bacon.

The low whistle issuing from his lips brought the man's face around. Naked fear shone in his icy eyes, his freckled shoulders peppered with gooseflesh.

"Stay still, don't move," Dominic murmured. He whistled again and dangled the bacon from his fist. The dog's head turned in his direction, head cocked, ears pricked. Satisfied he'd gained its full attention, Dominic took a couple of swift paces and hurled the bacon as far down the street as he could. The dog bounded after it. Locking eyes with the stranger, they took off down the alleyway in the opposite direction, slipping in the mire. His companion kept up a low-voiced swearing.

"By all the Gods," he grunted as he skidded on the damp cobbles, catching his own fall. "That wench was not worth the price, no matter what Dupliss said."

Lungs heaving with exertion, they slid to a stop when they reached the river. Oily water rushed southwards. A single-row boat bobbed at its place against the jetty. Lightning flickered in the distance as the storm moved on.

"My thanks to you and your quick thinking, Sir." The aristocrat executed a courtly bow, one hand pressed against a chest liberally sprayed with golden hair. His hair was gold as well, burnished as a newly minted penny.

"Wait, I know you," Dominic said, recognition dawning. "You're from Court. Are you not Jared Buttledon's brother, Thomas?"

"That little lack spittle. Aye. That I am." Thomas leaned on the low balustrade and scraped his hands through his hair. "Who are you?"

"I'm Dominic Skinner."

"Are you now? By the Gods. You're the Mage-Blessed lad who fleeced my brother, are you?"

Alert for danger, Dominic took a step back, one hand reaching for his dagger. Thomas roared with laughter, his breath rich with wine. "Nay, you don't have to fear me. Jared will learn the hard way what gambling means. Sure enough, I just have." He shivered.

"Here," Dominic fumbled with the strings of his cloak.

"Nay, nay!" Thomas held out a hand in mock horror. "I've no need of your clothes. The beauteous Maria Fitzherbert'll wrap me up between her sheets in two shakes of a lamb's tail. She only lives over the river." He nodded at the abandoned rowboat.

"Exercise'll keep me warm. What say you?" he added, on a wink that swept a blush to Dominic's cheeks.

Thomas grinned his amusement. "By the Gods, such an innocent. What are you doing outside a place like Tremble's, anyway? I can think of better places to look for a woman."

"I'm not."

Thomas frowned. "Gambling, then? Don't go in there for that. They'll cheat you as soon as they look at you."

"Not gambling, either." Dominic paused, wondering what he could say.

Thomas waited, one well-marked eyebrow raised in question. He seemed happy to withstand the chill wind against his naked flesh as Dominic struggled for words.

"Welladay, lad," Thomas said as the silence spread. "You don't have to tell me. What reason would you have to trust me? If you've dealings with young Jared, I can understand your hesitation."

The man's tone was mild, but there was a hint of frustration in his voice at the same time. "Causes more trouble than he's worth. Our sainted mother swears he'll turn her hair grey before the year's out."

"He's a friend of Guildford's, isn't he?"

Thomas fixed him with a penetrating glare that belied his ready humour. "You know he is. Thick as thieves."

"I'm looking for Guildford."

"And you think he's in Tremble's? Gods help him if he is."

"Did you see him?"

Thomas laughed. "Not likely. Tonight, I saw the inside of Aramida's chamber and a reminder of what it's like to lose a bet to a courtesan from the dark side of Oceanis. I won't tell you what she bet me. Your virgin sensibilities would be too shocked. Suffice it to say, nothing takes place in that establishment that is not planned between the two of them. Her, and Tremble."

He stopped and fixed Dominic with a warning stare. "Don't go in there, I beg you. Nothing good will come of it."

Dominic swallowed. "I have to," he said. "I think Guildford has the Queen's falcon."

Thomas's freckled cheeks paled. "Is this a jest?"

Dominic sighed. "I only wish it was. As far as I know, he's in debt. Thinks Tremble will take the bird in exchange for what he owes."

The older man's eyes rounded. "By the Gods, his debt must be huge. What is he thinking?"

Dominic's lips thinned. "I don't care what he's thinking. I just need to get the Grayling back. Guildford can get what he deserves for all I care. He causes enough damage just by existing."

Thomas's gaze softened. "Aye, lad. You've taken some knocks, I know. Jared boasted about the pasting they gave you. If it helps at all, I gave him a beating for it. Bet you didn't hear that?"

Dominic's lips twisted into an unwilling grin. "I hadn't heard that, no."

"'Tis a pity our father is no longer with us. As it is, I get the ruling of the boy. Much good though it does either of us. I'm not cut out to play the heavy-handed father." He shivered again as the wind rose.

"You should go, warm up," Dominic said. "My thanks for your concern."

Thomas glanced at the nearby row boat, bobbing at the jetty. "And let a youngling like you brave Tremble? Fine man I'd be to let you do that. I'll come with you."

He stepped away from the boat, pale eyes lit with determination in the glow of the scudding moonlight.

"Nay, Sir." Dominic threw an arm out to stop him. "They know you too well. There's an advantage to being me, sometimes. Just another serving boy, scuttling around in the gloom." His mouth crooked into a grin. "Not to mention you are barely dressed."

His companion snorted a laugh and gave him the benefit of his penetrating stare. "You're brave, I'll give you that."

Dominic shrugged. "Brave or desperate. What's the difference?" He held out his hand, and Thomas clasped it. Arm to arm. A warrior's blessing.

"Well then, this I'll say. They don't guard the back anywhere near as well as they should. A stripling like you should have no trouble slipping in. Gods go with thee." He turned to the river and the rowboat. Dropping easily into position, he reached for the oars. Dominic bent to help the man cast off, tossing the rope in a neat coil to him for use on the far bank. Thomas lifted a hand in salute and bent to the oars.

"Good Sir," Dominic called as he departed, "should I fail in this, tell the Queen I tried."

"Stay fast to yourself, lad," Thomas called back, his voice carrying clear across the choppy water. "'Tis all you can do."

CHAPTER FOURTEEN

The back of Tremble's gambling den lay in dank darkness, half hidden behind the overhang of the first floor. Faint lantern light flickered at the edges of peeling shutters on both levels. The yard stank of night soil and rubbish. Holding his cloak over his nose to stifle the stench, Dominic dodged the midden to press against the slimy wall. A lowering drizzle continued to weep from the sulky clouds, stirred up by a northerly wind. Crouching, he edged closer to the door, straining his ears for some clue to what lay within.

A jumble of arguing voices and the clunk and clang of stacking dishes trickled through the roughly hewn planks.

"Get moving, you lazy rascal, do ye want the customers pouring their own drinks?" Rough as stone, the speaker's tone grated on his ears. "And get back in here as soon as you're done. Tremble wants his money's worth tonight, and so does the lady."

"Aye," the underling's tone, sullen and sulky as a soot-choked fire-place, had Dominic biting his lip. He'd get no good welcome in that kitchen. He stepped back into the yard and strained his eyes in the dim light to see what other points of entry there might be. To his left, a door, hardly up to his shoulder, set low against the wall. A cellar, Dominic guessed, or storage for the use of the kitchen. No good to him. He tilted his neck and scanned the upper storey. Four chambers and four windows at the back that he could see. Three of them candlelit, one in darkness. He huffed a sigh, his heart sinking. Only one way in. He'd have to climb the wall.

The mere thought of it sent a shudder through him. He wiped his clammy palms on his cloak and peered regretfully at the battered back door. Chewing his lip, he edged his way to the far side of the building and surveyed the crumbling stonework. Flecks of old mortar speckled the soot-stained surface, as well as more treacherous moss. Wiping his hands again, he placed a trembling foot on the edge of the lower wooden sill and levered himself upwards, pressing hard against the rickety shutters. His fingers felt for the edge of the windowpane, his free foot waving wildly in the air for a second as he gained his balance. His pulse thudded loud in his ears as he crept a hand upward, searching for finger holds in the ancient stone. Above his head, the elaborately carved overhang of the first storey jutted, black as a dead tooth. He swallowed and reached for a handhold to his left. He'd have to aim for the edge of the building and go around it. His fingers found a crevice and clamped onto it. One foot, then the other, scrabbled madly for toe holds as he edged his way up. He froze as his new scabbard scraped against the top of the shutter. Sweat cascading down his back, he waited for someone to find him. Only a few feet off the ground, and already his bowel was twisting with dread. Pressing his cheek against the wet wall, he closed his eyes, flooded with the memory of another rain-filled night. His skull echoed with the never forgotten laugh of his older brother as he reached down for the new roof tile Dominic was supposed to pass to him. Except that he hadn't. Heaving the heavy slate against his chest and lifting it above his head, the rain in his face had stabbed at his eyes, blinding him. He'd wavered on the slippery ladder as he levered the piece upwards, arms flimsy as twigs, shuddering. Grinning, blond hair slick and dark with water, Gavin had lunged to catch it and pulled himself straight off the roof and headfirst onto the cobbles. Dominic could still hear the sound of his skull cracking like a fresh egg. Fingers still clamped into their handholds, he pressed his sweating forehead against the wall. Grit scraped his skin. His shoulders ached with grief. The memory of his brother's blood pooling on the rain-washed street that fateful night made his stomach lurch.

Somewhere above him, a window opened with a creak, and he hugged the cold stone closer as the acrid contents of a privy pot hurtled past him into the yard. The window rattled shut. Wiping his tear-stained face against his shoulder, stuck halfway up a wall, Dominic huffed a bark of ironic laughter that bordered on hysteria. Gavin would have earned drink after drink for this tale were he still alive to tell it.

"Slowly, slowly," he muttered to himself as he spread his knees and pushed upwards, left hand crawling, seeking blindly for its next secure position.

He mouthed a curse as his knuckles struck solid wood. The overhang. There was little to cling to. The carving crumbled under his fingertips, the wood slippery. It jutted over his head by a foot, casting him into its shadow. Swearing under his breath, he felt for more finger and toe holds. Bit by bit, he eased himself to the corner, where he could pull himself up and past the narrow boundary between the floors. He edged cautiously along it, conscious of the yawning gulf at his shoulders. He'd shuffled more than halfway along, aiming at the far room, where not a pinprick of light showed when his foot found a rotten piece and went straight through it. Flailing like a lure in a high wind, his arms shot out to catch at the casement of the third window. Shards of wood fell away to clatter against the cobbles below. At the front of the building, he thought he heard the hound bark, and sure enough, the mastiff's scrabbling claws sounded on the cobbles below. He risked a glance down and wished he hadn't. The dog squatted directly beneath him, head cocked, tongue lolling. It eyed him with interest, but strangely, it didn't make a sound. Instead, it panted. Quite happy to wait.

Dominic glanced to his right, stifling a groan. He still had several feet to travel, and the flimsy balustrade looked even more rotten at the centre. About to risk one more step, pain erupted in his forehead with a ferocity that took him completely by surprise. He winced at the blare of voices as they exploded into his mental hearing. They seemed to come from everywhere. From every building in his immediate vicinity and from much further away. A babble of disconnected thoughts, arguing, complaining, praying, hoping, despairing. They swarmed him like a wasp nest disturbed. Stinging him, demanding his attention. Overcome with fear, he shook his head to dislodge them. One foot slipped into thin air, then the other. He grabbed the window pane, fingers sliding uselessly down the lead panels. It was over. He'd fall. Just as he always knew he would.

"By the Gods, Dominic Skinner."

One female, disembodied voice, loud and clear, piercing through the clamour of the rest. A slim, sure hand darted from the window to his left and grabbed his windmilling elbow, dragging it over the Gods'-blessed sill. Desperately, he gripped it, the solid surface welcome under his clutching fingers, heaving breath into his panicking lungs.

His rescuer tangled both hands in the folds of his woollen cloak and heaved. Dominic tumbled headfirst, not to the dreaded cobbles but to the smooth wooden planks of an elaborate bed chamber. Panting with effort, he rolled to his back and opened one eye. His rescuer's face swam before him. White as milk, terrified. She cast a glance behind her, to the sumptuous bed hung in drifts of aqua silk. A loveseat, embellished with fine carving and inlaid with mother of pearl took advantage of the crackling fire. A light, salty scent hung in the air, fresh as the breeze wafting from the ocean, the essence of rain.

"Quick," Felicia said. "We don't have much time."

"What? You?" Dominic managed, blinking in the dim light shed by the fire.

"No time. Come on, Up. Up!" Felicia all but snarled at him. Her determined fingers hauled on his cloak. "Dominic, get up!"

Head reeling, he scrambled to his feet. Disembodied voices still circled in his mind like hungry vultures. He staggered, blundering against the wall, panelled and unusually sumptuous, considering the state of the rest of the building. Felicia dragged him to the door and cracked it open. Footsteps and the husky laugh of a practised courtesan breathed carnal promise from the nearby stairwell. Music and muffled voices filtered up from the gambling rooms. The same salty scent drifted towards them.

"She's coming, move. Come on!" Felicia hissed, herding him into the narrow corridor. Hugging the wall, she headed for the empty chamber Dominic had been aiming for from the outside. Drained, he followed her as she darted in, snicked the door shut, and turned the key.

"You make enough noise to wake the dead," she whispered, looking down her dainty nose at him, "and you stink." Fumbling in the dark for a flint, she held a light to a single candle. Its feeble glow illuminated plain panelling, a single chair, and one bed piled with slightly grubby blankets. A small fire flickered dully in a tiny hearth.

"You'd stink, too, if you'd crawled around the back end of a building through a midden where people chuck chamber pots out of windows," he said weakly. "What are you doing here?"

Face grim, the girl looked him up and down. "Same as you. Looking for Guildford."

Dominic rolled his eyes, struggling to shrug off the excess telepathy. It was difficult to hear her through the clamour. "How did you get in?" He looked her over. Her dress was damp but not as wet as he would have expected.

"Through the front door, like anyone else, you idiot."

"What, they just let you in? A young girl?"

Felicia's pale face pinked a little under his disparaging stare. He noticed for the first time that she'd unbound her usual neat braid. Her hair fell in luxurious waves over her slim shoulders. The bruise on her jaw had darkened over the day. "I told them I was something else."

She raised an eyebrow, waiting for Dominic's wits to catch up.

"By the Gods!" he exploded.

She shushed him, panic written all over her face. "It got me a bed for the night, you fool. Guildford's supposed to be here, but at least they won't disturb me if they think I'm with a…"

"By the Gods, Felicia, you're only just fourteen," he said. Despite the cacophony of voices, heat crept up his cheeks.

Felicia's eyes rolled. "I had to do something," she said. She took a seat by the fireplace and withdrew a muslin-wrapped package from her cloak. Dominic squatted on a nearby stool and pressed his hands into his head. His headache tightened to a vice. He swiped a hand across his face and realised his nose was bleeding again.

"I don't see why," he said through the pain. "He deserves everything he gets." He peered at her from under his brows. Her youthful face was hard with determination.

"He's my brother," she said, as if that explained everything. "Does it hurt, the settling of your powers?"

Suspicious at the sudden sympathy in her voice, he squinted up at her, watching absently as she placed an earthenware container over the fire and tipped some contents from her package into it. She topped it up with water hanging from a flask on her belt and sat back, regarding him warily from behind a cascade of dark blonde hair.

He nodded brusquely. "Yes."

She smiled, but it didn't meet her eyes. "Good."

Something about the precise derision in her tone triggered a recent memory that set the hairs rising on the back of his neck. "Wait." He stared at her, mouth open. "That was your voice in my head just before you opened the window."

Her jaw tightened. She hid her expression by peering at the contents of the flask. The pungent smell of herbs rose with the steam. He coughed.

She shrugged. A tiny movement.

Dominic rose to his feet with an effort and tugged her shoulder until she lifted her face to him. A peculiar mixture of pride, defiance, and fear played itself out across her fragile features.

"And it was you, in the Mews, this morning. Wasn't it? And the other day?"

She bit her lip. Another shrug. "You were going to run." Her voice was so quiet he had to stoop to hear her.

She put her hand on his, her fingers icy despite the warmth from the fire. Her eyes raised, crystal grey at the edges, golden with prophecy at the centre.

"He who holds the Grayling holds the crown. You can't run now, Dominic. If you do, the falcon will die. The kingdom will fall." She blinked, and the golden haze vanished from her eyes as if it had never been, leaving him staring at the familiar grey ice.

Startled beyond measure, he took a step back. "You're not just a telepath." He shook his head, not wanting to believe it. A traitorous Wessendean, a member of the Blessed. The thought made his skin crawl.

She shook her head. A tear traced a delicate line across her cheek. "Not just a telepath."

He stared at her slender hand where it rested, light as thistledown against his own. His skin tingled at the contact. "What else, Felicia?"

She shuddered a sigh. "A Seer, I think. It's all so jumbled, it's hard to know. I hate it! I hate it all!" When she looked up, it was to plead with him.

"Promise me you won't tell Guildford or my mother," she said. "They'll kill me."

CHAPTER FIFTEEN

Dominic pulled his fingers away at the mention of Guildford and stood up, putting distance between them.

"He is here, then?" he said, voice cold. "He has the Grayling. And you knew all along?"

The girl turned her face and busied herself with her potion, swinging the bubbling pot away from the flames. She didn't reply.

"Answer me, Felicia!"

She glanced up at him, scanned his expression and then turned away, shoulders hunched. "What's the point?" she said. "You won't believe a word I say."

He watched, frustrated, as she tipped a fresh batch of water into another flask and began brewing again. He recognised that smell at once.

"Valerian," he said slowly.

Another shrug. "What about it? I take it to help me sleep, otherwise, the bloody voices and visions don't let me rest."

He blinked, remembering the unusual lethargy of her merlin in recent days. "You drugged your own bird."

Her head shot up. "I did not!"

Dominic ignored her. He paced the room, his voice rising along with his rage. "You must have done. What were you doing? Practicing the dosage to use on the Grayling so he'd keep quiet when you took him?"

Felicia glanced at the door. "I didn't take him. Keep your voice down, you fool."

He glared at her. "I'm no fool. It's time you stopped treating me like one and told me the truth. What do you need the Heartease for?"

"It takes magic away." Her face glowed a dull red in the light from the flames. "I've had the visions for months. At first, I thought they were just waking nightmares. But the telepathy part took me by surprise. It's growing stronger all the time. Harder to hide." She stopped, her face twisted with anguish. Dominic narrowed his eyes.

"Oh, don't look at me like that," she snapped. "You must know what it's like being like this. Headaches, nosebleeds, and noise all the time that just won't go away! And then it does, and your mind just feels…empty."

Dominic shook his head. "Why didn't you confide in Terrence Skinner? He'd have helped you to get on top of it. There are techniques, breathing patterns, ways to block your own energy so that other telepaths can't pick up on it and use it." He huffed a laugh as the last words left his lips. "I did not know what you were, so you must have worked that part out for yourself."

"And have the world know I'm one of you? A Blessed? Tainted by evil? Tell my mother, who already hates me and hates magic more?" She gave an exaggerated shudder and turned her attention back to her potion. "I ran out of heartease. I don't know how to suppress anything. I don't want to be like this, so I block everything with Heartease. It's easier." She picked up the flask she'd left by the hearth and swirled its contents around. "Your health."

Dominic lunged for the steaming flagon as she tipped it to her lips. "Nay, don't, not yet!" He snatched it from her and held it behind his back.

Her skin paled. "Please, Dominic. If my mother finds out, she'll kill me."

The flask bled heat into his work-hardened palm. Wincing, he transferred it to the roughly hewn table and guarded it with his own body.

"Does Guildford know you're here?"

Her gaze turned inward. "I followed him out of the castle. He's not supposed to be here."

Dominic's chest clamped. "That's no answer. You'd better tell me what's going on, Felicia. If he harms a single feather on that bird, I will kill him. And if I don't, the Queen will."

Her mouth twisted. "He wouldn't tell me. Said I was better off not knowing."

Dominic's eyebrows raised. "You and him are closer than fleas in a mattress," he said, scorn lacing every syllable. "He must have told you."

"He didn't," she argued. "I'm just trying to stop him from getting his stupid throat cut."

She glared at him, defiance stamped across her face. Dominic stared at her, trying to see behind her expression to what lay beneath and failing miserably. His head thudded like the inside of a drum.

They both froze at the clump of feet marching along the passageway. Felicia swallowed, backing away to the far wall as the handle rattled.

"You finished in there, girl? There're more customers downstairs!"

Felicia stared at the door, horror in her eyes. Dominic gathered his wits and crossed to the bed. He threw his weight on it and jumped. Hard. The frame gave a satisfying rap against the panelled walls, so he did it again.

"By the Mage. Hurry it up!"

The owner of the voice thumped his frustration on the wooden panels, but his heavy footsteps receded.

Dominic chewed the inside of his cheek as he watched relief flood Felicia's face.

"Not the greatest of plans, was it?" he said, lying back on the bed and crossing his legs at the ankles. The pillow smelled faintly of cloves and sweat. "What are you going to do? Hide in here all night? And they know your face now."

"I'll think of something," she muttered.

"There's always the window," he offered.

"So full of helpful suggestions."

He sat up. "You stay here. I'm going down. Keep the door locked."

Felicia sent him a withering look that should have skewered him to the mattress. "What can you do? You look like death."

Dominic shrugged and levered himself wearily to his feet. "Good news. I'll fit right in," he said.

Bathed in shadows, the narrow corridor outside Felicia's small room echoed the sound of muffled voices. Ecstatic groans issued from behind the thick oak panel lead to Aramida's chamber. The grunt and rhythmic slap of flesh on flesh pounded through the walls of the remaining two. Drawn by the dim haze of pipe smoke and the rich smell of hops and wine, Dominic crept to the shallow gallery at the head of the stairs. Peering down, his eyes pierced the gloom. Of the giant who had thrown Tom out, there was no sign. Two sweating musicians, one armed with a sackbut and the other piping alternately on a recorder and banging a drum, livened the atmosphere. Several narrow tables hosted various card games. From where he stood, half hidden behind an oak pillar, Dominic spotted two games of Primero and another of Noddy. Several groups played dice. The clientele comprised an eclectic cross-section of Blade's finest. Gamblers all, no matter if they wore velvets or fustian. He recognised the breed. Red-eyed in the dim light, faces clenched in concentration, the shouts of the victorious. And their counterparts, slumped in defeat, called for more ale and prepared to try again and again to win back their wealth. His eyes widened at the sums of money in front of some players, and he fingered the hidden pouch strung around his neck. Part of him itched to try his luck until he spotted one gangly sort, sporting a tall hat and a thin, lacklustre beard, palming a card into his voluminous sleeve. His mouth tightened.

A small group of servants scurried from table to table, mopping at spills, collecting empty tankards, and returning them to the bar. Creeping further down the gallery, following his target, Dominic's heart sank. The giant loomed there, his greasy, rat-tailed head almost brushing the low ceiling. He pulled jugs and tankards from the barrels lining the wall, loading them up half a dozen at a time. Muttering orders at his staff, he took money and gave change without taking his attention away from the busy gaming tables. Dominic blinked against the smoke, mesmerised by the man's efficiency as he loaded his back with an empty barrel and strode with it to the kitchen. Taking advantage of his absence, Dominic darted downstairs and into the activity. Arming himself with a couple of tankards, he drifted around the room, searching for Guildford's golden blaze of hair, but with no success. Responding with alacrity to the clicking fingers of a Primero player, his heart all but stopped when he recognised the thin black moustache and high cheekbones of Count Dupliss. Swallowing hard, he stood at the man's shoulder and placed the tankard on the wine-spotted table. Holding out his hand for money, he waited until the man pressed a coin into the centre of his grubby palm. Dominic's fingers closed around it, and he backed away. Dupliss, here, at Tremble's. Jerking his hood up, he retreated to a shadowed corner, sheltered by the line of barrels standing on their dust-covered supports to watch.

Dupliss's narrow lips twitched minutely as he studied his hand and laid his cards with great precision on the worn table. Flushed with rage, his opponent forfeited the game and pushed another mountain of gleaming coins towards him. The older man's grunt of triumph at the outcome sent shivers of irritation across the faces of his fellow gamblers. His winnings glinted like a dragon's hoard in the dull light. Dominic didn't miss the curious mixture of relief and dread in his expression as he sorted the pile of coins into fastidious piles before placing them into his purse. Bowing courteously to his fellow gamblers, he stood. Dull lantern light flickered over his narrow face, highlighting the new silver at his temples. His tunic had seen better days. The lace at the neck was lacklustre and torn. Still, he wore his tattered clothes with a sort of rebellious pride. Shoulders straight. Thin mouth stretched taut with determination. A long, straight sword hung from a richly tooled scabbard at his belt.

Dominic watched from his corner as the man left the room through a narrow door. Glancing toward the kitchen, where the giant returned with an enormous barrel of fresh ale balanced on one sturdy shoulder and a keg of wine tucked under the other, he left his slim shelter and followed Dupliss from the games room.

CHAPTER SIXTEEN

A heavy silence hung in the narrow corridor beyond the gambling den. Ornate lanterns illuminated panelled walls lined with tapestry. Dominic squinted at the scenes so meticulously embroidered on the heavy fabric and recoiled at the savagery depicted there. Heads rolled free of bodies. Dismembered limbs formed interlinked borders of tales so grisly they turned his stomach. The owner of this artwork revelled in the grotesque and the macabre. Blood and brutal death appeared to be the dominant themes. He bit his lip, starring at the row of doors along the passageway. Guildford must be mad to think he could barter with the mind that revelled in sights as heinous as this.

A pewter decanter full of wine and two heavy glasses on a tray waited on the top of a carved table. Dominic glanced behind him, but no servant appeared to transport it to its destination. He pushed his hood back, attempted to smooth his wayward hair, and reached for it, ashamed of the tremble in his fingers. Dupliss had come this way. So Dominic would have to follow. Arabella, Dupliss, the twins. All of them bound together in some sort of plot too twisted to fathom.

"What are you doing with that?"

It was a woman's voice, hushed and thick with tension. Dominic froze on the ornate carpet, the skin on the back of his neck prickling in alarm. Turning to face her, the glasses rattled on the tray.

The young woman frowned at him. In the dim light, her skin shone like wax. A straggle of fine blonde hair tangled around thin cheeks, swollen and purple with bruises. She wore silk, but the robe swamped her narrow frame.

"Who are you? I don't know you. One of the customers? You shouldn't be here. This is private." She closed the gap between them and snatched the tray before Dominic had a chance to stop her.

"Go back to the main room. 'Afore he catches you." She glanced at the door leading back to the tap room. "Quick, before he comes."

"Before who comes? The giant?"

Her dark eyes darted. "Don't let him hear you calling him that. Touchy, he is."

"What should I call him?" He took a small step towards her. Her head cocked, wary, ready to take flight. She reminded him of a sparrow, all light bones and twitter.

She stepped back, eyes wide. "Norwood, that's his name. Not from around here, are you? Or you'd know."

Her turn to shake. A puddle of wine sloshed over the rim of the pewter decanter to pool in the tray like blood.

"Gods damn it. Now look," she put the tray down on the table, fussing with the jug, using her own kerchief to blot the spilt wine.

"Everything just so, that's how it has to be," she said, almost to herself.

Dominic's heart went out to her. "Let me help you. I'll take the tray. Who's it for?"

She swallowed, her tongue flicking out to wet dry lips. He followed her gaze to the far end of the hall.

"T...Tremble." The name was a whisper, and her eyes raised to his, filled with fear. Dominic screwed up his courage. Her terror was contagious. He reached for the tray, but she backed off to the wall.

"But he's expecting me. 'Tis my task. Wait on him and stir the fire and such..."

"I'll do it. Say you're ill. What's your name?"

"Rebecca, but he won't believe you. And then he'll send for the giant, I mean Norwood, and then..."

"Leave his service, then. Surely you don't have to be here. Go to the Sign of the Falcon. Tell Jacklyn Sommerton I sent you."

"I can't, Sir," her voice dropped still more, along with her red-rimmed eyes. "He'd send Norwood after me. I'm his daughter, you see."

"By the Gods." Dominic stared at her. One salty tear dripped into a glass as she sniffed. He took the tray from her unresisting grip and watched her mop her face with the stained kerchief. Her hand shook.

"Go back to the kitchen," he urged. "I'll take this, as I said. I have business with your father."

He hoped he sounded surer than he felt. She glanced up at him, eyes still awash, and nodded once, like a puppet. Dominic waited until the door to the taproom closed behind her and set off, bowels churning with dread.

Footfall muffled by the luxury of an imported carpet in shades of red and black, he paused at each closed doorway, straining his ears for some sign of life at each one. He heard nothing until he gained the furthest portal. The rhythmic click of Dupliss's voice filtered through the thick panel. Each word was bitten off with tight precision. A whisper of a voice raised in reply, the words muffled. Swallowing heavily, Dominic knocked and slid in.

The first thing to hit him was the smell. The copper tang of a charnel house. A plush, dark Argentian carpet covered most of the floor. Furniture comprised a low table and a single wooden chair. The atmosphere was thick for lack of air, the windows shuttered. Frowning, he realised that further carpet extended up the walls in place of panelling. The unnatural smell turned his stomach. His gaze flitted to the silhouettes of two men against the wan candlelight. Tremble's reputation was greater than the man himself, he realised, with surprise.

Dupliss' tall, narrow frame dominated him for height. Two heads shorter, Tremble cut an almost childish figure beside him. A smooth mass of pale blond hair swept to shoulder length under the rim of his fashionable hat. Expensive, Argentian lace decorated collar and cuffs. Candlelight glinted from several gold rings and the heavy, embellished belt that harboured his knife. There was something of the dandy about him, but Dominic doubted many would dare laugh. A twist in the surrounding aura turned the air turgid and dark with menace.

Both men turned to face him as he stood there, the glasses chinking together caused by the slight tremor in his hands. Dupliss passed his eyes over Dominic with mild recognition but no alarm. A slight frown creased his hawkish features. Dominic averted his face, looking at the smaller man. A colourful figure with dead eyes. Tremble jerked his head at a side table.

"You should know better to disturb me before I ring. Where's Rebecca?" he demanded.

"A stomach malady, my lord. Norwood sent me instead," Dominic replied, trying to keep his voice steady.

Bowing to keep his face away from Dupliss as much as possible, he put the tray down and turned to the fire, where a sulky flame flickered. He bent to it without asking permission and stifled a grim smile as the men continued their conversation over his head.

"You must take me for a fool, Dupliss," Tremble said. There was a chink of decanter against glass. Dominic's mouth watered at the rich aroma of Argentian wine as he poured.

"Not at all, good sir, not at all," Dupliss replied, quick to reassure. "But to injure my lord of Wessendean might anger the Queen. And I have her money with me. She is more than happy to pay the lad's debts. For now."

Laying fresh wood, Dominic huffed a silent breath over the remains of the old fire, listening for all he was worth. The Queen's money? That was good.

"The boy promised me her falcon. Magical, isn't it? Worth a fortune. That was the deal. Bring me the falcon, and I won't take his balls." Tremble sounded like a child deprived of a promised treat. Voice as sulky as his fire. Playing for time, Dominic pretended to encourage it with another shallow breath.

Another clink. This time from the purse of coin. Dupliss deposited it on the table with a heavy thunk.

"Perhaps this might make up for it?"

Dominic dared a quick glance upwards. Tremble held his glass in one hand, while he raked through the piles of coins with the other, his expression murderous. Dupliss watched Tremble, his face impassive, but Dominic was aware of the tension building in the surrounding air. He turned back to the fire and fussed with the wood, grateful for the warmth as it caught, all his senses on full alert.

"I suppose." Disappointment soured Tremble's tone. Dominic's lip curled. Tyrant in his own sphere he may be, but he still had a healthy regard for the Queen's reputation, it seemed.

"So we have a deal? The table is even?" Dupliss asked. Floorboards creaked under the carpet as he took a subtle step back. The atmosphere took a sudden dip that stood every hair on Dominic's arms at alert. He forced his attention to the fire, suddenly terrified to attract attention. Perspiration slid down his back.

"Aye, apart from this."

Dupliss uttered a single squawk of alarm. A flurry of movement and the sickening, decisive sound of a blade hitting the table caused Dominic's shoulders to hunch reflexively to his ears. He flinched as something flew past him into the merrily blazing grate. Dumfounded, his eyes fixed on Dupliss' little finger as it tumbled amongst the logs. The atmosphere thickened with the reek of charred flesh. He retched as the digit blackened and twisted beneath his fixed gaze. Blood dripped and spat on the freshly stoked coals.

"You, boy." Tremble's voice was more cheerful now.

Scraping his hand across his mouth, Dominic rose unsteadily to his feet. Dupliss clutched his bloody hand to his chest, face pale but composed. He seemed to deal with the situation much better than Dominic. Their gazes clashed. Dupliss' eyes widened, then narrowed as recognition dawned. Dominic raised his chin with an effort, thankful beyond measure to feel the welcome fizz of telekinesis returning to his fingertips. Only that enabled him to face Tremble. The man had re-sheathed his knife and whistled softly as he scooped Dupliss' winnings into tidy piles. His hands moved so quickly that they blurred. Open-mouthed, Dominic recalled something he'd heard months ago from his uncle about the natural strengths of the Eperans. Blessed or not, all of them moved fast. Tremble had obviously honed his ability to almost Blessed-levels of skill. He appeared oblivious to the harm he'd caused. Apart from the terrible stench of burnt meat and his guest bleeding into the carpet, the situation could be completely normal to a man like Tremble. Realising the sour smell permeating the chamber was old blood, Dominic had to stifle the urge to vomit.

"'Twas a blood debt,' Tremble said, apparently amused at the naked horror Dominic couldn't hide. "Someone had to pay it." He jerked his head at the door. "Show my guest out," he said. "And send Norwood to me."

Relieved at the dismissal, Dominic headed for the door, not waiting to see if Dupliss followed. Itching to retrieve Felicia and escape, he fidgeted in the passageway, but Dupliss had apparently stopped to chat to his tormentor. Shaking his head, Dominic stood to one side as Dupliss emerged, still calm. His calculating, clammy gaze roamed across Dominic's face. He nodded, a smirk twisting his narrow lips, and strode down the corridor. Dominic almost trod on the heels of his worn-out boots; such was his urge to leave.

About to enter the relative safety of the taproom, he froze at the soft whisper behind his left shoulder and shuddered at the long fingers that clutched his arm through the thick wool of his tunic.

"No guest should leave so soon. Come. For the Queen's man, our hospitality is, of course, on the house."

CHAPTER SEVENTEEN

All eyes turned to Dominic before dropping hastily away as he preceded Tremble through the crowded taproom. The sackbutt player stopped blowing momentarily and then restarted his tune on a wrong note. Norwood glanced at them from his station behind the bar. He glowered at Dominic and visibly shrunk as his master's eye fell on him. Despite his predicament, Dominic gloated inwardly. Clearly, the giant Norwood's failure to identify an outsider in the closed world of the den had been a grievous error.

He hurried upstairs, taking the treads two at a time in his effort to put distance between Tremble and himself. The man kept up a running commentary as they ascended. Something about the delights awaiting him in Aramida's room. Dominic couldn't bring himself to listen. His gaze strayed the length of the corridor to the room where Felicia had, hopefully, barricaded herself. No light shone under her door. Desperate, he searched his mind for her distinctive, withering voice. There was nothing. He prayed she hadn't taken the Heartsease. Stretching his senses into her room, he found only emptiness. The would-be princess had fled.

Outside Aramida's chamber, Tremble came to a halt.

"In here. There is no charge," he said, a smooth smile creasing his cheeks. Brow quirking at the man's manner and too terrified to refuse, Dominic stepped forward. Tremble held the door for him. Risking a glance into his ice-blue eyes was a tumble into the well of madness.

Here was a different man entirely from the dead-eyed monster with a taste for blood sport. He had time to wonder what Dupliss might have said of him to cause this extreme solicitude before his attention snapped to the sight that awaited on the bed. His ready blush swept heat equally from his chest to his cheeks and loins.

A knowing chuckle rippled through the smaller man's body. There was a pause, and the woman dipped her gaze in acknowledgement of Tremble's unspoken request. She blinked once, turquoise eyes lambent and luminous as sunlit sea and nodded.

"This is Aramida. Enjoy, my lord," he said and backed out. The door snicked closed behind him. And then locked.

Throat dry, Dominic's eyes darted around the room to avoid the woman who reclined gracefully upon the mattress. The window through which he'd fallen earlier was closed against the damp breeze. A fire burned in the grate, sprinkled with so many aromatics his head spun as if he was already drunk. A familiar, salty scent overlaid even the aphrodisiacs.

"Well, sir, don't be shy. Come, sit a while. Why don't I take your cloak?"

A rippling sea of undulating curves, Aramida unwound herself from her nest. Honey-toned hair cascaded down her back. Dominic couldn't say what she was almost wearing. Something silky and half transparent. She crossed in front of the fire, a study in female beauty, and strolled to the decanter of wine waiting on an inlaid table. Seating herself on a low chair, she waved him forward, long nails beckoning, a soft smile illuminating her features.

Caught in the web of automatic desire, Dominic stumbled forward with all the grace of a newborn colt, clutching his outsize cloak like a child's comforter.

The courtesan patted the chair next to her own. He stared at it and then her, overcome with a wave of lust so intense it blocked the cackle of disembodied voices currently playing in his skull. Her smile was sleepy and encouraging. Not a threat. No, not a threat at all.

He melted into the chair and, of a sudden, found himself presented with a large measure of blue Oceanian wine served in fine Oceanian glassware. Dolphins cavorted around the bowl. He stared at it, mesmerised by the combined aroma of sea berries and apples.

"Drink, good sir, or may I call you by your given name? What is it?" Her tone was gentle, but persistent. He stared at the wine, distracted by the pulse of desire throbbing between his legs. She raised his glass further.

"Drink, why don't you? Nothing will happen, all is safe..." Her voice in his mind was like nothing he'd experienced before. It wasn't telepathy, or at least, the way he understood it. More a feeling. A promise. Siren song, he remembered dimly, through the fog of enchantment. Oceanians loved their siren songs.

One carefully trimmed nail tipped the glass upwards, pressing it insistently to his lips. Her other hand curled towards his lap under the cloak. Gentle and insinuating as a summer tide. She stroked him. He groaned.

"That's right. Relax, all is well. Trust me..."

All is well. Who else had said that to him? Another woman. Lost in a sea of sensation, his logical mind grappled for the information. He strove to ignore the cunning fingers, the warmth of her breath as she leaned in to press her high, rounded breast to his shoulder. Another woman. Someone more important than this one.

Petronella.

The Grayling.

He straightened, pushing her hand away from his lap. The courtesan lifted her head, puzzled at his withdrawal.

Dominic avoided the plunge into her mesmerising gaze and tossed the contents of his glass onto the fire. Blue flames roared up the chimney, dispelling the fug of herbs, and he jumped to his feet, one hand reaching for his dagger.

Aramida's face twisted in exasperation, and Dominic backed away from her to the door, holding his knife in front of him. He felt for the handle, but locked from the outside, it turned useless in his grasp.

"You can't escape that way," Aramida said, stalking him, her knowing smile back in place. "And you won't get out of here without giving me what I want."

"And what is that? Exactly?" One hand behind his back, Dominic tried to concentrate on moving the lock without taking his eyes off the woman before him. Powers still at their lowest ebb; it was all but impossible. Frantic, he eyed the window.

She raised her delicate eyebrows. "Why you, of course. Your youth, your beauty." She undulated closer, and Dominic ground his teeth in frustration as her siren song reached inside him to play on his senses once more. His dagger drooped in his hand, even as other parts of him leapt upwards in rampant anticipation.

"That's right," she whispered, pressing her body to his. "No need to fight your desires..." She slid a hand behind his head, her pink lips parted. Her perfect breasts grazed his chest. Dominic gritted his teeth. He wouldn't kiss her. He wouldn't...

He kissed her. She tasted of honey and apples.

She sighed against his mouth, her sinuous body moulding completely against his. Still kissing her, Dominic gave up trying to manipulate the door handle. He turned with her, pressing her body against the door with his own. All heat and curves. Her hands wound deep in his hair. Eyes closed, she didn't see him gesture madly at the window. A chill breeze at his back told him he'd succeeded.

Sliding the dagger into its accustomed position at his waist, he untangled himself regretfully from her embrace and stood back. Her turquoise eyes shone with unquenched desire, deep and dangerous as the sea.

"By your leave, mistress," he murmured.

Then, he took three steps and launched himself out of the open window.

Aramida's cry of surprise echoed into the damp night as he cartwheeled madly from the first floor. The overhang to the ground floor caught his heel as he tumbled, and he ended up sprawled gracelessly across the disgusting contents of Tremble's midden. The stench was overwhelming. Clawing rotting vegetable peelings from his face, he staggered to his feet, wincing at the pain that shot through his left ankle. Aramida leaned against the casement, a ferocious scowl screwed across her face. The fresh air cleared the fog of herbs from his brain. The storm clouds had gone, chased away by the rising wind, and beyond the uneven roofline, stars twinkled reassuringly in the navy sky.

"You're a fool!" she yelled down at him. "I'm the best there is. A lad like you could never afford me!"

Regarding her with his head to one side, he shrugged.

"When it comes to it, mistress, I hope I'll never have to pay," he said.

She opened her mouth to reply, but he turned his back, sliding from the muck to limp across the filthy courtyard. The Mage must be with him because there was no sign of the vicious dog.

Chapter Eighteen

Plucking bits of stray rubbish from his grubby tunic, Dominic hobbled away from the shadowy back alleys of Blade to the principal streets. Glancing back over his shoulder, he limped with shoulders hunched, expecting the giant, Norwood, to follow. But it seemed only Aramida's pride was hurt. He was not in debt to the gambling master. Remembering the blackened stump of Dupliss' little finger as it cooked on the red-hot coals, he shuddered. Even more astonishing was the man's stoic acceptance of his fate. And on behalf of that bastard, Guildford, to boot. He frowned, filing the thought away for later consideration.

Patting his chest, satisfied that the rest of his money was still intact, Dominic discarded the filthy cloak at the first opportunity. Reeking of offal and slimy with filth, it was hardly the best disguise. Passing strangers had already moved out of his way as he approached. Bereft of its comforting embrace, he shivered in the night air as he navigated back to the upper end of town. Pain throbbed insistently from his ankle on every step.

Away from the distraction of Aramida's presence, Eperan voices chattered inside his mind. Irritatingly loud before dying away to a soft background whisper. The soft buzz of telekinesis came and went at his fingertips, tickling, teasing. Gritting his teeth, he tried to ignore it. He'd have to reclaim the Grayling with or without a magical advantage. Part of him still wondered at what point his powers would settle and in which direction. Would the Mage grant him a goodly measure of ability or a mere trickle? Only time would tell. A wry grin crossed his face at the last thought. Coming to education later in his life had certainly set him back. Even if he became a member of the Blessed elite, it was doubtful whether he'd ever command his gift with any degree of skill. Terrence would have his work cut out.

The market post-curfew was still trading, albeit with a slightly different type of emphasis. Small tents sprung up in the gaps between their more legal daytime neighbours. Wary traders stood ready to disappear at a moment's notice, their eyes alert for the Queen's Guard. Stray dogs nosed at rubbish. Snatches of song from the nearest taverns bellied towards him on the wind, along with the tang of ale and frying sausages. Ever hungry, he joined a small line of people at a food stall to buy a meat pie and a swallow of ale to wash it down. The food warmed his frozen stomach. He purchased another cloak, smelling faintly of sandalwood and pipe smoke, and huddled into the folds of its hood. Stifling a yawn with the back of his grimy hand, he left the market, lost in thought.

He almost missed the lunge of a small shadow out of the darkness of an alley on his side. Side-stepping, the figure twisted past him, and he drew his dagger in reflex, eyes alert. A shrill giggle followed the launch of another child from his other side. Skin prickling with danger, he turned. They'd encircled him whilst he daydreamed, slipping like skeletal ghosts from the shadows. Joining ranks, they paced around him. Eyes lit, menacing and calculating as wolves. One of the many thieving gangs to roam Blade's streets at night. Cheap daggers glinted from tight fists.

"Yer money, sir," a husky female voice advised from the darkness. "Or we'll take it from thee."

Hand tense on his own knife, he cocked his head. Something about the rasp and timbre of that voice. He'd heard it before.

"Is that you, Meridan?" he said, as a slender form advanced into the halo of light shed by a torch bracketed to the side of a cobbler's shop. Her ragged shirt fluttered in the breeze. Fine hair, lighter than thistledown, wafted around a face characterised by high cheekbones sharp as knives and a delicate, pointed chin.

At the sound of their leader's name, the circle halted, wary. Dominic threw back his hood and let his grip on the dagger relax.

"Master Skinner, 'Tis you?"

The girl's voice was quiet, but distinctive. Deep and gravelly for one so young.

"Aye, what are you about? Thought you'd given up thieving. Am I not paying you enough at the tannery?" Dominic asked. He stood with his hands on his hips, shaking his head.

"Well, yay..." Meridan said, glancing back at the ragged crew behind her. "But well, there's these others, see. None of us with parents anymore, like. An' they don't have work like me."

"Shut up, Meridan. Don't talk to him." An older lad strode forward, dagger in hand. "He doesn't care about the likes of us, with his job at the castle and all."

Dominic frowned, the boy's voice almost drowned out by the press of voices swelling inside his mind. His shoulders tensed in response. Waiting for the settling of his Blessed gifts was like standing in the snarl of a gale from the northern mountains. The power alternately pummelled him and then faded, both distracting and painful. He rubbed his forehead, glancing round at the gang of thieves. They numbered about half a dozen. Ranging in age from around six to his own. Children. Orphaned by the sickness, no one to apprentice them. No one to look after them. He sighed. First things, first.

"Anyone think they're Blessed?" he asked, looking around.

The smallest, a young girl with a face like a grimy flower, stepped towards him. "Me," she said, sticking her tiny thumbs in the waistband of her baggy breeches. "They need me. I can tell 'em sometimes who's not paying attention. Like you, just then. Not always, though. It comes and goes." She scowled, obviously considering this a great inconvenience.

"Right. Anyone else?"

Silence. They looked at each other, shuffling their feet. Meridan scanned her group. "I think Pieter could be a mentomantist," she said, looking at the oldest lad.

He glared at her. "I am not. I'm a Citizen. Bloody Blessed. Who'd want to be that? All that book learning and praying you have to do."

Dominic grinned. As far as he knew, book learning was mandatory. Praying, much less so. He said as much, and Pieter glowered at him from beneath his tattered fringe.

"What do you know?" he said, sneering. "You're just like us."

"No."

Dominic breathed it quietly, and a small part of his heart clenched at the wary step back all the children took.

"But you own the tannery," Meridan said, her forehead creasing. "You're just a Citizen, like your ma and pa were."

"That's not how it works," Dominic said. "Anyone can be Blessed. Just because parents are Citizens doesn't mean the same for their children or the other way around. The Mage chooses who carries his power. He can choose to take it away, too."

"Magic's evil." Pieter's face closed colder than the ice in the northern mountains.

The youngest girl's face crumpled. "I'm not evil!" she said. "I'm not!"

Meridan rounded on the boy. "Shut up, Pieter," she said. "Magic's not evil. Little Bird's not evil. Dominic's not evil. He looks after us at the tannery as much as he can."

Pieter drew himself up to his full height, eyes flat in the starlight. "He works at the castle for the Queen. And she don't care about us, either."

The group gasped as he spat in Dominic's direction. "That for you and the Blessed and the blasted Queen," he said, wiping spittle from his dry lips. "She let us starve once she was safe on her throne. Watched us die. And now, we steal for our food. Her taxes are too high. All the Citizens hate her."

Dominic took a step back as if someone had hit him. His hand curled once more around his dagger, head thumping. Memories long buried surfaced and disappeared, forming and dissolving like clouds under the sun. Petronella, the Grayling, and the defeat of the Dark Army. And after that, her desperate negotiations with Oceanis. The anxious wait as carts lumbered up the Fool's Road laden with life-giving food. He'd been part of the army of volunteers to direct the carts onward into the depths of Blade, high into the hinterlands and the remote mountain villages. And then the sickness swept across them. It came with the carts. Some said it was the Oceanians seeking their revenge. Others that the Shadow Mage cursed the food. And the carts were slow. Too slow on the mud-clogged paths.

He clamped a fist against his heart, aware of the still-crushing weight of grief. "My parents died, too, Pieter," he said.

The boy stared at him, chest heaving against his ragged shirt. His jaw worked. He looked at Meridan for confirmation.

"Did they?"

She nodded shortly, her face grim. "I've told you before. You just don't want to hear. The Starving didn't spare anyone, Citizen or Blessed."

"So, how come he's still alive?" Pieter jerked his sparsely bearded chin at Dominic. "Course he had something to eat. Lives at the castle, doesn't he?"

Dominic shook his head. It was a mystery to him, as well. "I don't know, Pieter," he said. "We sent everything we could to the people. I would have taken my parent's illness myself rather than lose them, just as you would."

Pieter locked eyes on him, and Dominic stared back, pressing a hand to his forehead where his headache pounded between his eyes. The child thieves muttered to each other. Meridan put her arm around Little Bird's shoulders. Fresh tear stains washed the dirt from the child's cheeks. She glowered at Pieter from her place at Meridan's side.

"You're not kind, Pieter,' she said, her shrill voice cutting the tension. "All our families are dead, else we wouldn't be here. 'Tisn't the Queen's fault."

"I know what I think," Pieter said. He stared at the group and then at Meridan. Something passed between them. She raised her chin, fists clenched, but said nothing. This was an old argument, Dominic realised. He chewed his sore lip and remained silent. A muscle ground in the lad's jaw as he stared at the group, and the tension grew.

"Enough of this," he spat, finally. "You can keep your Blessed and their magic, Meridan. Carry on with the likes of him," he nodded scornfully at Dominic, "see how much they care about you. I'm for the Citizens. Enough of us there are to make a stand against them and take our dues. Who's with me?"

He raked the group with his glare. The children shuffled. Only one, a girl with a lopsided face and one shoulder higher than the other, left the circle. She pushed past Meridan and went to stand with Pieter, who did little more than raise an eyebrow at her defection.

"Anyone else?" he demanded. "What about you, Rosa, or you, Will?" The two named stepped closer to Meridan and folded their arms. Pieter's face twisted. He'd obviously hoped for better.

"You've had your say," Meridan said, "and about time, too. You're welcome to go. Don't let me keep you." Acid edged her voice.

Pieter shifted his weight. Dominic hid a smile behind his hand. Now that it came to it, the boy seemed somewhat reluctant to leave. "You're a fool, Meridan," Pieter spat.

The gang leader kept her eyes on him and shrugged. "Stay or go. It's up to you."

The group waited, the chill breeze ruffling the rags of their clothing. Little Bird huddled closer to Meridan. Will coughed. A harsh, sudden sound that broke the impasse.

Pieter's expression hardened. "Let's go," he ordered his only recruit. He turned on his heel, vanishing toward the market. The hunch-backed girl sloped after him like a faithful hound. Neither looked back.

"Welladay, good to see the back of 'im," Meridan said, but her eyes were bright in the dim light, her tone artificially brisk as she herded her gang off the street. "Come on." She glanced back at Dominic, regret sparking in her expression. "Don't worry," she said harshly. "I'll still be at work come the morn."

Startled, Dominic shook his head. "Bring these others with you. If they want. Talk to Master Sherringham. Tell him I sent them." He fumbled a coin out of his purse and flicked it to her across the narrow gap between them. Meridan's grubby fingers shot out to catch it. She held it up to the dim light of a torch, her mouth falling open.

"Go to the market. Buy them food. Warmer clothes. And you, too. Light the fire in my parent's home."

"Truly?"

Dominic nodded briskly to hide the pain in his heart. "I'll try to find 'prenticeships for them. But no more thieving. Do you hear me? Or I'll turn you in myself."

CHAPTER NINETEEN

S till thinking about the plight of Blade's orphans, and panting for breath, Dominic hobbled at speed across the rain slicked cobbles of Guild Square. Grey stoned civic buildings lined the space on four sides, each a proclamation of permanence and wealth. At this time of night, their windows were shuttered. Torchlight illuminated the handsome porticos. A solitary watchman lingered in the gatehouse of the Merchant's Guild. Huddled in his cloak, he marked Dominic's limping progress with little interest. Dominic ducked his head, following the road north to the wide streets that housed Blade's most illustrious families. It was the only part of the city unfamiliar to him.

At the head of Broad Street, he stumbled to a halt, his mouth hanging open. No wonder the poor of Blade hated the Blessed and the wealthy alike. Every residence boasted its own forecourt, hemmed with embellished stonework. The houses of the rich featured elaborate carved porticos. His awed gaze climbed the solid stone walls. Chimneys were sumptuous affairs, the status symbols of wealth. Each finely decorated stack proclaimed the owners could afford to heat the interior. No shops at ground level. Every gallery and window frame curlicued and carved. Candlelight glowed from behind expensive glass, but many houses were unlit, their occupants already abed. Chewing his lips, Dominic surveyed the height of some of them and cursed his luck, dreading the idea of more climbing. And which one was the Wessendean mansion, anyway? Pushing his hood back, he scrubbed his hands through his hair, eyes gritty with fatigue. The wind tugged at his senses and dragged his gaze upwards to the sky, where steel grey clouds raced onward, driven by the remnants of the storm. At roof height, pennants fluttered, their vibrant daytime colours silvered by the wan moonlight. His eyes widened as he recognised the bear and beaver emblem of the Buttledon family on the house closest to him.

Emboldened, he shuffled onwards, scrutinising each rippling banner, trying to ignore the pain in his left ankle. In the end, the Wessendean manor became apparent only because no pennant billowed from its roof top. Leaning on the gate, Dominic pressed his face against the hard, cold iron and searched the frontage for signs of life. The manor lay in darkness. In marked contrast to some others he'd seen, where laughter and music crept softly from chinks of shutters to liven the dull night.

The gate swung open at the touch of his hand with nary a creak. He raised an eyebrow as he entered the grounds. Four years should have been enough to rust little used hinges. Trying to keep to the shadows cast by a series of tall trees that lined a short drive, he crept up to the shuttered house.

He listened. Silence. And not just from the absence of external sound. With a jolt, he realised that the clamour of voices keeping him company most of the evening had also vanished into the ether. Shaking his head like a dog, he listened again, but nothing. No voice, no prayer, no disembodied curse or exclamation interfered with his own thoughts. A smile creased his cheeks, even as a slight dizziness washed through him, causing him to lean against the nearest support. More alarming was the complete absence of telekinetic ability. No prickle of energy tingled at his fingertips. Biting his lip, he tugged his dagger from his belt, hefting its familiar weight. This would have to do instead.

The front of the mansion lay in darkness. Dominic made his way to the corner of the building, where the boundary wall of the neighbouring property bisected their joined grounds. The gap between wall and house was narrow and clogged with ivy. He made his way as silent as a burglar, one hand on the wall of the manor, his knife hand forcing a passage through the suffocating strands of twisted vegetation. Halfway along, he stopped. The skin between his shoulders pricked and he frowned, certain someone was watching him. Twisting as best he could in the confined space, he glanced backwards over his shoulder towards the road, but there was no-one there. Somewhere in the grounds, an owl hooted. A mournful note in the night. Gritting his teeth, Dominic plodded on, his feet making little sound on the soft ground.

The manor was much longer than it was wide, but the builders had taken no account of the meandering boundary wall. Squeezing himself with difficulty along the last few feet, Dominic poked his tangled head around the corner and surveyed the back of the house.

Moonlight bathed the shadowed space in patches, highlighting a meticulous knot garden close to the rear, and extensive grounds beyond. Several figures that he mistook for people before identifying them as marble statues, stood sentinel at various points on the gravel paths. His jaw flexed. Gravel meticulously raked. Not a weed in sight. In the air, the nighttime aroma of herbs from the knot garden mingled with the scent of tobacco from a recently smoked pipe. So much for banishment. Lady Arabella Wessendean may not be strolling the streets of Blade, but she was certainly occupying the private quarters at the back of her manor, hidden from the road.

A blur of voices, raised in argument, erupted from the nearest window. Dropping to his hands and knees, Dominic crawled closer, hugging the wall, still faintly warm from the heat of the day.

"You absolute fool. I told you to bring the bird straight here, not decide to bargain with that madman who controls every gambling den and card house in Blade. Look what Dupliss has done for you. He's still bleeding!"

Arabella's voice. Thin and sharp, something about it had always reminded him of needles. It cut through the half closed pane with pointed clarity. His fist clenched on his dagger. Guildford muttered something. It didn't sound much like an apology.

"Leave the boy alone, Bella. "'Tis done with. Tremble would have had his balls if I hadn't won enough to pay him off." Dupliss this time. His clipped tone was equally memorable, albeit tinged with fatigue. Dominic wondered briefly how much blood the man had lost. He scowled in the darkness, remembering Thurgil's blanched face against the rough flags of the castle mews. However much it was, it wasn't enough.

"But your finger! Guildford, you will make retribution to your stepfather. Fetch my sewing case and clean cloth. Felicia, bring honey and wine. There is mandragora in the garden. I will need to stitch the wound."

Dominic clapped a hand to his mouth to hide his gasp of shock and missed Guildford's sulky reply. He jumped as the window opened more fully and a coil of pipe smoke curled through the air. Arabella had married Dupliss? He blinked. He'd have to tell the Queen about this.

Clutching his dagger, he raised himself to a half squat, balancing awkwardly on his sore leg, and peered through the lowest diamond shaped pane. Clothed in her familiar silver grey, Arabella paced restlessly across his vision. Her children took after her, although Arabella's hair gleamed flaxen blonde, styled in intricate ringlets that bounced as she walked. Dupliss sat on a chair half facing the fire, his narrow face waxy and clenched with pain. He still clutched his injured hand to his chest. There was someone else in the room. The edge of a shoe was visible beneath a long robe. Dominic crept further along the window, but whoever it was had taken a stance next to the window to smoke another pipe. Blue haze softened the scene, shifting slightly in the draft.

Caught up in his surveillance, trying to make out the identity of the shadowy figure, Dominic barely registered the back door open. He whirled at the tap on his shoulder, knife up and ready.

Felicia glowered at him, her expression a curious mix of resignation and alarm. She glanced at the open window and gestured grimly at the shadowed gardens, one finger pressed to her lips. Ankle aching, Dominic allowed her to lead him away, still scanning the interior for the Grayling. There was no sign of the falcon anywhere in the room.

The girl knew the grounds well. She hopped over the knot garden wall, skirted the pruned hedge that outlined a maze, and pushed him bodily into a summer house, well out of earshot. Cushions mottled with damp lined shallow stone seats. A long-ago stone mason had enjoyed himself decorating the window and door lintels in a riot of curling vegetation. No sign of the Mage here.

"I might have known you'd turn up. All of this is your fault. I hope you're satisfied." Felicia growled. Her nails bit through his sleeve like talons.

"Me? What have I done?" He stared at her. The white disc of her face was pale in the moonlight, eyes shadowed but still furious.

"You took all Guildford's money, you idiot. He owed Tremble. And now look. Dupliss is injured. My mother's furious."

Dominic's temper flared. "Your precious brother should have thought about that before he gambled with me. And Dupliss deserves to lose much more than a finger. Where's the Grayling? I know he must be here."

The girl raised her chin, mouth flattening into the stubborn line he was beginning to know too well.

"Felicia…" he said, raising the knife.

She cut him a scathing glance. "Oh, put that away. You know you're never going to use it."

"I need to get that bird back safe to the castle."

She rolled her eyes. "The Queen's precious falcon. You can stop worrying. It is safe for now."

Blood drained from Dominic's cheeks. "What do you mean, 'for now'"?

Felicia turned back to the garden, settling her slender shoulders.

"My mother has a scheme to use it to persuade the queen to reinstate her."

Dominic waved a hand at the mansion and the elaborate grounds. "Not doing too badly, uninstated as far as I can see," he said. "She's not even supposed to be in the city."

Felicia scowled. "She belongs at court. She's going mad, shut up here. And she misses Guildford."

Dominic noticed she didn't include herself, but his sympathy evaporated before the rage that boiled in his chest. His scowl matched her own. "Let her back so she can cause havoc again with her gossip and her pathetic ambition? Your mother plotted against Petronella and was happy to watch her die. She poisoned Princess Alice. She deserves every punishment she gets. The queen looks after you, Felicia. You're well kept, clothed. Given an education. I can't believe this is how you repay her."

The girl rounded on him, flint grey eyes sparking. "Yes, we're looked after, but under her rules. No status. No prospects. Just bargaining chips for our mother's good behaviour. Our father was the king. We are heirs to the throne."

He frowned, forehead creasing in pure bewilderment. "What are you talking about? The queen has a husband and a family. They are the heirs to the throne."

"Not for much longer, when Dupliss and the Citizens have their way. " Guildford said, from the garden. His light tenor sent shock waves spiralling through Dominic's bowels.

"What?" Dominic stuttered, hardly able to believe his ears.

Felicia glanced at him. For a fleeting moment, he almost glimpsed an apology in her eyes as she stepped aside from the door. In her place, her brother's broad shoulders crowded the narrow entrance. He moved with an animal grace. Light on his feet. A gentle, menacing smile lifted the edges of his mouth. He exchanged glances with his sister, who shrugged. Alight with malice, Guildford's pale eyes turned to Dominic, Dominic's skin prickled with alarm. His heart rate increased. Swallowing, he rubbed his hand against the rough cloth of his cloak, regaining his grip on the precious dagger. He lifted it, ashamed of the way it shook in his sweaty grasp.

"Felicia, what are you planning?" His shoulders hunched. Brain flooding with the memory of every beating he'd received from the younger boy's brutal fists, he took a cautious step back. Felicia watched his progress with something that looked a lot like regret. She bit her lip as Guildford squared his shoulders.

"That's for us to know. You shouldn't have come looking, Skinner. Didn't you know I would pay you back?" Guildford said, closing the distance between them. "Curiosity always kills the cat. That's what they say, isn't it? All I can tell you is the queen's days are numbered, and her progeny with her." He rolled his shoulders and removed his crimson doublet, folding it neatly before placing it to one side. Somehow, the slow deliberation of his actions bred more terror in Dominic than the rage of a mad rush.

Throat dry, Dominic's eyes darted to Felicia. She'd turned her back. Her skirt trailed behind her like the sloughed skin of a snake as she took a position a few feet away, facing the house. For a second, he thought he caught the edge of her thought, but no telepathic message made it through the dull emptiness left in his mind.

He swallowed, body already tensing against imminent pain. He lunged with his knife, but lost it when Guildford forced his arm down, twisting his wrist until he groaned, forcing him to drop it. Wrenching himself free, his eyes darted around the confined space, but there was nothing there to aid him. He flexed his fingers, willing his power to wake and drag his blade to him, but the Mage's gift remained silent. As unreachable as the moon. He backed further, eyes locked on his tormentor, clawing for the unfamiliar hilt of his new enchanted dagger in its elaborate scabbard. Too late. The back of his knees collided with the edge of the stone seat.

"Too weak." Guildford's face filled his vision, twisted with contempt. "Puny. Useless. Queen's. Pet." Guildford's heavy fists exploded against his stomach with each grunted word, knocking him back against the mildewed cushions, driving the breath from his lungs. Gasping, he struggled like a bird on a wire, twisting away. The young princeling hauled him back to his feet and threw another systematic punch to his jaw that snapped his neck back and made his head swim. Through the roaring in his ears, he heard Felicia's voice, hushed as a falcon's wing.

"Please don't kill him, Guildford," she said.

Blood boiling with sheer hatred, Dominic twisted violently to avoid another blow, snatching himself away from Guildford's grip.

"I know what you are!" he shouted at her hunched back. "When are you going to tell him you're a member of the Blessed?"

His words were lost under the hail of blows to his head, his chest, to his back. It was almost a blessing to pass out.

CHAPTER TWENTY

"I told you not to kill him." Felicia. Exasperated.

"He's still alive, isn't he? What did he mean, you're a member of the Blessed?" Guildford. Accusing.

The two voices crossed each other and echoed around his head, blurred and out of focus. Something soft cradled his swollen cheek. His searching fingers found wool. Warmth. A bed of sorts, but no mattress. The tightly strung cords of its base dug painfully into his abused muscles. They'd moved him. The room smelt faintly of damp plaster. Musty. Neglected.

His thoughts floated, much as their distant voices. Somewhere in the air above his pounding head, unreal and untouchable, an argument raged.

"You're one of them, and you never said? That's despicable." Pacing. Floorboards creaked under a pair of heavy feet.

"Guildford…"

"You know what mother's going to do when she finds out. She'll kill you." The boy's voice rang with vicious satisfaction.

"You can't tell her! Promise me you won't!" Frantic pleading. The part of Dominic that still knew what was going on allowed itself the satisfaction of gloating. His eyes cracked open, then shut again, as a lamp loomed closer to his face.

"He's waking up. What will we do with him? He knows too much."

"Guildford, answer me. Are you going to tell her?"

A pause. The lamp light against his closed lids dulled as the boy removed it to look at his sister.

"What have you got?"

The derision in his words made the Mage's blessing sound like an illness. A plague. Something nasty you caught. Every part of his body ached, and Dominic's face stung as a solitary tear trickled from the corner of his eye to his split lip. The returning tingle of telekinesis at his fingertips was no consolation. He knew if he'd had the use of his Blessed abilities during the fight, he would have used them against this boy. This Citizen. Anything to avoid the pain and humiliation he'd suffered at his hands. The Mage would have shunned him. Unworthy. Dishonourable. Just as he'd always thought. Another bleak tear trickled down his cheek to be blotted by the cloak, serving as a pillow.

"Telepathy. Farsight." The girl's voice was hushed, weighted with dread. "It's not always there. I'm too young. It hasn't settled yet," she said, in a rush, hastening to reassure. Hardly daring to breathe, Dominic could only imagine the contemptuous expression on her brother's face.

Guildford took his time to reply, but when he did, his tone was implacable. "Blessed or not, you must pick a side," he said. "I have to know for when we fight. Whose side will you be on?"

"You're my brother. Of course, I'm on your side," Felicia said. Her voice trembled.

Her twin snorted. "And yet you run after him. The Queen's lap dog, Sir Skinner, blessed by the Mage. What do you see in him, Felicia? He's a peasant, no matter his fancy title, and you're the daughter of a King."

"The illegitimate daughter of a dead King," Felicia pointed out.

"Still with a claim to the throne," Guildford persisted. "Doesn't matter whether we're Blessed. The Eagle blood still runs in our veins, and Terrence Skinner told me once that's all that matters. And we have the people on our side. They don't want the Blessed lording it over us again."

"Petronella doesn't lord it over anyone," Dominic mumbled through swollen lips, unable to help himself.

He shrunk into the bedstead as Guildford whirled towards him, fist raised. "No one gave you permission to speak, you snivelling little pissant," he hissed.

Felicia clamped her hand on her brother's arm before it descended.

"Leave him alone. He's not going anywhere. Look at the state of him. What can he do?"

Dominic forced himself to keep his eyes open as the younger boy glanced at him. The contemptuous expression on his face was the same as the castle cook's when she discovered weevils in the flour.

"Pathetic. Not much use, is he? As for you," Guildford jerked around and made for the door. "I'll never be on your side. I want nothing to do with you or your sort. You're tainted. Poisoned. One of them. Like him."

Felicia gasped. "I didn't ask for it. Don't tell her, Guildford. Please don't." Her soft voice was pitiful to hear, smudged with tears.

Silence. Guildford stared at her, uncertainty clouding his expression. The door clicked shut, leaving them alone.

Felicia's image blurred before him. A slight figure, pale-faced in the lamp glow. She wiped her wet cheeks on a pristine kerchief and lifted a shallow bowl from a low table. The bed dipped as she seated herself at his side.

He winced at the touch of cool liquid against his battered face and turned his head to stare at the wall. Rough plaster. No fine guest room, this.

"Leave me alone. You're a traitor." His voice came out as a croak. Even breathing was painful. He'd probably cracked a rib. Maybe two.

Felicia ignored his words. "This will help. It's comfrey and arnica."

Whatever the infusion was, its touch soothed his swollen skin. He mumbled something incoherent as she rolled him over, unlacing his tunic with the dexterous fingers of an experienced sempstress. She hissed under her breath at the sight that greeted her and continued her ministrations.

"He really did his best to you this time," she said, reaching further around his body to track the swollen path of the bruising.

"No thanks to you. You just stood there and let him do it."

A faint flush stained the smooth skin of her cheeks. She bit her lip. "I couldn't have stopped that. He's been wanting to beat you to a pulp for months. Better to get it over with."

Dominic tried to pull his battered body away from her and failed. "Better to get it over with? Are you serious?"

She shrugged and continued chasing the injury pattern under his skin with the cloth. The bruise on her own jaw had purpled over the day. Dominic put his hand over hers, halting her. His fingers tingled at the contact.

"He hit you as well, didn't he?"

Shamefaced, her eyes lifted to his. "He took the Grayling on our mother's orders. She told him to come straight here, but he wanted to go to Tremble's with it instead. I waited for him at the spring. We argued. I tried to snatch the bird's cage. He hit me and then rode off. He took my horse with him."

Dominic frowned. "So how did Dupliss end up at Tremble's instead?"

Felicia huffed a laugh. "He used to be Falconridge's second, remember? Still has spies in every camp, friends in the Queen's Guard. There's a reason he drinks at the sign of the Black Eagle with the soldiers. He and my mother have been livid about Guildford's debts for months. You know Guildford. It's easy to follow the track of his mind. All Dupliss had to do was intercept him and remind him that even with money, Tremble would still want his share of blood."

Dominic clenched his aching jaw, eyes watering at the dull thud of pain.

"Dupliss was a fool. He should have let Guildford go in. Find out what it means to be on the losing side for a change."

Felicia rolled her eyes, dipped her cloth into the infusion, and held it against his cheek. "My brother holds grudges almost as much as Tremble does. I tried to warn you. Don't move, not yet," she added as Dominic's body jerked in instinctive denial.

Silence bled between them. Dominic's headache blazed between his eyebrows, and the endless chatter of mental voices returned to blare through his mind once more. Sighing, he levelled his breathing, trying to bring the gift under control.

"What hour is it?" he asked her.

Felicia shrugged. "Around midnight," she said.

He nodded, overwhelmed with fatigue. It was near time for the Mage to decide.

"Your mother married Dupliss?" he asked, half asleep.

Felicia's hands jerked. "Match made by the Gods." Her words were light but held a wealth of meaning. Dominic's battered wit was not up to the task.

"Why were you at Tremble's?"

She smiled. Despite the bruise, the expression transformed her face. "Oh, that's easy. I had to be there. Someone had to stop you from falling off that wall."

Dominic gaped at her. She used the cloth to close his swollen jaw. 'Tis erratic, but Farsight can be useful," she said, her breath soft against his cheek.

He shook his head. "I can't work you out," he said. "You tried to stop him at the spring but refused to tell me what's going on. You stop me falling to my death, but let your brother half kill me. And now you're here, patching me up. Whose side are you on, really?"

She paused, cloth suspended, grey eyes flickering to gold in the dim light. Dominic lifted a hand to wipe splashes of potion from his chest. She seemed to have forgotten where she was, thoughts a thousand miles away. His skin prickled. He touched her damp hand.

They both jumped as the door opened. Felicia blinked and dropped the cloth with a splash into the bowl as her brother entered.

"Properly awake now, is he? And you tending his wounds. So loyal to us, Felicia," he mocked, crossing the room to loom over the makeshift bed. Felicia stood, returning the bowl to the table with a thud that slopped liquid over its edge.

"You've beaten him to an inch of his life, Guildford. What more do you want?" The golden light of Farsight disappeared from her eyes. She settled her hands on her hips, and Dominic drew the laces of his damp tunic together, attempting to sit and failing.

Guildford looked him over and smirked. He shrugged. "One skinny peasant's life, more or less. What does it matter?" he said. He jerked his chin at the door. "Our sainted mother wants you. Don't worry," he added at Felicia's stricken expression. "I didn't mention your affliction. Or him. Yet. Want no more hysteria from mater."

Felicia glowered at her brother as he ushered her out. At the door, she turned. Her gaze clashed with his.

"Get out of here before Guildford finishes you for good. Drink what's in that jug by the window. It will help, I promise."

Dominic's eyes narrowed. His mental voice chased her down the passageway, following the disappearing footsteps.

"What's in it?"

"Poison, of course."

"Felicia..."

He could almost see the despairing glance she sent to the ceiling.

"By the all the Gods, it's for pain, you complete idiot. Don't do anything stupid."

Her voice vanished. Dubious, Dominic twisted his head with difficulty to the window on the far wall only a few feet away. The room had grown chilly. The cord bed underneath him was cushioned only by his own cloak. Gritting his teeth, he prised himself upright, perspiration breaking out on his forehead. He pulled at the laces of his tunic, tightening it against his battered ribs as much as he dared. Rough plaster walls swam around him as he gained his feet. Bracing himself against the edge of the bed, he raised his hand to the earthenware jug on the floor. At a low ebb, power prickled at his fingertips, and the flagon scraped reluctantly towards him across the rough floor.

"Come on," he willed it, "By the Gods, I can't come to you."

It took time, but somehow, he raised the wobbling flask to grabbing height. Suspicious, he sniffed at the contents, only to be greeted with the familiar herb-green scent of willow bark and tassel bane. He tested it with his tongue, but it seemed Felicia had not been lying to him this time. Just a simple pain relief potion, albeit a hefty dose.

He saluted the door.

"Your health, maid of mystery," he muttered, lifting it to his lips.

The strength of Felicia's potion almost knocked him sideways. Fighting a gag as it threatened to erupt from his stomach, he blundered painfully around the room, searching for water to rinse the acrid taste from his mouth. One circuit was all it took for his tongue to numb, and there was no water. He stumbled against the narrow cot, clutching his heaving belly, and willed the medicine to stay where it was. Sweat broke out across his forehead. Every muscle ached.

Outside, the owl called. A solitary two-note melody played on a mellow flute. A stiff breeze played through the half-open shutters to touch his sweating neck. Aware of being watched, his bleary gaze lifted to the window, and a chill crept down his spine. A white owl perched on the sill. Silent. Huge yellow eyes focused and hypnotic, feathers pure white. It glowed with a light all its own.

Lured by its majestic beauty, Dominic approached, mouth dry, marvelling that the bird showed no fear. The tangle of voices in his head grew louder, the bird's gaze more compelling. The tingle of power in his fingertips increased to alarming levels of intensity. It climbed from his fingers into his palms. Further up his arms, to his chest. The voices in his head swelled. Shouting at him, demanding attention, and he fell to his knees, clapping his fizzing hands to his ears in a vain effort to reduce the pressure. Blood trickled freely from his nose, and still, the bird stared, dragging him out of his own skin and into the vastness of a world beyond. Dominic felt himself float, grateful to leave his pitiful, hurting self behind in the tiny, dank room. Alive and lighter than a feather, he flew beneath the determined gaze of an all-seeing God. Soaring through the cool night sky. Turning beneath the dizzy stars, the Mage toyed with him, keeping him aloft and buoyant on the updraft of his own creation. Dominic circled higher and higher still. Until the city of Blade lay remote below him. Turning his head, he saw the world stretched below him in every direction. Pin pricks of light scattered the surface of the land. Other Blessed souls going about their daily lives with a touch of mage-magic in their veins. Safe in the hand of the God, Dominic felt their presence. Bonded to them in a way he had never believed possible. He could see the connection between the Blessed of Epera. It danced in the cool air, a wave of pulsing, silver light. It found his heart. Sought his mind. The pressure built to a painful blur of noise and sensation, heat and cold, so intense he could hardly bear it.

Somewhere, a decision was made. Agreement was sought. A contract forged. Tears streamed down his cheeks as the communication dimmed, and the voices in his mind faded to a manageable level. The buzz of telekinesis settled in his palms, warm and comforting. Constant, as it had never been before. The room turned around him. He could have been kneeling there, locked in painful, glorious communication with this power for centuries or seconds. He couldn't tell.

The great white owl blinked. The spell broke. Dominic scrubbed his sodden cheeks with his sleeves. He remained kneeling even when the bird swept silently into the night, staring at the space it had occupied, his mind in turmoil, dull with fatigue.

One by one, he turned his hands over and studied them. Filthy with grime and blood, they looked no different. Biting his lip, he extended his hand to the bowl of potion Felicia had left. Her soaked kerchief floated effortlessly towards him, and he hooked the cloth from the air. The potion soothed his hot cheeks, and he used it to wipe blood and sweat from his face. Climbing stiffly to his feet, he limped to the bowl and washed his hands, blinking at the unfamiliar pink of his freshly cleansed palms. There. If he looked closely. The sign of the Mage pulsed faintly beneath his skin. He glanced back at the window and hobbled to it, leaning on the sill, searching the night for any sign of the great white owl in the midnight sky. Nothing, except the cool hush of wind through the trees and the silent gaze of stars. Strangely terrified, his memory replayed in gut-wrenching detail the never-forgotten face of his older brother as he tumbled to his death. His hands tightened on the window frame.

"You've made a mistake. I'm not worthy," he whispered.

CHAPTER TWENTY-ONE

O vercome with exhaustion, Dominic eyed the door impatiently, waiting for Felicia's potion to do its work. He found his old dagger tucked into his belt, probably returned to him by Felicia at some point. More curious than ever now his Blessed gifts had settled, he slid his new enchanted blade from its elaborate scabbard. It shone in his palm. Mage-light chased the delicately etched runes of its razor-sharp surface. He traced his fingers over them before returning the knife reluctantly to its leather cover. He did not know how to make it work or what it would do, and he'd better not risk finding out.

Another few minutes and the ache in his ribs dulled enough to allow easier movement. He shook out his cloak, refastening it around his shoulders. Felicia had even collected his satchel. He found it pushed under the narrow bed. Brow quirking with bemusement, he shrugged it over his shoulder and cracked open the plain wood door.

The shadowed service corridor smelled dimly of roasted meat and honey. Stone flags led the way into the manor kitchen, silent and dark. A carefully banked fire glowed sullen red in the dark. Dominic crept like a sleepwalker in the unfamiliar space, hands out in front of him, feeling for obstacles. A door in the far wall led up a short flight of stairs into the main part of the house. He pressed his ear to it but heard nothing through the thick oak. Taking the deepest breath he could, he closed his eyes and cast his mind out to the wider environs of the house. Felicia's thoughts were a river of fear that he couldn't let himself swim in. She was the only other telepath in the vicinity. Nothing to pick up from any other inhabitants.

But the Grayling was here, somewhere. He had to be.

Slowing his breathing was hard. Slumped against the rough wood, Dominic's head drooped on his shoulders as he extended his mind to reach across the manor. There. A pinprick of awareness. His heart raced, and he cursed as he lost the connection. Panic wouldn't help. Steadying his breathing, he forced himself to relax, uncurling his fingers, letting his arms dangle from his shoulders.

"I'm here. Show me where you are."

The Grayling's signal was so faint he could hardly trace it. His mouth thinned. The bird was upstairs somewhere, still hooded and blind. Hungry. Afraid. Near death.

Jaw clenched, Dominic searched the dark kitchen for food. One door led to a pantry full of goods. A wheel of Blade's finest cheese stood no chance against his dagger. He dropped a hefty wedge into his haversack and grabbed the heel of a loaf from a plate. At a pinch, the Grayling would eat cheese, but somewhere, in a manor this size, there would have to be a hanging larder. Sweeping his hands across the shelves, trying not to disturb anything, his searching fingers encountered a jug. A quick inhale confirmed a welcome draft of small beer. He gulped it down, wiping his mouth with the back of his hand, and returned the empty flagon to the shelf, backing out of the larder in search of fresh meat.

He found the cellar steps by accident, stumbling over a sack of flour left by a careless servant. Cold air swept towards him, along with the sweet, ripe smell of hanging game. His lips lifted in a grim smile as he tiptoed down, one hand still pressed to his cracked ribs. Felicia's potion did a sterling job but could not entirely prevent the cutting edge of pain down his left side.

He felt his way between the stiff, dangling bodies with faint distaste, the smell of spilt blood sharp in his nostrils. His shrinking hands tried and tested each that blocked his way. Here, the blunt outline of a pig, a little further, a deer, yet to be skinned, its hide slick and damp under his palms. He swallowed nausea, making his way around the larger animals to the edges of the room. Feathers stroked his cheek, and he jumped, mind still stamped with the impressions of the mage attending his Blessing in the guise of an owl.

Blindly, he fumbled a small, fragile body from its hook. Pigeon, or something similar. That would do. He dropped it into his sack and edged his way back through the cold, dim room to the wooden stairs, glad to put the dead eyes behind him.

Creeping out of the kitchen, aiming for the stairs, Arabella's shrill voice floated to him through the half-closed door of the parlour.

"Is it true what your brother says? Answer me."

Dominic paused in the corridor, one hand on the smooth, burled wood of the banister rail winding its way upward into the gloom. The sound of a brutal slap and a muffled yelp of pain drew his eyebrows together like a thunderclap.

"Answer me, I said!"

"Leave her alone, Arabella. If she's Blessed, there's nothing to be done. It changes nothing. She knew what she had to do." Dupliss' icy tones sent a shiver across Dominic's shoulders. Spare, concise. As clipped and neat as the man himself.

"Felicia, are you well? What did you have to do?"

No reply. Dominic cast a yearning glance at the upper storey. He should leave them to it and find the Grayling, but the thought of Felicia in danger stopped him in his tracks. He moved closer to the wall and used a whisper of his power to edge the door further open, craning his stiff neck sideways to see past it into the room. Arabella's silk gown drifted across his narrow range of vision as she paced. Her shadow danced across the lamplight. Dupliss had not moved from his chair. The contents of Arabella's sewing basket littered a small table at his side. Her needle case lay open. The heavy scent of mandragora wafted out to meet him.

"Guildford is right, for once. We must hear from her own lips what side she is choosing to take in our fight for the throne," Arabella insisted, her tone harsh. Another slap, and a gasp from Felicia.

"I'll make you talk, miss." Alarm sparking in his veins, Dominic took an involuntary step towards the door.

"Don't use your needle, mother. Put it down. She's on our side. Aren't you, Felicia?" Guildford's voice held an imploring note. Dominic's sore jaw tightened. Unusually, the boy sounded frightened.

"I'll hear that from her own lips, or I'll sew them shut for good." A scuffle took place out of his range of vision.

"Mother! Put that down!"

"Arabella, what are you about? Stop it at once."

Guildford and Dupliss spoke across each other. Dominic's fingers dug painful crescents into his sweaty palms. He itched to blast the door wide open and confront them all. To do so would condemn the Grayling to whatever horrible fate they'd planned for him. As the argument continued, his body trembled with the need to contain his anger.

"You don't have to worry, mother. I've carried out my part." Felicia's soft voice cut through the tension. Dominic's jaw clenched. She sounded as if she was forcing the words out through gritted teeth. A pair of pale, narrow hands busied themselves at the low table, collecting the scattered sewing kit. Arabella's words were as sharp as her needles as she thrust the implements into the box. "You'd better do what you are told, or I'll make you pay for it. Nothing but trouble, Felicia. That's what you've always been. And now we know why, don't we? Blessed by the Mage, like our saintly Queen, Gods rot her." She slammed the lid shut.

"It could be a good thing, my dear," Dupliss said. "Do not be so quick to judge."

"Don't be a fool. Magic is never a good thing. Petronella killed my children's father with it. And then she killed her own father. Your friend." Arabella spat the words at her husband. "I don't know how you can forget that. And I will take her down. I swear I will. Nothing will stop me."

"There are a final few pieces to put in place, Arabella. I have despatched the message to the castle. Our forces there are waiting for our signal. Be patient. It is not yet time." Dupliss's tone bespoke his own impatience. His chair scraped as he stood, disappearing from Dominic's narrow view.

"Patient?" Dominic winced as Arabella's voice soared in pitch. "I've been patient for nearly four years, and still, I rot here while that bitch breeds more of her evil spawn. You promised me my boy would sit on the throne. And here you sit, still dressed in rags, your wealth stripped from you. And here I sit, imprisoned in my home, unavenged. My patience is at an end."

"One more day, Arabella. That's all. The Citizens are almost ready to march. We have the falcon. My message will lure Joran from the castle, and then what can she do? Left on her own up there, weakened by childbirth. Petronella's throne will topple, make no mistake about that."

"You see, mother. Everything is in hand. No need to panic."

Dominic's fists clenched at the smug satisfaction in Guildford's tone. Backing away as quietly as he could, horrified at what he'd heard, he crept to the stairwell and used the bannister rail to support his climb, cursing his injured ankle that gave way under him with painful regularity.

Below him, attempts to contain Lady Wessendean's ranting continued unabated. Arabella's voice hitched ever higher the more her husband added his point of view. Dominic shook his head. The woman sounded unhinged. His satchel bounced against his hip as he gained the landing and paused, glancing around. Bedchambers o this level, he guessed. Instinct dragged his eyes upward to the attic and the servant's quarters. A narrow stairwell at the end of the corridor turned in on itself and led to a sturdy door. He nodded in grim satisfaction, reaching for the iron handle. As he expected, locked.

"Felicia, where's the key to this room?" He projected the image to her along with his thought.

"My room. Second door on the left. You'd better hurry. She'll be asking someone to fetch the Grayling to her once Dupliss has calmed her down."

Not really expecting Felicia to reply, he couldn't prevent the tingle of satisfaction that shot through him when he heard her voice in his mind. He retraced his steps to the first floor. Felicia's room was much like herself. Small and almost obsessively neat. He hovered uncertainly on the threshold, letting the moonlight show him the contents. A washstand and basin occupied the area under the narrow window. Colourful woollen blankets covered the bed. A large oak trunk, much like his own, took up valuable floor space at its foot. A couple of cloaks hung ghost-like from wooden pegs in the wall. The faintest scent of valerian and Heartsease tickled his nostrils. He rubbed his nose, stifling a sneeze. No key on any of the visible surfaces, so trunk it would have to be.

He approached cautiously, almost embarrassed to open the lid. It seemed a terrible violation of privacy to go ransacking the contents of a lady's coffer. He reached out a hand, then snatched it away.

"Is it in your trunk?" he asked.

"You have my permission to open it, Dominic."

His mouth crooked into a crooked grin. That exasperated tone was more like the Felicia he knew. He raised the lid.

The smell of herbs lingered amidst the well-ordered contents. He bit his lip as he rummaged, conscious of the roughness of his palm amid the delicate frippery of a woman's life. Hoods and sleeves. A dish of pins. The crisp smell of freshly laundered linen. A spare nightgown.

At the bottom, his searching fingers closed on something more solid. The key.

Sighing with relief, he let the coffer latch shut and lurched back to the upper storey.

The key turned easily in the lock, and his hands trembled, his eyes darting around the open space of the attic. A chill breeze crept to him from a half-open window set high in the eaves. Thick oak beams criss-crossed the roof above his head, sensed rather than seen in the dim light. He stumbled forward, ears pricked. Heavy curtains hung at intervals from the beams, demarcating spaces large enough for a rough pallet and little else. This must be where the manor staff slept, he guessed. But now, the space felt almost unoccupied. Except for there. Pushed hard against the back wall. A bird cage.

He leapt towards it, almost forgetting the pain in his muscles, straining his eyes against the dim light.

The Grayling was sleeping, hooded head tucked into his feathers. Dry-mouthed, Dominic reached into his satchel for the dead pigeon. He whistled softly, and the bird came awake with a chirp of alarm, launching himself from his perch. He came up short from the jesses attached to it and bated, beak open.

"I know. You're hungry," Dominic said, sliding the cage door open. He plucked at the ties of the bird's hood, and the Grayling snatched at the limp body, tearing it from his hand and taking it to the bottom of his cage. Watching him devour the carcass, Dominic's shoulders relaxed for the first time in what seemed like forever. He lowered his forehead to the delicate metal bars, struggling to hold back tears of relief. The bird was there. Alive. Eating. All he had to do was warn the Queen and return to the castle.

.

CHAPTER TWENTY-TWO

Waiting for the starving falcon to eat, Dominic squatted by his cage and dropped his chin to his chest.

"Your Maj,"

Now he'd received the Mage's gifts in full, the telepathic connection between them thrummed with energy. He saw it as a delicate silver thread, reaching from his mind to hers. Accustomed to her instant answer, he frowned in the darkness, all his senses alert for danger.

There was nothing there.

He forced his head against his chest and tried again, pushing urgency to her through the ether. *"Your Majesty, it's me, Dominic."*

Still nothing. Not even a sense of her presence, let alone the sound of her mental voice. Throat dry, he swallowed. Panic fluttered in his chest like the wings of a dying bird. Had something happened? Was the birth too hard? Had she died?

"Petronella, please, answer me," he begged, struggling against the sob that clogged in his throat. *"They are coming for you. I've got the Grayling. Tell Joran to stay with you. He must not come to Blade."*

Nothing. Biting his lip, he tore his mind from his connection to her and concentrated on Joran instead. He'd never tried to contact the Prince using telepathy, and, sure enough, his mental quest bumped hard against a firm block. He scrubbed his hand through his hair. Unsurprising really. The last thing the Prince Consort would want was an open channel to any nosy telepath.

Clambering to his feet, he grabbed the cage. Still eating, the falcon eyed him from the remains of the pigeon and uttered an annoyed chirrup as his shelter lurched.

"Sorry, lad, we have to go," Dominic muttered.

Hoisting his satchel over his shoulder, he limped down the narrow stairs to the next floor. Heavy footsteps on the main staircase sent him darting for the dubious security of Felicia's room. Creeping in he pressed himself against the door, trying to muffle his breathing with his cloak. The Grayling hunched his wings over his supper and continued to eat. Pausing only long enough for the stranger to reach the attic stairs, Dominic crept to the ground floor, hugging the shadows, heart in his mouth. The conversation in the parlour had moved on. He caught random snatches of it as he retraced his steps to the kitchens. Something about infiltrators in the queen's guard up at the castle. And the number of Citizens ready to ambush Joran and whatever force he brought with him. He shuddered. The grubby taint of betrayal followed him to the kitchens, and he quickened his pace through the sullen darkness, stumbling over the knot garden in the cool, damp night.

Detouring further into the grounds to avoid being seen from the parlour window, his heart leapt in his chest at the scream of rage that echoed from the parlour, swiftly followed by Felicia's urgent mental command.

"Where are you? Get out of here, Dominic. They know he's gone."

He took off into the darkness, away from the manor, the Grayling's cage swinging wildly with his lurching stride, his satchel bumping awkwardly against his thigh. The wind sighed through the black tree-tops, bringing with it the scent of night flowers and rain. He splashed across a narrow stream, dodged round a final statue, and all but careered into the thick brick wall that marked the far boundary. Glancing back, he smothered a gasp as the wavering burn of several rush lights spread out behind him to swing in wide, sweeping arcs across the manicured space. Squinting in the dim light, he scraped his hand along the boundary wall; the bricks damp and solid beneath it.

"There's no way out, Skinner. You may as well give up!"

Guildford. The boy's laughter drifted on the breeze, smug with the certainty of success. He appeared to be heading the search from the middle of the hunting party. Scuttling like a five-legged crab along the rear boundary, Dominic renewed his efforts, but it appeared the young nobleman was correct. No back gate of any sort. Pausing under the spreading branches of an ancient yew, hidden by its bulk, he heaved a breath. Mage power bloomed from his fingers as he locked his gaze on the Grayling's cage. The bird chirruped uncertainly as his shelter rose smoothly into the air and drifted in a gentle arc over the wall. Chewing the inside of his cheek, Dominic turned his back on his pursuers to concentrate on a soft landing for the falcon on the other side. Satisfied no harm had come to it, he turned his reluctant gaze to the tree. Its twisting trunk offered a dizzying array of footholds. Thick foliage trembled only a few feet above his head. As trees went, it was almost inviting someone to climb it. Clenching his teeth, he stretched against the gnarled trunk, hissing at the pain in his abused ribs. His toes scrabbled for footholds as he edged his way upwards, too scared to take his eyes off the twisted, dusty bark mere inches from his nose. An orange glow flowed across the rough grass below his feet as rushlight pierced the shadows. Stomach muscles straining, he pulled his legs up, pressing uncomfortably into the scratchy, concealing canopy of leaves. Water dripped down his neck. He shivered.

"Come on, Skinner. I know you're here somewhere. You may as well give up. There's nowhere to go."

Guildford came to a halt under the yew. Hunching his shoulders, melting against the trunk, Dominic willed the tree to cover him. He almost lost his perch at the unexpected tickle of leaves on his exposed neck. Guildford's torch light dimmed as the yew quietly spread its foliage to shield him. Pressed hard against its ancient wood, Dominic breathed silent gratitude into the bark, his mind reeling with amazement.

"Anything?" Guildford called. He waved his torch in a frustrated circle. Dominic hid a smirk against his arm.

"Nothing my lord."

Guildford's companions joined him under the yew, the noise of their boots muffled by the soft ground. A waft of tobacco followed the familiar scratch of a flint. The heat from the combined torches warmed Dominic's chilled feet.

"He must have come this way," Dupliss snapped. "Look again, Goodshank. And if you don't find the boy, spread word to the others and be quick about it. That falcon is the key to everything. We must retrieve it."

"Yes, my lord." The light diminished a little as Goodshank hurried away.

Face crushed against the trunk, Dominic lifted one eyebrow in cynical acknowledgement. Goodshank. Of course. Yet another Citizen to throw his hat in the ring in the search for future riches.

Muttering their irritation, the pursuers moved off, and Dominic gradually relaxed as their torch light dwindled. The sheltering branch creaked swiftly to one side, and he moved gingerly to a higher position where he could gain access to the tall brick wall. Vertigo tugged him as he shuffled gracelessly from the nearest branch. Dropping to the top of the narrow boundary, he swayed, clutching for support, and risked a quick glance down. The Grayling's cage lay at a slight angle a few feet away, tipped slightly against the wall. A narrow lane ran off in both directions. The rear boundary of another house loomed in front of him. Lowering himself carefully, he slid the few feet to the ground, wincing at the pain in his ankle. The Grayling regarded him with his slender head on one side and pecked at the cage. The bars strummed like the strings of a lute.

"I know. You want out." Dusting off his hands, Dominic tugged at the hood of his cloak and picked up the cage. The Grayling already seemed brighter, his eyes alert. He poked his beak forward, and Dominic moved his hand with a skill born of practice as the bird snapped at his fingers.

"Not yet. You'll have to wait a little longer."

He pulled a fold of his cloak forward, shrouding the shelter in darkness, and set out for the market stables.

CHAPTER TWENTY-THREE

Weariness permeated every cell of Dominic's body as he lurched across the slick cobbles of Blade Market. Under his cloak, muffled in darkness, the Grayling dozed, silent. Determined not to let him go, Dominic clutched the iron handle of his cage so tightly the metal warmed in his grasp. Every shadow looming at the edges of his vision held the possibility of capture. He walked with shoulders hunched, tired eyes straining in the gloom, head continually turning, ears alert for signs of pursuit.

His Blessed gifts had settled at last. The warming buzz of telekinesis tickled his palms, controlled by the mark of the Mage. Experimenting with his telepathic ability as he walked, he found he could amplify or reduce the volume of mental voices. The constant headache and pressure bursting against his skull had quieted. A ravening beast finally tamed. He blinked with relief in the absence of it, able to hear himself think.

The last dregs of the night had sent even the nighttime revellers to their pallets. His limping footsteps echoed across the damp cobbles. Around him, the canvas awnings of the deserted stalls fluttered like sails on the stiff breeze. Starlight was fading; the darkness before dawn. Even so, tension in the air pricked at his senses. No sign of the Queen's Guard who should patrol the streets. He bit his lip, remembering the confident drawl of Tremble's bodyguard. "We own the Queen's Guard, my Lord."

He shook his head. Jacklyn Sommerton was right. The Queen should be more wary of dissent and more willing to use her God's-blessed power in defence of her throne. His hand clenched harder on the cage at the stealthy scuffle of footsteps approaching from his right.

Head slightly cocked, he shuffled onwards, all his senses on alert. Faint in the wind, the aroma of sweat and onions trickled like rancid oil towards him. His bruised face tightened, and he slid his free hand to the dagger at his hip. He recognised that noxious combination. The bear-shaped Citizen, Carl.

On his left, a telepath keeping pace opened their mental channel. Dominic strained his ears but could hear nothing. The mental signal was intermittent and unfocused. Whoever carried it was untrained. He gritted his teeth. Little Bird. It had to be. Her footsteps were so light, her progress went unheard.

"What are you doing here, Little Bird? Go back. It's dangerous."

Her reply came to him in fits and starts. He caught the name Meridan. And then something about Pieter. He shook his head in frustration. Her message was clearly urgent, but he couldn't capture it. The market stables loomed before him, a comforting smell of fresh straw and horse greeting his arrival. Quickening his pace, he creaked the door open and hobbled in. The layout of the livery was familiar; one long central corridor lined on each side by a series of stalls for its equine occupants. A low ceiling accessed by a rough wooden ladder at the far end led to the hayloft and would double as the sleeping chamber for the stable lads when required. Barrows and heavy metal shovels occupied a space to his immediate left. One horn lantern dangled from a secure hook near the door, shedding a dim light on the scene.

His low-voiced whistle prompted Kismet's familiar snort. Dominic had never been more grateful to hear it in his life. Ignoring the pain in his ankle, he approached her stall at a run. The Grayling woke with a jerk, his alarm call puncturing the silence. Around him, horses stirred and stamped, and Dominic caught the ominous sound of the Bear's heavy footfall behind him. He increased his pace and launched himself into Kismet's stall, running a hand over her sleek neck in greeting. She whinnied, pushing her shoulder against him.

Almost blind in the dark, he'd barely heaved her saddle onto her back when a heavy pair of shoulders loomed into view. His fingers blurred as he tightened the saddle girth. Long years of experience meant he did not need to look. Instead, he met Carl's narrow eyes over Kismet's smooth shoulder. Her bridle dangled from a hook on the planked wall. There was no way to reach it and no need. He could ride with her wearing a halter just as easily.

"You'll hand that bird over, you little runt," Carl growled, his voice as brutal and self-satisfied as ever. He pounded his meaty fists together in anticipation and Dominic scooped the cage from the floor. Pure adrenalin spurred him into a leap onto the saddle. The cage bumped hard against his thigh. The Grayling raised his wings in protest.

Tightening his knees, Dominic backed Kismet in the narrow space and sat back. "Up," he commanded.

On cue, Kismet reared, front hooves flying. Startled, Carl jumped back, and Dominic collected his mount underneath him, preparing to use the command again.

"Master Skinner," another voice said from behind Carl. The bearish man glanced aside and then stepped back, a satisfied glint crooking his thin mouth into a gap-toothed grin. Dominic's heart sank.

Pieter stood between Dominic and freedom. He held Little Bird hard against his bony chest, his cheap, deadly blade angled across her grimy throat. Tears tumbled freely down the young girl's cheeks. Her whole body trembled. Dominic read the apology in her reddened eyes with no need for telepathy and kicked himself for not trying harder to understand her telepathic message. His palms tingled.

"Put the knife down, Pieter," he ordered, trying to keep his voice calm. Kismet shifted uneasily under him. He balanced the Grayling's cage more securely on his thigh, cradling it with one arm.

Pieter's eyes narrowed. "Hand that bird over, or I'll stick the girl." He pressed the edge of his knife against her skin. Little Bird winced at the sting of its edge. A trickle of blood crept down her neck to stain her ragged shirt.

She looked at Dominic, delicate mouth set in a stubborn line, eyes almost crossing with the effort. *"Don't. Meridan,"* he heard.

"Give him the bird!" Carl's impatient shout echoed across the building, and Little Bird jerked in surprise. The blade scraped her neck. Blood welled from the cut.

"Don't move," Dominic begged her. His gaze leapt around the standing figures. Unnerved by the unfamiliar commotion, the horses in the nearest boxes pushed their chests forward against the low doors, ears pricked. Teeth bared, Carl strode forward, reaching a hand to Kismet's halter, and Dominic backed her away until her hindquarters collided with the back of the stall. She snorted and tossed her head against his restraint.

Praying he was breaking no Blessed rules, Dominic gritted his teeth and waved a determined hand along the row of stalls. A series of bolts shot open. A further jerk of Dominic's hand clattered iron spades and pitchforks to the stone floor, and the quiet stable erupted suddenly into a tangled mass of frightened, sweating horses with nowhere to go.

Carl staggered as one huge black stallion blundered against him, nostrils flaring. Pieter looked over his shoulder, and Little Bird twisted in his grip, dropping to the flagstones and sprinting for the door. She dodged the heavy hooves with impressive agility, her ragged shirt fluttering like a banner as she disappeared into the night. Dominic spurred Kismet onwards into the melee, clattering for the exit.

He came up short at the sight of his uncle. Terrence Skinner stood solidly in his path, dark eyes alert under his spectacles. Alone and as calm as an island in the churning sea of equine bodies, he raised his hand in Dominic's direction, and Kismet shuddered to a stop, her chest heaving. She tossed her head, mane flying, unable to press forward and not understanding. The loose horses crowded behind, equally confused, hooves pounding uneasily on the cobbles. Dominic risked a glance behind. Pieter and Carl loomed at the back of the mass, fists clenched, but Terrence's power held them still.

"Give me the bird, Dominic," Terrence said softly.

Dominic's hold on the Grayling's cage tightened further. He eyed the older man, hardly able to believe his eyes, jaw set in a stubborn line.

"I won't. I lost him, and it's my job to return him safe to the Queen," he said.

"How far do you think you'll get, lad? Dupliss laid his plans well, and the word has gone out. Joran is already heading this way."

"It's a trap! They want to kill him!"

Terrence inclined his head. "They do."

"I've got to stop them!"

A thin smile curved his uncle's mouth under his beard. "One frail boy against an army of Citizens set on revenge. I think little of your chances, especially when they are also after the Grayling," he said.

Stung by his uncle's light derision, Dominic squared his shoulders, sitting a little taller in the saddle.

"My powers have settled tonight. I have control of them now," he said, aware of the ring of pride in his tone.

Terrence's ghostly eyebrows raised, and he bowed slightly in his nephew's direction. "Indeed? Then my compliments to you, Sir Skinner," he said.

Dominic flushed, clenching his free fist on a rising flood of frustration. "I'm not a child anymore!" he said. "You cannot tell me what to do."

"I'm asking you to use your common sense. My powers have enabled me to travel unscathed and almost undetected from the Castle to the City tonight. Yours..." he paused for effect, eyeing Dominic's battered face. "Have not."

Dominic flushed. "How is the Queen? I have tried to contact her."

Terrence blinked. "She has given birth to a daughter called Theda, after her grandmother. It was difficult, and she lost a lot of blood. She is resting."

"But she's in danger! Terrible danger! I must get to the castle. I have to get there!" He urged Kismet onward, only to be brought up short once more. "Please, uncle. Let me go."

The older man's expression softened. "Work with me, Dominic. You're tired and injured. You've done a tremendous job finding the bird, but your chances are better without him. Give him to me. I will ensure his safety. You find Joran. Try to get to him before he arrives in Blade. That's the best use of your skills right now."

Dominic swallowed, twisting uncertainly on the saddle, his palm sweaty on the Grayling's cage. His mind reached once more for the Queen, only to be met with the same blank absence. Prince Joran's mind was still closed to him. Only physical contact would stop him now. His eyes drifted to his uncle, standing foursquare and commanding, holding back the shifting mass of bodies with just the power of his mind. He sighed. What could he do by comparison? Parlour tricks. So unsure of the line between what was permitted and what was not.

He lifted the cage. About to hand the Grayling over, he started when Felicia's mental voice exploded into his mind like a comet.

"Don't give him the Grayling, Dominic!"

He gasped, brought up short by the urgency in her mental tone. Terrence shifted his weight, one hand extended to receive the cage, a light frown creasing his brows.

"What is it, lad?" he asked, his voice gentle. "I'm your uncle. Your only living relative. Surely, you know the bird will be safe with me."

"He doesn't mean it! He's lying to you! Don't, Dominic!" Felicia's gabble ended in a scream of pain that rocked him in the saddle, almost pitching him off his narrow seat. He clapped his free hand to his ear in reflex.

"Ah, I see. Telepathy. Who was that? Young Felicia?" Terrence's eyebrows raised in polite enquiry. They might have been discussing magical matters in the library, surrounded by scrolls and ink.

Dominic blinked, heart still thudding at the thought of the girl in pain.

"She's been keeping it secret. How did you know?" he asked, his voice shaking.

Terrence chuckled, his broad shoulders lifting under his high-necked robe. "Dear boy. Of course, I knew. Headaches, nose bleeds, she kept trying to hide. Her interest in anything appertaining to Blessed powers, where her brother is so dismissive. I caught her trying to get into the Restricted section once." His smile widened, and he shook his head. "The Gods-forsaken, traitorous Wessendeans, Citizens all, have bred a member of the Blessed... Who would have thought it?"

Dominic swallowed. He glanced at the Grayling, hunched and quiet in his confinement.

"You know what the bird's fate will be, should the Wessendeans get hold of it," Terrence said, following the direction of his gaze. "They plan to use it to lure Joran from the castle, and then they will kill them both to weaken the Queen."

The blood drained from Dominic's cheeks. His eyes leapt to where Terrence stood with his head on one side.

"I hate to be the one to tell you," Terrence continued, tone as mild as if he was talking about the weather. "I know you want to trust Felicia of Wessendean. But you should know. The reason you cannot contact the Queen is that Felicia infiltrated her chamber early this morning and exchanged a jug of valerian to relieve pain in childbirth, with a huge dose of Heartsease tea. For now, the Queen's Blessed gifts are useless."

He waited, and Dominic's mind raced, his face grim. Pieces of overheard conversation nudged his awareness. Felicia's insistence that she had carried out her part of the plan. His jaw tightened. Now he knew what it was.

"Felicia, is my uncle telling the truth? Did you drug the Queen?"

He waited for her reply, dreading what she might say, praying his uncle was wrong.

"Felicia?"

He felt her hesitation before he heard her voice.

"I can explain..."

"No."

Heart aching with disappointment, he ended their mental conversation. Scrubbing his free hand across his mouth, eyes blurred with tears, he leaned over and handed the cage to his uncle.

CHAPTER TWENTY-FOUR

Terrence Skinner nodded at him as he received the cage. Deep in his eyes, Dominic spied a tinge of regret before he turned on his heel and marched into the shadowed market. At his retreat, the plunging horses calmed. Their huffs and snorts breathed oats into the chill air. Dominic felt their solid, curious presence behind him as they pressed uselessly forward.

Almost in a daze, Dominic nudged Kismet on, but it seemed his uncle had not yet removed his mental focus from the stable. The mare tossed her head, pawing at the invisible restriction, ears flat. Dominic risked a glance behind, where Pieter and Carl remained immobile as statues. Their angry stares sparked, muscles flexing with their attempts to break the silent spell.

"You'll be dead meat when the Citizens finish with you, Skinner," Carl growled, frustration in every syllable. Dominic ignored him, still craning his neck to follow his uncle's path, away from the market and to the right, toward the half-rebuilt Temple complex. He bit his lip and scrubbed his empty hands on his filthy breeches. The hand no longer holding the cage felt bereft. Doubt nagged at him. Joran's life was in danger. If that was now his mission, Terrence should no longer hold him here.

Even as he thought it, the barrier broke. Kismet surged forward, accompanied at a charge by the equine herd, eager to escape. The ancient market cobbles rang with the clatter of panicked hooves as the horses dispersed, barrelling around the empty stalls, jumping over stacked crates. Reining Kismet in before she joined the headlong rush, Dominic turned her in a tight circle. Pieter and Carl stumbled into a flat sprint, heading straight for him, and he wheeled north, uphill, away from the river towards Castlegate.

"Dominic!"

Felicia's mental voice pierced his mind as he rose with Kismet's brisk stride. He dared not canter the mare on the hard city streets. A trot was as much as he could allow. He scowled, even though he knew Felicia couldn't see him, and risked a glance behind. Pieter and Carl were closing rapidly. His best hope lay in outpacing them from the city and racing the mare on the grassy verge of the castle road. If the Gods were with him, he'd meet Joran's forces on the way.

"Dominic, you must listen to me."

"You never stop, do you? I won't listen to you, Felicia. You're a traitor, just like the rest of the Wessendeans. So handy with your drugs and potions." His hands hardened on the reins, and Kismet snorted, tossing her head until he relaxed his grip. The City walls loomed ahead of him, solid and imposing against the night sky. The heavy wooden gate was closed. He'd have to bribe the guard to let him through.

"Please wait, you have to know. Your uncle is not on your side. He wants the Grayling for something else. Something much worse."

Gritting his teeth, Dominic spurred Kismet to a faster trot. *"What could be worse than what your own mother and stepfather are planning?"*

A pause. Felicia's indecision thrummed through their mental connection. Exasperated beyond measure, Dominic prepared to block her.

"No, wait! There's something..." her frustration bled through the open channel. *"I can't see it clearly. Just snatches. But I know there's something wrong. Something about your uncle."*

Dominic rolled his eyes. *"You'll say anything to prevent me from doing what I have to do. Leave me alone."*

He'd reached the City walls. Petronella's standard fluttered in the breeze atop the solid stone towers that flanked the heavy gates. Drawing Kismet to a halt, Dominic shouted for the gate guard, one hand on his dagger. The puffing breaths of Carl and Pieter jogging up the slope in his wake sounded loud in his ears.

He frowned as two narrow figures detached themselves from the shadows and moved towards him.

"We be the guards," the larger man said. He strolled to the gate and put his back to it. His mirthless smile did nothing to light his scabrous features. Instead, Dominic's shoulders hunched at the ring of steel as the man slid his sword from his scabbard.

He twisted in the saddle as footsteps stopped behind him. Hands on his knees, glaring at him, Carl panted for breath. Pieter eyed him from under his ragged fringe, fingering his blade. Kismet jinked, back legs twitching, as the boy stepped closer. The second guard reached a hand to her halter and peered at him in the dim light.

"Yes. This is the lad Count Dupliss told us about. Scruffy, blond, beaten up. Skinner, is it?" he raised a thick eyebrow in question.

Dominic raised his hands, grateful beyond measure for the power that lingered there.

"You'll step back and let me through," he said.

The second guard huffed a laugh through his nose. "Ha, hear that, lads? Step back, shall we?"

"See boy, we know you can't use your Blessed power against us, mere Citizens, like," the first guard explained.

Dominic's eyes narrowed. "Depends on what I do with it really, doesn't it?" he said. Sitting deep in his seat, he commanded Kismet to back up. Pieter jumped out of the way to avoid her. Still bent over his knees trying to catch his breath, Carl was not so lucky. Encountering something unfamiliar behind her, the mare lashed out with a hind leg.

Carl crashed to the cobbles. A flick of Dominic's fingers tore the royal standard from its pole, and he used his ability to wrap it around the second guard, pinning his snaking hands to his side. Eyes bulging, the first guard stood his ground. Dominic used his heels. Snorting, the mare jogged towards the gate.

"See? No harm done." Kismet halted. The guard raised his sword, but he wasn't quick enough. At Dominic's quiet command, the mare reared, her hooves punching the air. The guard ducked automatically, dropping his weapon with a clatter to the ground.

Dominic reached past him to the heavy barricade lowered in place every evening. Power hummed around him as he lifted it from the iron brackets that supported its weight. He grunted. Even with the Mage's power now settled, the solidness of it dragged against his mind. He nudged Kismet with his knee and she moved sideways, crowding the first guard against the wall. The man grunted as she squeezed the breath from his lungs.

"Don't go through the gate!"

Felicia's voice again. He ignored her, concentrating on moving the heavy doors. They creaked open.

"Dominic, Kismet!"

She shrieked at him, nearly deafening his mental channel. His gaze snapped forward. Braced in the space outside the heavy gate, bow raised, Dupliss' face glowed with hatred as he fired. The arrow whistled at him out of the darkness. He only just threw his hand out in time. The projectile missed Kismet and he bit off a scream as it took a chunk out of his leg. Pain blazed through him and instinct took over. He whirled her about, heading for the relative safety of the city, knocking Pieter out of the way as he retreated, pushing Kismet into a desperate, unwise canter back down the hill.

Swaying in the saddle, clutching his leg with one hand as blood oozed through his fingers, he barely remembered the mad ride through the twisting back streets to his father's tannery. His mind raced, counting the disasters of the evening. Dupliss's plan had dropped into place bit by bit. Joran and Petronella were in mortal danger. He, trapped in Blade, could not warn them. But his uncle had the falcon. He bit his lip. He'd do as he'd said and protect the bird, wouldn't he? Threading Kismet as fast as he could through the quiet streets, he tried not to remember Felicia's voice in his head. His lips hardened. Wessendeans were traitors. She had drugged the Queen. That's what he knew as a fact. But still, his heart disagreed, and the battle waged.

In the tannery courtyard, surrounded by the familiar stink of blood and ammonia, he half fell from Kismet's back, stumbling into a pile of buckets. The acrid aroma from the tanning vats filled the narrow space. A rat ran over his foot, and he levered himself upright. The low walls of his parents' humble home twisted in front of his exhausted vision as he staggered forward, fumbling for the door. He leaned against it, taking comfort in the feel of the aged wood against his forehead, almost too exhausted to stand.

"Master?"

A rushlight lowered, casting its warm glow around him, and a thin, but sturdy arm circled his waist.

"Meridan?"

"Aye. Steady now, lean on me..."

She raised the latch. The narrow door creaked open, and they shuffled in. Their joined shadows shifted uneasily across the unadorned stone walls as she led him to a bench by the roughly turned table. She lowered him and fixed the torch to a nearby bracket. It highlighted the sign of the Mage carved into the wall. The vocational alcove below it contained a single, unlit candle. The humble hearth glowed with heat.

"Bar the door and light the candle." Dominic could only manage a whisper.

Grim-faced, she vanished. Overwhelmed, and wishing only for sleep, Dominic slumped to the table.

He roused to find not only Meridan, but Little Bird, Rosa, and Will all crowded into the small room. Little Bird sat opposite him, her face propped in her tiny hands, questions in her eyes. Someone had wrapped a rag around her injured throat. She wore it jauntily, like a bandana. Will dumped a bucket of water and a heap of rags on the floor. Rosa waited behind him, one hand on her knife, the other clutching a small wooden cup. The votive candle flickered gently under the symbol of the Mage, as it always had in the days of his youth. A distant comfort.

"Can you sit up?"

Meridan again. The girl turned him round on the bench and snatched out her own blade, reaching for his breeches. She glanced up at him. Shadows ringed her pale blue eyes.

"Sorry, Master, I need to see the wound."

He let her slash at the garment and bit his lip at the deep gash across his leg. Meridan reached for a rag and gestured Rosa forward. Her dark eyes were ringed with shadows, peeping at him like the wary eyes of a fox from beneath a tangle of russet hair. The sharp scent of brandy tickled his nostrils.

"Have some of this. But leave some for your leg," she said.

Dominic took the cup from Rosa and slammed half the contents down, gasping as the stuff bit his throat. Meridan took back the cup, soaked a rag, and laid it gently across his skin. His entire body leapt as the alcohol seared the wound. A flash of Felicia's soothing potion swept across his mind. Somewhere, he could hear her mental voice tugging at the back of his brain, but he closed his mind to it, biting his tongue until the sting died away and the alcohol warmed his stomach.

"Is the door barred?" he mumbled.

"It is. We went to the market for food and clothes, like you said." Head down, Meridan reached for another rag, dipped it into the bucket, and busied herself cleaning the blood from his skin. "But it was strange, wasn't it?" She glanced at her crew. Little Bird leaned forward, dragging her ghoulish attention from his leg, and nodded. Blonde hair tangled in front of her eyes. "It was like they were all waiting for something. And then people started walking up Castlegate."

"Like some sort of signal," Will added. He shifted from one foot to the other, and wandered to the window, a mere hide shutter. He pressed his ear against it. "Nothing to hear, so far," he said.

"Kismet?" Dominic asked, wishing he had more brandy.

"She's fine. I put her in the stable, gave her some feed," Rosa said. "What's going on? Do you know?"

Meridan ripped a rag into strips and wound them around his leg. She looked hard into Dominic's face.

"You know, don't you, Master?" she said.

"Call me Dominic. I'm no Master," Dominic said. He looked around at their serious, grimy faces, heart clenching in sudden dread. His leg throbbed in time with his pulse and he winced as Meridan tugged the bandage tight.

Her shoulders twitched. "What's going on? We need to know."

He sighed. "The Citizens want to remove the Queen and put Guildford of Wessendean on the throne. They stole her falcon to lure Prince Joran from the castle and plan to ambush him. Those people you saw are part of that. They must be. I have tried to contact the Prince using mind talk, but I cannot make a connection. The Queen is not answering me, either. However, the Citizens don't have the falcon now. My uncle, a powerful member of the Blessed, has him."

Uncomfortable at the mention of Blessed gifts, the children exchanged glances.

Rosa avoided the subject. "There were guards, and all sorts," she said, lips thinning. "Traitors."

Meridan's eyes were enormous in her narrow face. "Pieter's part of it, isn't he?" she said.

Dominic gave her a jerky nod, his eyes sliding to Little Bird's bandana. "Yes, he is. I'm sorry for it," he said.

Meridan shrugged, her shoulders hunched under her woollen shirt. "His parents were some of the first to die in the Starving," she said. "He was only ten years old, and there was no one to help him. He never got over it, not really." Her face softened as she looked at him. "You should try to rest, Master," she said. "There's little else you can do."

Dominic glanced at the only other room in the humble cottage, the bedchamber. Staggering to his feet, he limped reluctantly towards it, throwing open the door.

The rising dawn cast the room in grey shadow. His parent's narrow wooden bed stood hard against the far wall, blankets folded neatly at the foot of its straw-stuffed mattress. Staring at it brought tears to his eyes. In his mind, death stalked the chamber, the small room haunted by ghosts. After his fatal fall, his brother had lain there, face pale, a mask of surprise etched forever across his handsome features. Tangled in each other's arms, thin and red-faced with fever, both his parents had gasped their last breaths there, too. He rubbed a hand across his aching chest. Even overwhelmed with fatigue, he could not bring himself to sleep on that bed.

His mother's coffer still stood sentinel at its foot, and he shuffled towards it. Kneeling shot a heavy thud of pain through his injured calf, but he lowered himself enough to heft open the heavy lid. The familiar smell of mint drifted towards him. His mother's favourite scent, used to combat the everlasting stench of blood and faeces from the tannery that dominated her life.

The coffer was empty, except for one small ornament, abandoned in a corner of the trunk. He picked it up, turning it in front of his tired eyes until the image became clear.

The wooden carving of a falcon. Burnished to chestnut brown, its delicate lines painstakingly carved. He stared at it, grim-faced, transported to a distant time of cheerful firelight and brotherly teasing. "Here, Dom. For your name day. It'll bring you luck." Surrounded by tiny slivers of wood and a precious tin of expensive beeswax, Gavin had tossed it to him across the width of the cottage. The constant pounding of wet hides in the courtyard had formed the backdrop to their conversation. "You'll be glad to leave here, Dom. Less smelly in the castle stables!"

"You should come." Dominic remembered his hopeful, piping voice with dreadful clarity. And Gavin's cheerful reply. "Nay. Some un's got to help Pa with the business. 'Twill be mine one day. You go up to the castle with the gentry. Make yer fortune!"

Returning to painful reality, he crushed the carving in his hand, welcoming the hard edges as they dug grooves into his skin. Gavin had fallen to his death the next day. He had a sharp memory of standing in this exact place, his mother's arm around his shoulders, both of them crying at the sight of Gavin broken and lifeless on the bed. The heavy weight of her grief had pressed guilt deep into his heart. No longer worthy, he'd let Gavin's gift tumble into her coffer. He rubbed the heel of his free hand across his cheeks. A dull murmur of conversation drifted across his worried mind, dragging him back to painful reality. He opened his fist. The pressure marks caused by his grip overlaid the faint silver glow of the Mage's sign. The carving sat prettily in his palm. Was he worthy of it now? He shook his head. But still, his brother's cheerful voice, the light in his pale blue eyes. "Here, Dom. For your name day. It'll bring you luck."

He cast one last look at the empty bed and returned to the main room, Gavin's last gift to him clutched firmly in his fist.

CHAPTER TWENTY-FIVE

"Can ye not sleep?" Meridan asked. She'd been busy in his brief absence. The table contained a wooden trencher of bread, a crock of butter, and several meat pies. His mother's favourite earthenware jug oozed condensation and the comforting aroma of small beer. A selection of cups and tankards waited to be filled. Gravy smeared Little Bird's cheeks as she rubbed her hand across her face.

"Want some? There's plenty," Meridan said, filling the cups.

Half dazed, Dominic leaned in and grabbed a pie. It was cold but delicious. Saliva burst into his mouth, and he took another bite, reaching for a drink.

"I need one of you to take a message to Sir Thomas Buttledon," he announced. "Any of you know him?"

Rosa shifted uncomfortably in her seat and shot a glance at Will. Little Bird giggled, spraying crumbs. Meridan shot her a look, and she clamped her lips shut with an effort, shoulders jerking with mirth.

Dominic stared around at them. "You robbed him, didn't you?"

Little Bird giggled again, choking. Meridan hammered her back until she stopped, eyes streaming, and reached for the jug with both hands.

"Too easy for words, he was," she said, between gulps. "Not looking where he was going at all. Walked right into us, didn't he?" She looked at the older children for confirmation. Will eyed her steadily from under his blond eyebrows, his square, freckled face serious.

"You're not supposed to talk about it, Bird," he said. "If they catch us, we'll hang."

"Well, Dominic won't say anything, will he? He's much too soft to turn us in," Little Bird said. She stared up at him, navy eyes entreating. "You're on our side, aren't you, Master?" she prompted. "We're on yours, aren't we?" She looked round at the others.

Meridan's eyes narrowed. "Of course we are. Don't be daft, girl. Eat your supper."

Dominic huffed a reluctant laugh. "From what I know of him, he'd not take much persuading to be robbed by children," he said. "You could have just asked him for money."

Rosa sat up, affronted. "We're not beggars," she said. "Robbing is skilled work."

Will nodded, and the three younger children fell to arguing their various skills.

Brow quirking, Dominic glanced at Meridan. She looked at him and shrugged, her pale face slightly pink. "Had to make it into something for them," she muttered under her breath.

A half smile crossed his face, and he looked at Meridan with new respect. She had all the makings of an outstanding leader.

"You've kept them safe. Given them some hope. 'Tis more than many," he said.

Her brow creased. "You meant it when you said they could stay here?" she asked. "But I'm not sure how interested they are in tanning."

"I need no more tanners. But if we get through the next few weeks, I'll try to find positions that are better suited," Dominic replied. "Tanning's a filthy job, even for an adult."

Meridan frowned her acknowledgement. "Aye, that it is. Do ye know where this Sir Buttledon bides?"

"Last I heard, he was heading for Maria Fitzherbert's house, wherever that might be." He helped himself to more beer. "If not there, you might find him at his manor up on the north side. Their emblem is the bear and beaver.'

She nodded. "I know of it. I'll find him. What do ye want me to say?"

"I need him to get out of Blade and up to the castle. He needs to warn Prince Joran not to leave for Blade, no matter what he's told. It's a trap. There are traitors in the castle. The Queen is not safe. He should tell the Prince the message comes from me, and that I tried to warn him at the joust. Then Joran will know the message is true. No one else overheard that conversation."

Meridan's eyes rounded, but her grubby face was doubtful. "Will Sir Thomas believe me, though?" she asked. "Last time I saw him, I had a knife at his kidneys."

Dominic shrugged, hoping he was right. "He was prepared to help me earlier this evening. I believe he's on the side of the Blessed, even though he's a Citizen. If he doubts you, tell him he was right about the back of Tremble's, but he owes me for failing to mention the midden. That should do the trick."

The table jerked as Meridan stood. She glanced around at the squabbling children and bit her lip.

"I'll keep them safe," Dominic assured her, his voice rough.

The gang leader slid her blade into her belt and turned for the door. "Where will you be?" she said over her shoulder. Dominic followed her to the door.

"I'm going after the Grayling. If the Wessendeans get him, they'll start their coup. I can't let that happen. I think my uncle took him to the Temple. He says he'll keep the bird safe, but..." His voice tailed off as doubt crowded his mind. He sighed. "I'll just feel better if I'm the one looking out for him, that's all."

Meridan put her hand on his arm. "I'll see you there." The votive candle fluttered in the draft as she left. Massaging the back of his neck, conscious of the tension there, Dominic conjured up an encouraging grin for his young companions. Full of food, they lolled at the table. Little Bird's eyes almost crossed with tiredness. Rosa's gaze drifted longingly to his parents' bedchamber.

"You can stay here, but you'll be on your own," he remarked, stifling his own yawn with an effort. "Meridan's on a mission to save the Queen. I'm sure you don't want to be left out."

"But it's morning. This is when we go to bed," Rosa objected.

Dominic raised his eyebrows. "Sleep then, but you might not like the world you wake up in," he said.

Rosa shot him a resentful glance. She looked at Will. "Are you going with him?" she asked.

Will stood up, spilling the remains of his tankard down his shirt. "Of course. This is important. If Meridan's helping, then we must, too." He held out his hand. "Come on."

"I'm coming. You're not leaving me behind." Bandana fluttering, Little Bird scrambled from the table and reached for Dominic's hand. The warmth of her tiny palm was comforting in his. "We'll do it together, won't we?"

The first rosy hues of dawn spread delicate fingers across the eastern sky as the tired, ramshackle group crossed the noxious courtyard. Dominic's tannery workforce opened the shutters of their lofts and climbed stiffly from their beds to start work. Their curious gazes pressed against his back, but Dominic didn't wait to see how many might have crept away to join Dupliss' rebel forces in the night. The thought turned his stomach. Instead, he led the way through the quiet pre-dawn streets, hugging the walls and hoping that his trust in his uncle was justified.

Their quiet passage took them into the centre of Blade, through the lesser-known alleys. Cats hunted amid rubbish left over from the day before, their lamp-like eyes gleaming from secret hiding places behind loose planks and shadowed windowsills. Blade's many shops stood silent, waiting for their owners to unbar their doors and ready their wares. Hand on his dagger, Dominic kept a sharp lookout for trouble, but the City lay strangely silent, almost as if it was holding its breath.

He bit his lip at the sight of the Black Eagle. It had never closed in all his years. Even during the fierce Eperan winters, the outer doors stood open. The small group exchanged confused glances at the sight of the closed shutters.

"Where are the soldiers?" Little Bird asked, mouth agape.

"Part of Dupliss' army, mayhap," Will said, his lips tightening. He shot a glance at Dominic. "Do ye think, Master?"

Dominic grimaced in reply. He glanced northwards towards the castle. Somewhere out there, huddled together in the damp, tangled forests that lined the castle road, an army waited, headed by Dupliss, an experienced and demanding commander of men. He shook his head. Thomas Buttledon would have to keep his wits about him to avoid them and reach the Prince. Quickening his stride, he bit his lip at the shooting pain stabbing up both legs. *"Petronella, answer me!"* He put all his power behind the mental signal, but it was like shouting into the wind. Nothing in reply. His fists clenched in frustration as they left the soldier's tavern behind, angling away from the market stable towards the temple complex. He frowned. The sun was up. The streets should be bustling by now. Where were the carters, and merchants, and tradesfolk? He raised his gaze to the pale pink sky, patched with soaring birds and unstained by Blade's smoking chimneys. His shoulders clenched. Something was wrong.

The deathly sound of a drawn sword snapped his head towards the strangely quiet market. Little Bird gasped, pressing closer to him.

Rosa and Will stopped in their tracks, automatically reaching for their daggers.

"Well met, Skinner." Guildford's voice lacked some of its normal smugness. Shadows crept under his pale eyes, but the sword arm did not waver. Morning light glinted off the blade. Elegantly attired in her favourite pale grey, not a hair out of place, Arabella stood at his side. Only the rapid tapping of her foot under the fashionable gown betrayed her agitation. She eyed the group with disdain, the corner of one thin lip lifted in a faint, triumphant sneer. Goodshank flanked her, sword raised. He glared at Dominic, daring him to move. Dominic stared stonily back, trying to see behind him for the shorter figure of Felicia. Skinny Aldric lingered at arm's length. New bruises decorated his pale skin. The hatred Dominic saw in the young boy's eyes as he glowered at his master was no surprise.

"Where is the bird?" Arabella said.

Dominic didn't blink. "I don't know."

"Oh, I think you do." Arabella gestured at Goodshank, who reached behind him to jerk Felicia to the fore. Little Bird gasped. Dominic clamped down hard on his shock, energy fizzing in his hands, demanding release.

Her gown was in tatters. Blood marred her downcast cheeks and matted her hair. Aghast, he reached to her through their mental connection. Nothing there. One long finger tapped a flask hanging from her belt, and Dominic understood. Heartease. They'd made her take it. Or she'd chosen to. Either way, her gift had gone for now, but that was not the worst of it. His heart clenched as she raised her face to his, eyes streaming with tears.

An ugly crisscross of black stitches, horrendous in their neatness, marred the delicate symmetry of her face. Arabella had sewn her mouth shut.

Chapter Twenty-Six

"Βy the Gods, you evil bitch."

The words leapt from his tongue before he was conscious of uttering them. He herded the children away, pushing them backwards with the force of his gift. Will uttered a cry of protest, trying to stand his ground. Little Bird tried to stifle her sobs. Breaking through her panic was hard, but Dominic managed a single mental command. *"Little Bird. Find Meridan. Temple. Go."*

He risked a quick glimpse around. It was enough. Hardened by her years on the streets, the young girl stiffened her heaving shoulders and met his determined gaze. She grabbed at Rosa's hand, and they retreated, dragging Will reluctantly with them. The ragged group slunk into the shadows like alley cats.

Swallowing down his relief, Dominic rounded on Arabella.

"How could you do that to your own daughter?"

Arabella's jaw narrowed. "I do not have to explain my actions to a peasant."

Blazing with anger, Dominic drew his dagger. "You may have to explain it to the Mage."

Sword raised, Guildford took two quick steps forward. Fuelled by fury, Dominic batted the weapon from his grasp with a single twist of his wrist and the force of intention.

"Your mother is insane. How could you stand there and let her do that?"

Guildford dropped his gaze. His feet fidgeted against the damp cobbles. Guilty as charged. Dominic's fury rose to new heights. He lunged.

Pale eyes lit with the prospect of battle, Guildford dropped into an easy crouch with the ease born of hours of practice. His own dagger, slim and deadly, appeared in his hand as if by magic.

"Come on then, Skinner. Now we're equal. Let's see what you've really got."

Despite his bulk, he was as quick as a cat. Hampered by injury, Dominic stumbled backwards as the blade lashed out. Its savage edge missed his stomach by a mere inch. Guildford followed it up with a swift kick that sent Dominic to his backside in the dust. His dagger flew from his hand and skittered uselessly across the cobbles.

Guildford advanced to stand over him, legs apart, hands on his hips. "You've got nothing, Skinner. Tell us where the falcon is, and I might just let you keep your life."

"I told you, I don't know!" Dominic's shout echoed off the stone buildings and sent pigeons fluttering to the sky. Shuffling gracelessly backwards, panting for breath, he scrambled to his feet. He raised both hands, his palms itched to strike back. How fair was this, really? Not an even fight indeed. When his own physical prowess stood no chance against solid muscle and steel.

He twisted his wrists, reaching with his power to the high neck of Guildford's brocade tunic. It tightened against the boy's throat, and he dropped his dagger in shock, eyes wild. Still holding tight to his mental grip, Dominic advanced, eyes narrowed, teeth bared. Guildford clawed at his neck, face crimson.

"Not pleasant, is it?" Dominic ground out, still squeezing, the pleasure of revenge singing sweetly in his blood.

"How dare you? Leave him alone!" Arabella took a step forward, murder in her icy glower, but seemed reluctant to engage. Dominic smirked at her, still holding her son effortlessly in his mental grip. Out of the corner of his eye, Felicia moved, distracting his attention for a fraction of a second. Dominic glanced round in horror as Goodshank reached out one long arm and yanked young Aldric towards him.

The boy yelped, kicking against the iron grip.

"Release his Lordship and tell us where the falcon is, or I'll end this child right here." His elbow tightened, and Aldric gasped, dark eyes raised in panic and supplication. Goodshank let his sword clang to the cobbles and stretched his long hand, spider-like, against Aldric's soft hair. His fingers crawled almost lovingly against the child's narrow skull. Black eyes smirked at Dominic as he repositioned his grip.

"Look how easy it is to break the necks of little birds," he hissed.

His hand jerked, but Dominic moved first. Releasing Guildford, he lashed out with both hands and Goodshank's own neck snapped around so hard, his entire body twisted with it. Aldric dropped to the floor. Goodshank crashed beside him, dead black eyes staring at nothing. Paler than chalk, Aldric stumbled away. He took one horrified look at his former employer and broke into a run, the sounds of his drumming footsteps fading on the cobbles. In the sudden, shocked pause, Arabella laughed, the sound harder than iron.

"Well, look at that. The peasant had murder in him after all," she said.

Dominic barely heard her. He stared, aghast, at the damage wrought by his own hands. A tremor of shame shook his body. He stood with his fingers clenched, head bowed, chest heaving. The Mage was already seeking the return of his Blessing. His hands and head ached with the inexorable withdrawal of his God's-blessed power. It siphoned from him, dragging fiercely at his mind and his blood. The swiftness of its going left him empty, his senses shocked and bereft. The silence after the storm. A tide going out.

Eyes still locked on the dead man's blank stare, He didn't bother looking up at the sound of Guildford's boots striding towards him. The force of his fist took him to his knees.

After that, darkness was easy.

CHAPTER TWENTY-SEVEN

"He knows where the falcon is. I'm sure of it."

Arabella's shrill voice pierced Dominic's ears. His eyes flickered open to find her looming over him, icy eyes narrowed with spite. He turned his head from her, inhaling the familiar scent of soiled straw, but not before he'd seen the light of madness buried deep in the shattered crystal of her stare. His blurred, terrified gaze didn't travel far before it bumped into a thick wooden wall. A single oil lamp hung on a hook above his head. His shoulders ached. The scratch of rope at his wrists behind his back accounted for that. They had taken no chances during the latest pummelling. He huffed a half laugh under his breath as he flexed his fingers. Nothing. He'd broken his contract with the Mage. His powers were gone. He winced at the slap of Arabella's hand against his cheek.

"Look at me, boy. You've seen what I'm prepared to do."

He glared at her from under lowered brows, mouth set in a stubborn line, and she lashed out again. One of her rings slashed the tender skin of his lips. His tongue flicked out, tasting blood.

"I'll beat it out of him," Guildford took a step forward. He sounded eager to inflict more damage. Arabella rolled her eyes.

"You've already tried that, and somehow, the boy keeps breathing, and still refuses to talk." She stood, poking his cracked ribs with her dainty, slippered toe. Dominic ground his teeth on the pain and glowered at her in silence.

Somewhere in the shadows behind her, a man cleared his throat. "My lady?" he said. "I bring news from your husband."

Arabella straightened to her full height, chin raised. "And?"

The messenger paused, taking in the scene before him, scrubbing a hand across his stubbled chin. "He says to tell you that all is in readiness. He requires only to know that you now have the bird safe in your possession."

Arabella launched her foot. Dominic grunted as it slammed into his cracked ribs. "Thanks to this vermin, we do not have the bird. My people are looking for it even as we speak. We know it is in the possession of this boy's uncle, a powerful member of the Blessed. We do not know where."

"But my lady..."

Arabella rounded on him. Coiled around his pain, Dominic rejoiced at her discomfiture. "Tell him we will send the signal as soon as we have the bird," she snapped. "'T'will not take long. This boy will tell us."

"It needs to be soon, my lady," the man warned. "The queen's powers will return to her when the drug wears off."

"Enough!" Arabella slammed her hand against his chest, shoving him away. "I have told you of the situation. I am well aware of my lord's plans. Tell him what I said."

Dominic's sharp ears pricked at the sound of the messenger's receding footsteps, and the slam of a large door some distance away. His eyes wandered once more around his cell, latching on to a hay filled manger, and the heavy ring embedded in the wall. A wooden bucket stood in one corner, a heavy iron shovel in the other. He blinked. A bull pen. Surely they hadn't brought him back to the market livery?

Arabella bent to him, jabbing a sharp thumbnail under his throat to survey his face, slanting his head this way and that. Parched in his throbbing skull, his brain rolled like a marble.

"Where's Felicia?" she snapped over her shoulder at Guildford. "Surely she's had enough time by now."

Straw rustled as Guildford left the small space. Dominic breathed slightly more easily in his absence. He ran his tongue around dry lips, tasting only dust.

"Thirsty, are we?" Arabella jeered. "Felicia's brewed something special for you." She leaned against the planks, folding her arms around her slim waist, one slippered foot tapping her impatience against the cold flags.

Thankful that Arabella had apparently no more to say to him, his mind roamed. How long would it take before Petronella's vast store of power reopened to her? Would Joran even realise she had lost it? Perhaps not, if the birth was as bad as his uncle had said. Perhaps Joran wouldn't even tell her that her precious bird was missing. He'd just set out to get it back so as not to worry her. Had Thomas reached him? Desperate to take action, his body twisted painfully against the ropes that bound him.

"About time. Come here, girl."

His eyes cracked open. Herded by Guildford, Felicia hovered uncertainly in the doorway. Her poor lips had swollen around the neat stitches, but she'd washed the dried blood from her cheeks. She carried a large jug in one hand, eyes cavernous in the dim light. Her terrified gaze clamped to his.

Arabella reached out and jerked her forward.

"Move, get in here!"

Felicia resisted, wrenching her arm away. The jug tipped, spilling some of its contents to the floor.

Her mother tutted. "Careful with that. We need it. Kneel."

Felicia had no choice but to do as Arabella commanded. The woman dragged her down by her hair, one scruffy dark blonde lock coiled firm in her fist.

"Alright." Arabella's gaze took them both in. Her face was white, but hard with determination. Guildford's feet were a foot away from Dominic's head. To his surprise, he saw that the powerful legs in their expensive boots were literally shaking.

"Mother..."

"Shut up, Guildford. If you want to sit on the throne, it has to be done."

Unbelieving, Dominic watched as she withdrew a long needle from her embroidered bodice. Its sharp point seemed to grow in his horrified vision until it was all he could see. A long, black thread dangled from it. The match of the cruel row of criss cross stitches against Felicia's rosebud mouth.

He swallowed, a tremor starting from his toes all the way to his own battered lips. Arabella braced her daughter against the wooden planks and tipped her head back. Chest heaving, Felicia whimpered, Dominic's bowel clenched in utter horror.

"Now, let me be very clear. The jug contains poison. I know you have some idea where that God's damned bird is," Arabella said. "And if you don't tell me, you can watch me sew her eyes shut before you die."

Above him, Guildford retched. "Mother, don't, I beg you!"

Eyes narrowed with concentration, Arabella took a firm grip on her needle and aimed it straight at Felicia's left eye. Sweat broke out across Dominic's face.

"No! Stop! He's somewhere in the temple complex. That's all I know! I swear it!" Dominic yelled it at the top of his lungs.

Arabella stopped, the needle a thread's breadth away. Felicia shivered where she knelt, blinking frantically. Arabella stared at him. "Are you sure that's all you know?"

"Yes, yes, let her go!"

Arabella dropped her daughter's hair and pushed her over to Dominic.

"Guildford. Start the search."

The boy needed no further urging to quit the premises. He left at a sprint. Felicia sobbed softly, her tears dripping onto his face. He looked up at her, longing to wipe them away. His hands strained ineffectually at the ropes that tied him, cutting into his wrists.

Arabella nudged Felicia with her foot. The contents of the jug shuddered.

"This will teach you to disobey me, miss," she said. "He's served his usefulness. Give him the potion."

Felicia shook her head, but she raised the jug. Her hair fell across his face in dusty torrents, shielding him momentarily from Arabella's fierce gaze.

He blinked, trying to focus on her grey eyes at such a short distance. Tears of his own joined with hers. She breathed something through her shuttered lips he couldn't make out and tipped some of the potion onto his mouth. Even without Arabella's stitchery, he clamped his own mouth closed, shaking his head. Her eyes widened, boring into his. She tipped a little more onto his face. He inhaled, choking as it sloshed up his nose. She frowned, exasperated, and widened her eyes even further. Dominic eyed her cautiously. His tongue flicked to test the liquid, and he tensed. Hidden by her hair, the corners of her lips stretched into a painful, pinched smile.

"Felicia, I mean it." Pulled once more by her own hair, the young girl's disfigured face rose slowly from his own. Still shaking, she tipped the jug against his lips. Dominic did his best to pretend extreme reluctance and bodily anguish. It wasn't hard.

Arabella's satisfied smirk bored hard into his face until he turned his head and writhed across the fetid straw.

"Good," she said. "That will finish him. Come."

She jerked Felicia upwards. The girl dropped the jug and climbed slowly to her feet, her whole body shaking. Arabella leaned across the narrow space to snatch the oil lantern from the wall and slammed the door shut. He heard the rattle of the heavy bar dropping in place, and the sound of their rapidly retreating footsteps.

He swallowed, dropping his chin to wipe the last of the potion from his face onto his filthy tunic, thanking his lucky stars for Felicia's startling audacity.

Far from poison, she'd given him an enormous infusion of valerian. All it would do would make him sleep. He blinked in the darkness, marvelling at her quick thinking as the sharp edge of his pain receded. As with many of Felicia's brews, the strength of the drug was irresistible. Already the potion was numbing his hurts. Lunging to claim him.

Alone in the dark, on the verge of consciousness, Dominic closed his eyes, battling with his own emotions. Where was Thomas? Had Meridan found him? Was the falcon safe? His mind yearned for its lost ability to connect. He called once more for Felicia, longing to beg her forgiveness. He tried the Queen. Joran, even Little Bird. But the Mage would not relent. He'd destroyed his bond. The delicate silver threads had been just that. Delicate. To be wielded with discretion. No wonder the queen was so sparing in her display of power. He had failed. Arabella would find the Grayling. Dupliss's army would march. He was on his own. A puny boy, unworthy of the faith others placed in him.

He rolled his face into the acrid straw, tears blotted by the dust on the ground, the thudding pain in his body matched only by the searing knowledge of failure in his heart. Felicia's potion laid a gentle blessing in his veins as he tumbled headfirst into sleep.

CHAPTER TWENTY- EIGHT

C hased by nightmares of needles and fists, Dominic hovered on the edge of wakefulness, his mind unwilling to make the full leap to painful reality. The power of Felicia's potion wrapped peaceful arms around him, swaddling him in the safety of slumber, whilst the demands of his battered body begged him to rise and attend to its needs.

Pain punched him awake as the last of the drug released its hold. Wincing, he rolled to his back on the soiled straw, staring at the low roof of the bullpen, trying to make it out in the pitch darkness. His fingers were numb, his shoulders stretched. He blinked, longing for light. What time of day was it? His straining ears caught no hint of sound. If he was in the market livery, the place was unusually quiet. Not even the soft snort of a drowsy horse. What was occurring? Was there some sort of curfew in place, keeping the folk indoors?

"Hello, is there anyone there?"

His voice was a croak, swallowed by the sturdy walls of his prison. Working moisture into his dry mouth, he tried again, head cocked, desperate for a reply. Nothing. Gagging at the pain in his ribs, he rolled himself to his stomach and from there to his knees. Disoriented, he swayed, swallowing nausea. He nudged his arms sideways, fumbling blindly for his new dagger, still encased in its elaborate scabbard. Useless to him now. With his hands fastened hard behind his back, unable to feel his fingers, reaching it was impossible. He'd have done better with his old dagger handy in his belt. He bit his lip at the memory of it sliding across greasy cobbles. But he couldn't stay like this. He had to get free somehow.

Shuffling sideways to the wall, he used it for support to edge himself upright, cursing when his shoulder caught the metal edge of the manger. A gentle waft of sweet-smelling hay tickled his nose. Alright. That meant the door was on his right. His head twisted, remembering the layout of the stall, and snared on the image of the sharp-edged shovel standing in the corner. Biting his lip, he sidled towards it in the darkness, feeling carefully with his feet. There! Standing awkwardly on one leg, he hooked the handle with his free foot, lowering it slowly to the floor. His vision blurred for a moment, and he leant against the wall, nudging the tool across the angle of the adjacent walls. Lowering himself to the floor again kicked agony at his ribs. Gritting his teeth, he closed his eyes against the pain and shuffled backwards to the sharp iron edge of the blade. The see-sawing motion of his tied wrists sent icy jolts of distress through his body. Face clenched, he worked his bound hands faster against the metal, heartened at the harsh sound of fraying rope. The relief as the strands finally parted sent his head to his chest as he dragged his arms forward. Abused muscles protesting, pins and needles shot through his clawed fingers as blood returned.

Blinking tears out of his eyes in the darkness, he looked at the door. He bit his lip, remembering the thud and rattle of the heavy bar coming down. The citizens of Blade didn't just keep bulls in here, he remembered. It was a cell. A place the Queen's guard would dump a drunk overnight to sleep off his excesses. The place they left people before they met the hangman's rope. He shuddered. No one knew he was here. Arabella had left him to die.

The after-effects of Felicia's sleeping potion still tugged at his senses, waiting to pull him down once more. Dragging himself to his feet, he roamed the perimeter of the cell, tracing its solid outline and rubbing life into his limbs. A slight breeze tickled his fingers when he pressed them against the planks, but no light permeated from the wider environment. Perhaps it was night, he reasoned. He stopped pacing, wondering with a jolt how long he'd slept. Surely not the whole day away?

The thought clawed panic at his chest as realisation dawned. Too much time had elapsed. Arabella must have found Terrence and the falcon by now. What would happen then? Tall and spare as he was, even at his advanced age, Terrence could probably fight better than Dominic. But the Grayling was still vulnerable, and Guildford would show no mercy. He never had. Not even to save Felicia from a terrible fate. As for their mother. His stomach roiled with the acid burn of righteous anger. The woman was mad. More ruthless and vindictive than anyone he'd ever met before, playing her children as pawns in a dangerous game of power and revenge.

Jacklyn's wise, concerned face moved across his inner vision, pragmatic to his soul. "Kill Arabella if you must, just don't use magic," he'd said. Dominic's shoulders jerked as he pounded his frustration into the thick wood. Too late. He would have lost his powers willingly for the chance to kill Arabella. But then, Aldric would have died. His drumming fists slowed, and he scrubbed his hands through his hair, tugging at his scalp. A tremendous sigh erupted from his chest as he stood there, understanding as he never had before, his queen's perpetual balancing act to juggle the immense power granted to her by the Mage. The delicate balance she rode between justice and mercy.

"There are many who still yearn for the days when magic was banished. If we persecute them, all we will do is prove them right in their assumptions," Joran had said just a couple of days ago. Dominic's lips thinned. The Citizens understood the Queen's magical power and resented it. No matter that she had never once used it against them, there was always the lingering feeling that she could. It made sense that they might be happier with Guildford on the throne. Another

Citizen, just like them, with all the normal faults and failings of an ordinary person.

To them, the Queen was merely a mortal blessed with the strength of the gods, a prisoner to her own abilities. A falcon with clipped wings, vulnerable to attack.

Pressing his fists against the wood, he lowered his head against them, grinding his knuckles into his forehead. This was his fault. He should have taken his duties more seriously. Guarded the Grayling more closely. Focused less on his desire to best Guildford of Wessendean and more on building up his physical strength. He groaned aloud at the memory of Marjorie's rough advice and his rejection of it. He should have taken up the sword and not waited for his powers to come to fruition. The coward's way. The easy way. So proud he'd been of his Blessed gifts. And now they were gone.

Memories danced across his mind. His awe on the damp night he'd first seen Petronella up close on the night of her escape. Shadows had crowded her navy eyes and lingered under her high cheekbones. Scrawny as a peasant in her rough garb, she'd been as hungry as him back then. As hungry as all of them. Risking everything to save the life of a friend and her kingdom, she'd ventured into the unknown with no hope of success. He remembered her raising him from his knees with wry humour, something about her quiet determination commanding his instant respect. Biting his lip, his shoulders stiffened. The twelve-year-old Dominic had been proud to assist. Had transported her to safety, brought the Grayling to her side on a whim. If he hadn't, the kingdom would have fallen to Darius and the dark power of the Shadow Mage. He kicked out at the boards, wincing at the extra pain in his right foot. She'd trusted him. Elevated him to the nobility in gratitude. Gifted him status and security, even a place at the High Table during supper. And he'd repaid her by spending his nights gambling and drinking and feeling sorry for himself.

And now her life was in danger again. He gritted his teeth so hard his jaw clenched. Raising both fists, he pounded again at the forbidding wood, yelling at the top of his lungs.

"Someone, help me! Get me out of here!"

And this time, to his flooding relief, someone answered.

Chapter Twenty-Nine

"Master Skinner?"

The voice on the other side of the door was a thin, harsh whisper. Dominic closed his eyes and pressed his face to the rough planks.

"Who...?" he started.

"Aldric." The boy's voice dropped so low Dominic strained to hear it. Relieved as he was to know someone was there, part of his heart sank.

"Can you lift the bar?" he asked.

"I'll try." Doubt stood clear in Aldric's voice. No great wonder there. The boy was skinny as a twig, much like Dominic's younger self. He cursed softly as his mind delivered another unwelcome image of his own ten-year-old weakness and its deathly consequences. Gavin's cheerful face flashed across his mind's eye. He cleared his throat, trying to keep the frustration from his voice.

"Try, please."

The answer was a grunt of effort and the dull thump of heavy wood returning to its bracket. Aldric leaned against the door, his voice a little louder.

"I'm sorry, Master. I'll fetch help,"

"Find Rosa or Will, of Meridan's gang, or Meridan herself," Dominic said before the boy could scuttle off. "Don't trust anyone else. Do you hear me?"

"There's no one much around, Master," Aldric replied. "Dupliss' troops have locked down the city. There's a curfew."

Dominic's eyes widened in the dark. "Has he marched on the castle?"

"I don't know. It's very tense. Goodshank's still lying on the street where you left him. No one's moved him yet. There're troops patrolling."

Aldric's voice was carefully neutral, but Dominic caught the note of fear within it.

"Well then, be careful. Keep to the shadows. Meridan's gang should be somewhere near the temple complex but keep out of sight. Do you hear me?"

"Aye. I'll get 'em."

Hushed on the cobbles, his light footsteps pattered away. Dominic slid wearily to the floor and braced his head against his hands, heart pounding in trepidation. He ran his tongue around parched lips. Feeling around in the dark, his fingers closed on the jug Felicia had left. There was still a shallow draft left in the bottom. Grateful to find it, he tipped the jug to his dry mouth. Hopefully, there was not enough there to knock him out again.

Slumped against the planks, waiting impatiently for Aldric's return, he nearly fell out of the door when it finally opened.

Eyes watering in relief, he blinked up at the circle of light cast by a horn lantern. Rosa and Will stared down at him. Alarm creased the shadows under their eyes. Will reached an arm to him, determination etched across his square, freckled face.

"Can you walk?"

Dominic ignored the arm and heaved himself to his feet, pressing his hand against his side. "Just. What's going on?"

Rosa and Will exchanged glances, uncertainty flashing between them. Will extended a bracing arm again as Dominic staggered.

Accepting it this time, he glanced between them. "What?"

Rosa's face twitched. She drew a breath. "We've been taking turns watching the temple complex all day," she said, ushering him forward. The row of horse boxes stretched empty to each side of them, the open doors gaping like hungry mouths. "Yer uncle came out once, but there was no sign of the falcon."

Dominic cast his eyes upwards in relief at her words. At least his instinct had been correct. His uncle had moved the Grayling to hallowed ground. But did that mean he was safe? He tried to ignore the nibbling doubt chewing at the edges of his mind. Felicia's wide eyes, misty above him as she encouraged him to taste the contents of her potion, flashed across his inner vision.

"Meridan found Thomas," Will continued. "He left as soon as he could. We've heard nothing from him since."

"Good." Despite his doubt, a prickle of hope sparked in his blood. "What of Arabella? They were searching the temple."

Rosa snorted as they reached the livery door and cracked it open. Dominic inhaled, drawing a painful breath of fresh air into his beleaguered lungs.

She allowed herself a harsh chuckle. "Aye, they did search it. Looked all over."

"But they didn't find him? How can that be?"

Rosa shrugged. "Don't know. It's a curious thing. We know he's there, but we couldn't find him either." She peeked through the door. "All clear, come on."

As a group, they slid into the dark night. Dominic's gaze flicked automatically upward. There was no moon tonight. Instead, a blaze of starlight swept the sky, rendering it as gauzy and transparent as Aramida's shift. An eerie silence prevailed. No blast of laughter and good cheer filtered through the tavern windows. No calls from the midnight market vendors hawking their wares or the rumble of wheels on cobbles. The surrounding buildings loomed solid, their windows shuttered and blind. He blinked. It was like waking into a dream, where eyes watched, silent and judgemental from shadows, and the future waited on the flick of a coin, twisting through its choices but yet to land. Watching the wheeling stars, he swayed where he stood.

Will squeezed his arm. "They've hurt you bad. Meridan said to bring you back to the tannery," he whispered.

Dominic squinted at the boy's freckled face, serious in the dim light. He shook his head, his gaze lifting to the distant city walls and the castle road.

"Arabella had a message earlier on. Dupliss is waiting for her signal to start the march on the castle. He won't move unless he knows she has the falcon. There's no bargaining chip without it." He stared around at the group. "And if she hasn't found him. We still have time."

The children looked at each other, their faces serious. Dominic screwed his hands into fists at his side. Some army, this! Rosa's face shuttered and remote, Will's twisted with worry. Skinny Aldric stared at him with a mixture of fascination and soul-deep fear. He frowned.

"Where's Little Bird?"

"We've been taking turns at the temple. She's still watching," said Will.

Rosa took the lead, and they hurried along streets made unfamiliar by their quietness. Every hushed footfall sounded loud in the night. Somewhere, a cat yowled, lonely in the scudding breeze. They almost stumbled across Goodshank's stiff body. The man's corpse sprawled across the cobbles near the market entrance, one arm flung north and pointing at the castle like a warning. Dominic averted his eyes, his gaze clashing with Aldric's. The boy crept towards him and extended his hand. Something glinted within it, and Dominic's stomach shrunk automatically at the sight of the blade curled in the lad's fist. He stopped. Aldric opened his fingers. Dominic's trusty dagger lay in his palm.

"I found this," the boy said, his hand shaking, his dark eyes huge.

Dominic took it. His fingers closed hard around the familiar pommel. The worn wood hilt lay in his grasp like the hand of a trusted friend. He saluted the boy with it and returned it to its accustomed place in his belt.

"My thanks, Aldric. And for finding me."

The lad nodded, jerky as a sparrow, his eyes drifting to the body of his former employer. The faint miasma of decay already rose from his corpse. "I'm glad he's dead," he said, his voice shrill. "He was cruel. To me and his birds. Everyone." His own hands went to his face. "The Queen's Guard will do me for stealing," he whispered from under them. "I went back to the shop. Let all the birds go, ate all his food. They'll hang me." Shamefaced, he dropped his hands and stared at the damp ground.

Will grinned. "You're one of us, now," he said. He gave the boy a shove. "Welcome, brother thief."

Wincing at the effort, Dominic thumped Aldric's shoulder. "You did the right thing, but the Guard would have to catch you first," he said. "And I don't think Goodshank will be the one telling them."

One corner of the lad's mouth lifted, and they hurried onwards, Dominic hissing at the pain in his ribs, clutching his side, steadying his limping gait against walls and fences.

The journey back to his childhood home seemed to take forever. Much as Dominic longed to rush to the temple, Meridan was right. He couldn't afford to dash in with no plan. It wasn't just his life at stake now. He glanced round at his tired companions, marvelling at their tenacity. All day, they'd watched, despite their own need for rest. His eyes lifted, piercing the gloom towards the distant temple. Wooden scaffold crawled around its outer walls, a delicate border softening its blocky outline. Dark shadows against the silvered sky, the twin spires soared above the skyline of Blade. Another narrow wooden scaffold bridged the yawning gap between the two graceful towers. Just looking at it from a distance made his toes curl. He lost sight of the temple as they entered the tangle of narrow back streets to the tannery, but his mind wandered. Somewhere in that vast stone complex, littered with fallen masonry and broken tiles, his uncle had the Grayling. Whether he could be trusted remained to be seen. Biting his lip as a loose slab twisted under his sprained ankle, he considered his options.

Desperate to get control of the Grayling, Arabella would lurk there, waiting to snatch the bird for herself. Guildford would back her up, along with Carl, Pieter, and any other citizens she'd prised away from Dupliss' mob. He shivered, his whole body braced in denial. To return to the fray in his condition was a fool's journey. He stood no chance. And if Felicia was right, and Terrence was involved... His mouth twisted, his skin pricking with the memory of his uncle's bleak face, eyes black, one fist clenching and unclenching in his effort to keep the Shadow Mage at bay. And his hushed confession. "I battle him to stay in the light every day of my life."

Turning the corner to the Skinner tannery courtyard, unmistakable by virtue of its ever-present stench, his gaze hardened, and his hand drifted to his dagger. Uncertainty still nagged at his gut. He had no power. But Thomas was also right. He had to be true to himself. Pushing open the door to his childhood home, the gang herded him to the nearest seat. Meridan glanced up from her stool by the fire, relief clear in the tired lines of her face. Shaking her head, her lips compressed in a solid line as she took in his fresh injuries. She rose, already reaching for salve and water. Medicinal brandy.

"By the gods, I'm glad to see you," she said.

Wincing at the bite of alcohol against the deep rope burns on both wrists, Dominic glanced at the ring of faces. Will, sturdy and serious. Rosa, dubious, somehow detached. Aldric, watching him with a mixture of trust and awe. Meridan, taking charge, watching out for them. Watching out for him.

He sighed, the breath shuddering through his bruises and battered ribcage. On the wall, the votive candle flickered in its alcove. The

206 CHRISTINE CAZALY

rough carving of the Mage's symbol above it seemed to undulate in its small, uncertain light. He bit down on a huff of laughter.

Felicia. So fond of calling him a fool. His brain snared on the image of the girl, mouth sewn shut, ensuring his survival at a terrible cost to herself. Admiration for her soared, along with the memory of her soft voice and eyes golden with prophecy.

"He who holds the Grayling holds the crown. If you run, the falcon will die. The kingdom will fall."

His fists clenched on his knees, and he lifted his chin. One more time, then.

He wouldn't run.

CHAPTER THIRTY

M eridan's mouth tightened along with the bandages she wound around his wrists and waved at his torn tunic. "Will, help him get that off. We have to strap him up."

Stifling an enormous yawn, Will moved forward with good-natured grace. Dominic groaned aloud as he lifted his arms, cold sweat breaking out across his skin. The touch of Meridan's cloth against his skin was soothing, although her milder brew held none of the instant pain relief of Felicia's.

"Will says you found Thomas?" he asked, as she used a dry rag to dab him dry, tutting at the damage, and began binding his ribs.

She nodded. "At Maria Fitzherbert's house, nose deep in a draft of sack, making merry with her ladyship. He wasn't best pleased at being disturbed."

Dominic chewed his lip. "But did he listen?"

His amateur physician shrugged, her thin mouth pursed. "Aye. Eventually. Mistress Fitzherbert sent him on his way. Seems like she's on the Queen's side, thank all the gods."

Dominic said nothing, and the girl met the quiet question in his worried eyes with a bare shrug. She shook her head. "He's had plenty of time to get there and back. There's no sign of him. I'm sorry."

His shoulders slumped. He turned away from her to stare into the flames, his fingers massaging the ache in his thigh muscles.

"So, we're on our own. That's a blow," he said. His forehead creased. There was no way of knowing if Thomas had been successful on his mission or not.

"Aye. Seems so." Meridan laid a sympathetic hand on his shoulder. "Here, put this on." She handed him a shirt and another tunic. "Stolen specially for you by Little Bird," she said.

"When did she have time to do that? Hasn't she been on watch at the temple all day?" He reached for the garments and accepted Will's help in getting them over his head. They smelled of strong soap and stone dust.

"She volunteered herself as a water bearer so she could keep watch on the premises. The labourers always need children like her, willing to work for a penny. Said she found the clothes drying on a block of stone in the sunshine. Handed them over to me when I checked on her."

Dominic snickered, fingering the rough fustian. Freshly washed linen had become something of a novelty in the last few days. He glanced at the front door. "Where is she now? It's black as pitch out there. She's not still keeping watch?"

He jumped as the front door cracked open and Little Bird stumbled in. Dust turned her pale face more ghostly still. Her hair stood on end. Meridan extended an arm, and the smallest thief leaned against her. Up close, the resemblance between them was startling, although Little Bird's hair was lighter in hue. He blinked.

"You're sisters," he said, realising it for the first time.

"Aye. Rosa and Will are brother and sister, too. Our cousins." Meridan pushed her sibling to the table, with a silent nod at the leftover meal waiting there.

Little Bird settled over it, elbows braced like the hunched wings of a hungry hawk, and snatched at a loaf. "We'll have to go soon," she announced, between bites. "There's something strange happening."

Rosa joined her at the table, hands on hips. "What do you mean, strange? You're always talking nonsense, Little Bird. What could be strange?" she said,

Little Bird eyed her dismissively and returned to her food. "What I said."

"Go on, Bird," Will said, "We're all waiting now. Tell us what you know."

The girl grinned around her mouthful, and Dominic hid a brief smile at the boy's manner. He'd clearly got the measure of the youngest member of the gang. Hero worship blazed in her eyes as she looked at him.

"I worked all morning. After the noon bell, it was. All the stone men just disappeared and didn't come back."

"P'raps they've joined up with Dupliss," Will suggested.

"Or the start of the curfew," Meridan said, packing her bandages and potions into a wicker basket and stowing them safely on the narrow shelf that still contained his mother's precious collection of pots.

Little Bird's brow quirked. She shook her head, her dusty curls brushing her cheeks. "Maybe, but they're not all for Dupliss. Some of 'em are still devout. I saw 'em in the morning, going into the temple. They've left offerings to the Mage in there, even though it's all still half fallen down." She threw an arm out in Dominic's direction. "Even that tunic. Look, it's got the sign on the Mage on it."

Dominic glanced down at the faded brown fustian. Little Bird was right. A subtle embroidery of the same coloured thread wove a delicate figure of eight around the frayed cuffs. He traced the edge with a dirty finger.

"So, what do you think it means?" he asked her. "Did you see anything else?"

She looked at him over her bread, navy eyes huge. "I saw him. Your uncle." A shudder rippled through her narrow frame. "He's scary. Those black eyes."

"Black eyes?" Clutching the wall for support, Dominic lurched upright, transported back to the castle library, to his uncle's bleak, forbidding stare in the grip of the Shadow Mage. He rubbed perspiring palms down his breeches. "Did you see the Grayling? Is he alright?"

"Only saw your uncle," Little Bird corrected repressively. "He came out of the temple when everyone had gone. He didn't see me. I was hiding."

"So, he's there. What's strange about that? We know he's there," Rosa scoffed. She took an apple and bit into it, spraying juice down her chin.

Little Bird frowned. "That's not the strangest thing. This is the strangest thing." She paused, looking around at them, debating their reactions. Her gaze came to rest on Dominic.

"Your uncle's not alone," she said. "There's someone with him."

Dominic dipped his head, giving her the point. It was possible that Terrence had conscripted others to his side for whatever purpose he'd chosen. "More than my uncle. Alright, good information, Little Bird," he said, still worrying over her description of his uncle's eyes.

"No." The thin face screwed up in thought. "See, I could see there was someone with him, standing at his side. But the strange thing is, I don't think he knew she was there."

Silence greeted her words. A sputter of derisive laughter from Rosa jerked their faces to her. "She's talking nonsense ghost stories again. All for attention, isn't it, Little Bird?"

Little Bird chewed her lip and looked at the table. Her shoulders tightened. "Knew you wouldn't believe me," she muttered. Picking up a knife she stabbed it deep into the heart of a cold pie. Gravy oozed around the edge of the torn pastry. A sweep of gooseflesh chilled Dominic's shoulders.

"Did you see her clearly, this woman? What did she look like?" he asked.

Rosa marched from the table to the fireplace and kicked a log further into the grate. A shower of sparks leaped up the narrow chimney. "You can't take any notice of her. She's always making things up."

Little Bird slammed her knife down and glared at Rosa's back. "I do not," she said, slim jaw squaring. "I steal things. I don't lie."

Rosa turned, eyes blazing with animosity. "Yes, you do. Always saying you can hear what's going on in people's heads. It's all rubbish. You just want to be special, that's all. A member of the Blessed. Like him." She jerked her chin at Dominic. Startled at her animosity, Dominic looked at Meridan. The gang leader's face hardened.

"That will do, Rosa," she said, steel in her quiet tone. "You had the chance to leave with Pieter. If you feel like this, why did you not go? He expected you to."

An ugly flush stained Rosa's cheeks. "I would have gone," she said. "Pieter wanted me to. But Will wouldn't leave you and Little Bird, and I don't want him corrupted by her tales of magical power. You're all rotten. All of you Blessed people. The Citizens should wipe you out. You're dangerous. Look what he did to Goodshank, just by thinking about it." She jerked her chin at Dominic, face as hard as stone.

"Goodshank deserved it," Aldric said, his voice small. Rosa skewered him with her glare. Fingers twisting with agitation, he raised his chin and stood his ground as if nailed to the floor.

Will took a halting step forward. Dominic's heart contracted at the anguish written across his freckled face.

"You can't mean that, Rosa," Will said, eyes wide in the firelight. "Please say you don't."

Rosa drew herself up. "I love you. You're my brother, but I can't help what I think. You're just a Citizen, like me. Come with me."

The two young people stared at each other. Dominic and Meridan exchanged a long look. She quirked an eyebrow at him, a silent question in her eyes, and he returned it with a rueful nod of his own.

Meridan cleared her throat, breaking the silence. "Then I'm sorry, Rosa," she said. "If that's what you think, you must leave. I'm a Citizen, too, but I'm loyal to our Queen, and the Mage."

Will whirled towards her, clutching at her cambric sleeve. "No, Meridan, don't make her go! Please. She doesn't mean it? Do you, Rosa?"

His sister nudged the log in the grate once more, sending dull sparks up the narrow chimney. She glared at Little Bird across the narrow space. Mouth twisting, she glanced once at her brother and stooped to hook a small satchel of goods from the floor.

"I mean it, Will. I'm sorry."

The boy's arm lowered to his side as she marched past, shoulders stiff, refusing to meet his piteous expression. The fire flared in the draft as the front door slammed.

Swallowing her mouthful, Little Bird scrambled from her seat to position herself in front of Will. The boy stared into space, his arms hanging, face white with shock under his freckles. Dominic grabbed the medicinal brandy from the table and passed it to him. Will swigged automatically, a harsh gasp torn from his throat as he threw it back. Tears burned in his eyes.

"I am truly sorry, Will," Meridan said. "If you want to leave and go after her, we will understand."

"No, don't go, Will, please don't!" Little Bird turned her face up to him, burying her head against his stomach. Will's hands tightened around her delicate shoulders. He closed his eyes, cheeks wet, and rocked the young girl against his boyish chest.

"You know I'll never leave you, Bird," he said.

The girl stood back, rubbing the heels of her hands against her grubby cheeks. She glanced at him, apology in her eyes, and leaned across to tug at Dominic's sleeve.

"What does it mean, what I saw, Master Dominic?" she asked.

Dominic scraped his hair back from his face, rubbing at the tension in his neck.

"I don't know, Little Bird. My uncle is a tortured man, haunted by his past actions."

"More to the point, what does he want with the Grayling?" Meridan said, cutting to the practical.

Dominic's shoulders rose in a painful shrug. "Don't know that, either." He looked around at the group. Without Rosa's solid, if doubting, presence, its fragility seemed even more apparent.

"Whatever we decide, we need to do it quickly," he said. "Every minute we waste now gives Dupliss the advantage."

Little Bird's brow quirked. "You know, I watched that horrible woman and her people poking around," she said. "They must have looked everywhere. Shouting, and pointing at each other. They found nothing. Same as us, when we looked. It's a mess. Broken stone where some roofs fell in. All dirty and weeded up. Ropes and pulleys and platforms. It takes a lot to move that stone." She stared around at them, the beginnings of a smile on her face. "But when I saw Master Dominic's uncle, and that woman, or ghost, or whatever she was, they came out of the Temple of the Mage."

"I don't understand," Will said.

"Ah," Dominic said. He winked at Little Bird, who ducked her head, shuffling her feet on the flags. "The other night at the stable, you saw what my uncle can do, didn't you?" he asked, knowing the answer.

She nibbled her lip, darting a glance at him.

"What?" Meridan demanded, losing patience.

"Arabella would have taken one look at the Temple of the Mage and thought it was empty. But there are catacombs underneath it. The entry is right under the altar. My parents are interred there.

Meridan shrugged. "So? There's no way into the catacombs. We saw it. It's covered by what's left of the roof. The lightning strike went straight through. That's why it's such a mess."

Dominic pushed himself away from the rough wall, the answer twinkling in his brain. "But what if you originally trained as an architect, and you can lift heavy objects with the power of your mind?"

CHAPTER THIRTY-ONE

"**H**ow does that help us? Can you lift something that heavy with your mind, too?" Will asked,

"Not at the moment," Dominic said. He averted his shamefaced gaze from the gang and stared hard at his shoes. Little Bird's grubby palm slipped into his, her fingers sticky.

"Is it because of that man you killed? Did the Mage take your powers, like you said?" she asked. She stared up at him. Dominic risked a glance at her, but there was no judgement on her grimy face, just vast curiosity.

His hand tightened on hers. "Aye. He judged me unworthy." He squeezed her fingers and banged his free fist against the wall. "Much good I can do us," he said. "You can all fight better than me if it comes to it."

"Doesn't matter about your powers," Will declared stoutly. "If that's where he is, hiding under the temple, he'll have to come out for water or food. We just have to be there when he does."

Meridan paced in a small circle. "And then what? Just march up to him and ask him nicely to give the bird back?" She arched a scornful eyebrow at Dominic, who tried to ignore the flush of embarrassment that flooded his cheeks.

"He's my uncle," he muttered, conscious of how weak that sounded.

"And he's still got his magical abilities," Meridan pointed out. "If anyone can keep the bird safe from Dupliss and the Wessendeans, surely he can?"

"Felicia of Wessendean told me not to trust him," Dominic mumbled, his face scarlet.

"Oh yes, so of course that must be true." Meridan glared at him. "She's a Wessendean, Dominic. Of course she's going to say that."

Dominic met her glare with one of his own. "She also saved my life at least twice in the last two days."

Meridan stopped pacing, fists clenched at her sides. "Why? Why would she do that? So you'd do the Wessendeans work for them?"

Dominic huffed a tired laugh. "Hardly. I've done nothing but get in their way, and now they don't have the falcon, just when they need him."

The gang leader slumped to the table and reached for a decanter of small ale. "So why are we so worried about getting the bird back?" she asked him, taking a hefty swig directly from the jug. "Your mentomantist uncle has the Grayling. The Wessendeans don't. That's good news." She flicked a disparaging hand at him. "They also know their chances of getting the falcon are much better if you have him. Look at the state of you."

Dominic sighed. She had an excellent point. But still. "Felicia of Wessendean is a Seer, Meridan," he said, choosing his words with care. "And she told me, if I run, the Grayling will die, and the kingdom will fall. So, the question is, does the fact she's born a Wessendean outweigh her gift from the Mage? He, at least, believes her worthy. Powerful, too. She's only fourteen."

Meridan looked him up and down. "Are you sure you're not thinking with your...heart?" she asked pointedly. "Because you're asking us to help you. And these are my friends. My family. My job is to keep them safe."

He closed his eyes, tipping his head back against the wall. "I know, I know. You don't have to help me. None of you do."

"I want to help," Will said. He avoided Meridan's angry glare and stepped forward, a small, stalwart soldier.

"And me," Aldric added, brown eyes bright. "I've got no one to tell me what to do now, have I?"

"Me too," Little Bird said. "I know I'm not very good at it, but I do hear people's thoughts sometimes."

"By the Gods," Meridan stared over the top of her tankard at the row of warriors. "What are you thinking? You could all die."

"Have to die sometime," Will said, settling his shoulders. "My choice."

"You can't tell me what to do," Little Bird said, her chin jutting at her sister.

"I can," Meridan rejoined crisply. She slammed the jug down. "You will stay here."

Little Bird's navy eyes narrowed. "Won't."

"I've had an idea," Aldric said, inserting his bird-like form between Meridan and Little Bird as they glowered at each other across the narrow room.

"Go on," Dominic said. "Let's hear it,"

"Those catacombs under the Temple of the Mage. How big are they? Are they the same ones that go under the Temple of the Empress? You know, the one the Argentians worship in?" he asked.

Dominic blinked. "I guess they probably are. My father said the catacombs travel all over the north of the city. Seems to make sense the city founders would share their use across all the temples. Why?"

"Well, after The Starving, they repaired the Temple of the Empress first. It was the least damaged. My mother's buried there, in our family crypt." He looked around at the group, firelight flickering in the depths of his dark eyes. "Why can't we enter the catacombs from there?

Delighted with the idea, the youngest members of the group put their heads together. Meridan stared hard at Dominic, reservation writ large across her narrow face. He sighed, reaching for his bag.

"I will go alone," he said.

"You're injured. You can't." She got to her feet and bundled the remaining foodstuffs into napkins, wrapping them carefully, wiping off Little Bird's abandoned blade. The decanter shuddered as she forced a lead stopper into its neck.

Dominic put his hand on her arm. "You don't have to do this. None of you do." Her eyes sparked with tears as she looked up from her task, and she rubbed the end of her nose with the heel of her hand, sniffing them back. She shook his hand from her arm, fixing him with an icy stare that raised the short hair on the back of his neck.

"We do," she said through gritted teeth. "But if anything happens to Little Bird, I swear to the Mage I will kill you."

He nodded in recognition, his gaze shifting to the youngest thief's blonde curls and jaunty bandana as she elbowed Aldric in the ribs, eyes alight with laughter. "If anything happens to Little Bird, I'll let you," he said.

CHAPTER THIRTY-TWO

H ugging the shadows, Dominic led the group towards the temple complex as fast as his injuries would allow. Dim candlelight crept out in the gaps between shutters and walls as they slunk through the winding streets. Eerie tension still gripped the city. Dominic glanced upwards at the circling stars. The dead of night. His shoulders pricked with alarm at the call of an owl, and he glanced up to see an enormous barn owl watching from the recesses of a nearby workshop. Was that the Mage? Watching? He shook his head like a dog, shaking off the golden-eyed stare boring into his skull as they progressed. Turning a corner onto Market Street, he waved everyone back, hand on his dagger. Meridan crushed Little Bird against the wall. Will took a pace forward to stand at his side, a small but sturdy presence.

The sound of marching feet approaching from opposite directions echoed clearly on the cobbles. Hardly daring to breathe, Dominic exchanged glances with Meridan. A dagger gleamed in her hand, her lips drawn back against her teeth. He blinked at the feral determination on her face. She held the knife as if she'd been born to it.

"Where's the signal? Dupliss is waiting! We've got word that the prince is heading out with his soldiers from the castle. Now is the time for our forces inside the castle to strike!" Agitation quivered under the approaching soldier's deep voice.

"We are looking for the falcon. It is somewhere in the temple complex. Once she has it, my lady of Wessendean will order the signal fire lit in the tower," the leader of the second group replied, his voice brisk with irritation.

"Then she'd better hurry. Dupliss is having trouble convincing his forces to stick fast to their course. They are not soldiers, most of 'em," the first man said. "And he needs that bird. It's his bargaining chip in case it all goes belly up."

"We'll find it." The second man's voice dropped to a growl, low and threatening. Even flattened against the wall and unable to see, Dominic registered the imminent danger lurking within it.

"Are you all stupid down here?" Dominic winced at the words. This would not end well. "One old man and one bird in a cage. How hard can it be? Dupliss said to say you've got 'til cock crow. After that, it's too late. The Queen's powers will recover from the drug. She's ripe to pluck now."

"We'll find it, I said."

"There's a gibbet waiting if you don't. He said to tell you that, as well."

"Oh, he did, did he?"

The harsh sound of swords leaving scabbards drew Dominic's immediate attention. Burning with curiosity, he pushed his nose around the corner. The two groups of soldiers faced off only a few feet in front of him. Both leaders had drawn their weapons. Their combined breath twisted in the chill air. Animosity charged the atmosphere between them.

"Think you know it all, don't you? Just because you drink with him at the Black Eagle." Jaw jutting, lips thin with ire, the leader of the search party settled into a fighting stance.

"You're under orders. Do as he says!"

"Or what?"

Dominic raised his eyebrows as the tension between the two sets of troops stretched tighter. The lower ranks eyed each other, alert and watchful as a pack of wolves. He risked a glance at Little Bird, the whites of her eyes just visible from her cramped position behind her elder sister.

Her face screwed into almost comic lines as she concentrated. She nodded to him. "No one's looking," she whispered.

A clash of steel snapped his gaze back to the warring men. The quiet street was suddenly alive with the blur of angry shouts, grunts of pain, and ringing steel as the two groups exchanged blows.

Intent on the fracas, no one noticed them as they crept from the narrow street and disappeared into the further patch of shadow granted by the tall market wall. Dominic gritted his teeth against the sharp pain lancing through his ribs as he limped onward, leaving the warring soldiers behind. Beyond them, the high walls of the ancient temple complex commanded attention. Patches of much paler stone stood out in the old boundary, replacing damage to the original structure. Passing through the magnificent stone arch, the group headed instinctively for the nearest patch of shadow. Eyes wide, Dominic stared around. Growing up under Arion's reign, he'd never set foot here. Back then, the complex was all but abandoned. To worship or even enter this hallowed ground meant risking your life. The size of the vast courtyard almost overwhelmed him. Almost a city, within a city. Four magnificent temples, erected in honour of the Four Great Gods, occupied the corners, each different in style. Decorated in temporary wooden scaffolding, the Temple of the Mage leapt skyward, its twin towers stretching for the clouds. In contrast, the domed roof of the Temple of the Empress, beloved of the Argentians, hugged the earth. A series of shallow steps led to its many-layered entry, inviting worshippers to the comfort of its interior. Twin statues of the Empress stood sentinel on either side of the stairs. Her serene features and rounded belly beckoned worshippers to wander within. Intricate carvings of trees and foliage decorated its exterior walls. A freshly planted garden stretched around it, the sinuous outlines hugging the curve of the building.

At adjacent corners, the Temple to the High Priestess of Oceanis stood open to the moon and stars. Still undergoing repair, the vast fountain in the shape of a cup loomed silent before its entryway. Turning his head, Dominic crooked his head in amazement at the Temple to the Emperor, the god of Battonia. The building stood foursquare, with four spires at each corner, twisting like flames themselves. A golden light glowed permanently in its interior, perpetually aflame in honour of the Battonians' blessed gift of fire.

Clustered around the vast well that served the complex, the detritus of a busy stone yard littered the central courtyard. The remains of several smaller constructions, once shops or service buildings, lined the walls between the temples. The space in front of the Temple of the Mage was an organised mess of half-hewn stone, mason's tools, buckets, platforms, hoists, and pulleys. Stacks of neatly piled wood and coils of rope waited to be pressed into use. The smell of stone dust and damp mortar crept across the space, driven by a rising wind.

"I hid over there," Little Bird whispered against Dominic's ear. She waved her hand at a group of barrels near the temple entrance, currently bereft of its magnificent double doors. "Your uncle came out for water, and then he went back inside again."

"Shall we look?" Will said.

He'd taken one lurching step forward when Dominic grabbed his arm and yanked him back. "We are not alone here. Look," he hissed. Subtle light bobbed uncertainly within the dark maw of the temple's yawning entrance and then disappeared. "We can't go in. The soldiers are there. Or Arabella." His body shuddered at the memory of her cold, hard face. "We'll try the Temple of the Empress like Aldric said."

"The soldiers could be there," Meridan said, her face harrowed. She glanced at her sister. Little Bird shrugged, fingering her knife.

"You don't have to worry about me. I'm small, but I'm quick, and my blade is sharp," she said.

Rough, muted voices floated to them across the quiet space, punctuated by Arabella's shrill tones demanding immediate action. Dominic heard the mention of ropes and pulleys.

"They've worked it out, at last," he said. "Come on, let's go."

Pursued by the sound of argument and the creak of windlasses being dragged into position, the group crossed Temple Square. Dominic's shoulders twitched once more at the sensation of being observed. He glanced upwards at the crenelations and intricate crevices presented by the various churches. Any shadowed alcove could contain the Mage in the shape of a watchful owl, but distance and low light defeated him. Head down, he scurried with the others up the shallow set of stairs leading to the Temple of the Empress.

He paused on the threshold, eyes adjusting to the flickering torchlight set at intervals around the circular walls. Expecting stone, the sheen of polished wood stretching away into the near distance at his feet surprised him. The immediate feeling in the church was of warmth and comfort. He inhaled an earthy scent of flowers and honey, and his nose twitched in recognition. The same beguiling aroma followed Lady Fortuna de Winter, Prince Ranulf's Argentian nurse, as well. At the front and centre, an enormous statue of the seated Empress rose from the floor to the low, domed ceiling. Her lap was a mass of flowers donated by her followers. The wall at her back comprised the graceful branches of a tree. Its trunk plunging deep into the earth under the temple. Carved rabbits and other woodland creatures lingered at the feet of the Empress; their necks hung with ribbons in the familiar Argentian colours of green and gold. Rather than benches, the congregation enjoyed the luxury of padded chairs, their low backs picked out in gilt.

Aldric lurched forward, kneeling at the feet of his goddess and bowing his head to the rich brown wood. Torchlight reflected the gloss of his black hair. Dominic jumped as Little Bird slipped her hand into his, her small fingers warm in his chilled grasp.

"There's someone else in here," she said, standing on tiptoe to whisper in her ear.

Every hair on his body prickling upright, Dominic jerked his attention from the young boy's devotions. Prostrate, Aldric took no notice of the shuffle of feet at his right-hand side. Dominic hefted his dagger and then relaxed as an old woman emerged from a low door underneath the spreading branches of the tree. She wore the green and gold of the Empress's colours, her silvered hair long, and threaded with flowers.

"The Empress' blessings upon you, seekers," she said, her voice tremulous with the patina of age. "What do you wish?"

Aldric leapt to his feet and bowed once again, touching her wrinkled hand with his forehead. "Why, Aldric Haligon," the priestess said. "What do you here at this hour?" She turned to look at the small group lingering at the entrance and gestured them in. "Come, come," she said. "The Empress will not bite you."

Exchanging glances, the group shuffled further into the building. Little Bird's eyes were enormous as she looked around. Meridan kept her dagger in her hand. Will's eyes turned in every direction, looking for traps. Dominic's gaze kept being dragged backwards over his shoulder to the Temple of the Mage, where distant shouting percolated through the night.

"Madam Priestess, may we beg a boon from you and the Empress?" Aldric asked before Dominic could open his mouth.

The priestess regarded him with her head on one side, brown eyes patient and wise. "Tell me what you wish," she said.

Aldric glanced at Dominic. He cleared his throat and stepped forward, Little Bird still clinging to his hand like a burr. "We seek passage through the catacombs to the Temple of the Mage, mistress," he said. "We must retrieve the Queen's falcon at all costs."

The old woman cocked her head as if listening to something Dominic could not hear. "At all costs, you say," she said, her tone musing.

"At all costs. Tonight. Now," Dominic repeated, impatience adding a roughness to his voice he did not at once recognise.

"Her mouth was sewn up," the woman said, as if continuing a different conversation with a person no one else could hear.

"What?" Dominic stared at her, his heart beating a rapid tattoo inside his chest. "How do you know that? Have you seen her?"

The edges of a smile curved the ancient face into a mass of wrinkles, the press of time against living rock. One hand dipped into the recesses of her robes and withdrew a parchment bound by a simple blue ribbon.

The Priestess held it out to him. Fingers trembling, Dominic took it.

"What is it? What does it say?" Little Bird crowded close to him as he slanted the vellum toward the nearest torchlight. Felicia's ever-neat handwriting jumped from the page.

Dominic stared at the spare message, his mouth falling open, his heart a sudden vice in his chest. "It's from Felicia. It says 'He who holds the Grayling, holds the crown'."

Meridan flapped a disparaging hand at him. "And so? A message from a traitorous Wessendean. We've had this conversation before."

"There's something else," Dominic muttered. His skin crawled with dread as he looked up at Meridan. "She says the Shadow Mage is here."

CHAPTER THIRTY-THREE

F ar from the start of unease that chilled his blood at the brief message, his companions greeted the announcement with an array of puzzled faces.

"Who?" Meridan said, tightening her grip on her dagger. She moved towards Little Bird, one hand on the smaller girl's shoulder, piercing eyes searching the temple for danger.

"The Shadow Mage, you say?" the old priestess said, her rheumy gaze sharpening. "Who brings this evil to our temples?"

"Evil?" Will echoed, his voice a thin whisper, almost lost to the softwood walls. "What does she mean?"

Dominic swallowed against the dryness in his throat. "The Shadow Mage is the dark side of our God," he said. "Petronella fought the Shadow Mage to regain control of her crown. She flew in the Grayling's mind to battle his power, and united the rings of justice and mercy to banish him from our midst. She returned our country to the light side of the Mage."

Meridan turned her pale face to his. "Then the stories are true? She really can do magic? Proper magic?"

Dominic's heart turned over as he looked around the group. Citizens, for the most part, he reminded himself. Alone in a world turned upside down by the abrupt ending of one brutal regime and the terrible decimation of sickness at the start of the next. With no parents, and no schooling. How would they know what really happened? Or what to believe? Thanks to the brutality of Lord Falconridge, there were so few of the Eperan Blessed left to tell them.

He nodded, his face grave. "Our Queen is one of the most powerfully Blessed Eperans of our age," he said. "She had a grandmother who was a Seer of Epera, bestowed with Farsight. Her mother was Blessed with the powers of illusion and transformation. The Queen's telepathic gift extends far beyond mind-talking. If she chooses, Petronella can walk into your mind. Experience your thoughts and memories with you. See your world as you see it. It is a formidable gift."

The child thieves gaped at each other. Will shifted uncomfortably, his eyes darting to Little Bird. She drew her shoulders back, navy eyes shining, clearly pleased at her inclusion in the ranks of the Blessed. Her ready smile lurked at the edges of her wide mouth. Aldric raised thoughtful eyes to the immense statue of the Empress. Her benevolent presence continued to extend its aura of peace and comfort around them. "Does the Empress have a shadow side?" he asked the old woman.

The priestess's mouth tightened minutely, along with her shoulders, but she inclined her head, giving him the point. "She does, young man. All our Gods possess a shadow side," she said. "But now is not the time for a lesson on theology. If the Shadow Mage is here, there is no time to lose. Come with me."

She turned on her heel, leading the way to the far recesses of the temple. Meridan put her hand on Little Bird's arm to draw her back as the girl made to follow. Little Bird shrugged out of her grip in one sinuous movement.

"What? Let me go," she said, face twisting into a glare.

"You will stay here. It's not safe. We know nothing about this Shadow Mage, or what it wants."

"I can help." The young girl's tone was determined. "The Queen needs me, Meridan."

Meridan sighed. Little Bird scampered ahead. Her older sister followed, her face a grim mask, lowered to the burnished wood floor.
Dominic brought up the rear, his thoughts a whirlwind of memories
and apprehension. Every hurt in his abused body seemed to beat in
time with his crazed heartbeat. How could he even attempt to rescue
the Grayling from the power of the Shadow Mage? Just the thought of
his uncle's ability sent spikes of anxiety through his blood. But the idea
of the Grayling's wild innocence crushed and in thrall to the Shadow
Mage, the danger to the Queen...No. He could not bear it. His chin
rose, his thoughts snapping back to connect with the real world. He
nearly bumped into Meridan's back as she stopped with the others at
the entrance to the temple catacombs.

"He who holds the Grayling holds the crown. These are also the
words of a Seer." The priestess' voice quivered. "And the young man
is correct. Queen Petronella once flew in the Grayling's mind. A small
part of her soul essence remains within the bird. The Shadow Mage
would delight in connecting with that. 'Tis an entry point to the
heart of a good queen, and from there, a mere heartbeat to the soul
of the kingdom." She looked around at them, one hand lingering
on a curtain of green brocade embroidered with sheaths of wheat.
They clustered around her, Meridan still eyeing Little Bird with deep
trepidation.

Nut brown gaze as shrewd and piercing as that of a squirrel investi-
gating a clutch of acorns, the old woman took a moment to look deep
into their eyes. "If you wish to prevent the return of the Shadow Mage
and save the soul of your queen, act with haste, and good intent," she
said. "All else plays into his hands."

She opened the curtain with theatrical grace. A multi-layered archway, jubilantly festooned with a repeating motif of flowers and foliage,
led the way to a cool, dry darkness.

Dominic gained the lead, taking a torch from a golden bracket
hanging at the head of the steep staircase. Its solid glare illuminated

the panelled walls. The comforting, autumnal scent of decaying leaves drifted upwards from below.

"The blessings of the Empress upon you," the priestess said as they passed her and descended, their fingers trailing the shapes of branches. "Look after each other. Your biggest trial is yet to come. I will watch and guard." Pausing at the foot of the stairs, Dominic turned at the sound of her fingers snapping. The dull glow of his torch lit the stairwell. His eyes widened at the transformation of the brocade curtain into a thick panel of painted wood.

"Which way?" Will said as Dominic thrust the torch forward to reveal a broad, well-trodden passageway, with several narrower entrances, almost burrow-like, leading off it. Each rounded arch contained a bronze plaque inset within it, etched with the names of prominent Argentian families.

"Go straight ahead," Aldric said. "These other entrances lead to family shrines, especially the ones closest to the temple."

They trooped forward, huddled under the glow of the torch, heartened by its light. Little Bird shivered in the cool breeze that shuddered through the adjoining passageways. "There's not ghosts down here, are there?" she asked, crowding closer to Will.

Aldric snickered. "Don't believe in ghosts," he said. "Back to earth, that's what we believe." He jerked a thumb over his shoulder. "That's our family shrine. The Haligon's," he said, as they passed it. "Come from a long line of farmers, I do. The first one ever who wanted to be a falconer. Just goes to show what a touch of Eperan blood can do."

The passageway twisted, the panelled walls giving way to packed earth veined with the skeletons of ancient roots, and then to solid stone.

"Still straight ahead?" Dominic asked as they came to a crossroads. Standing in a huddled group as they paused, he heard running water. A column of stone rose, damp and solid, on their left. "That's the central well," Dominic said.

"Neutral territory," Meridan's voice was hushed in the gloom. "Which way, Aldric? Do you know?"

"Aye," the lad's tone held a note of certainty. "One thing I got from my ma. A good sense of direction underground. Still straight, then left."

They pressed onwards. The air grew colder, the stone walls damp with moss. Dominic's head twisted on his shoulders, more aware than ever of the sensation of being watched. The skin on the back of his neck prickled. His shoulders twitched in sympathy. Alert for activity in front of him, he stopped short, holding his hand out to halt the others. His ears had caught something. Not running water this time, but what sounded like a low chant, a droning note, lilting but atonal, full of minor keys and unfinished phrases. The song made him sweat.

"Do you hear that?" he asked in a whisper. In answer, Little Bird's hand crept into his, her palm damp with nerves. "There's something here," she whispered. "Watching us. Can you feel it?"

He squeezed her fingers. "Aye. Can you see anything with your gift?"

He felt her shake her head, but her grip tightened and remained.

"I'm letting the light go out," he said, his voice as low as he could make it. "Watch out."

He heard Will gulp as he pressed the torch against the rock wall, rolling it across the damp stone until all that remained was a trickle of smoke and darkness. The wrongness of the distant song seemed strangely louder in the absence of light, pressing uncomfortably against his ears. He shuddered, trying to shake off its insidious melody.

"What is that?" Little Bird muttered fretfully. "It's horrible inside my head."

A shiver brushed the length of Dominic's spine. Taking a step forward felt like moving through mud. He huffed a sigh, his breath frosting in the air. "It's my uncle," he whispered in reply. "I think he's calling the Shadow Mage."

He forced himself onwards, battling against the invisible force that pressed against his injured legs, and fought to compress his lungs. He'd leaned off a cliff at Raven's Gulch, high above the Castle of Air once, just after his parents died. Closed his eyes and begged the ground to take him. The wind had howled back, denying him, and he'd screamed his fury at it. His loneliness, his deepest despair. Tears pricked his eyes, and he blinked. Why was he remembering this?

"I miss my mother," Little Bird's voice ached with want.

"So do I," Aldric said, on a sob.

"It's the Shadow Mage playing with us," Dominic hissed fiercely. He pressed his hands against his ears. "He sees everything. All our hurts, all most secret thoughts. Try not to listen to the song."

Bit by bit, the small group edged forward, heads down, spirits crushed. Will swore, a low-voiced babble of anger as he argued with someone only he could see. Meridan's silence was dreadful by comparison. Dominic edged a glance at her, but couldn't make out her features. Her breathing came swiftly in the dark. Panting like an animal in pain. He screwed his fingers into his palms. Little Bird sobbed, her clutching fingers clammy as she reached for his. Why, by the Gods? Why had he brought them here? Subjected them to this torment?

They stopped at the far edge of a circle of dark light, and his heart leaped in his constricted chest. Terrence stood in front of them, his arms raised to shoulder height. An upturned block of black granite served as a makeshift altar. The horrific, atonal chanting sounded from his throat without cease, his head was thrown back, locked in a trance. And the Grayling. Dominic's terrified gaze locked on the bird's cage, lifted above the altar and circling slowly. Within it, the bird bated, wings outstretched, battering his delicate feathers against the solid bars of the cage, pecking at them. Clawing at them. His shrill distress call pierced Dominic's heart like the ice-cold blade of a knife. His eyes flooded with tears he couldn't prevent.

"Dominic, he's taking him. He's changing him. Hurting him. Do something, Dominic!" Little Bird's high pitched screech echoed savagely around the tunnels. She shoved at him, her fingers like talons.

But he was already running, forcing himself forward against his uncle's divided attention.

Crossing the circle of dark light was a descent into madness. Ghoulish shapes loomed over him as he pressed onward. Skeletal fingers clawed at his attention. Every doubt, every loss battled for control of his mind. His breath froze in front of him. Clamping his gaze on the precious falcon, willing himself onward, he fought back. Each step weighed as heavy as a block of stone bound by lead. Jeering laughter, the thud of a fist against his battered body, the sneers of the nobility, all accompanied his halting progress. Biting his lip till it bled, muscles aching, jaw locked in a lifelong battle with his deepest fears, he struggled against it all. Somehow, his knife was in his hand. He had no recollection of how it had got there.

Lips bared, he only had two words as he plunged through his own world of darkness and raised his blade. His arm juddered with the effort. It felt heavy. Too heavy.

"No!" he gasped. "Stop!"

Terrence's face in the dim light was terrible as he lowered his obsidian gaze and flung out an arm. Unable to move, Dominic skidded to a halt, screaming for breath as his uncle closed his fist to suck air from his lungs. He collapsed to his knees on the dirt floor, battered legs protesting. Eyes streaming, he looked up at Terrence. Wrapped completely in the grip of the Shadow Mage, he appeared even taller and thinner than Dominic remembered. Eyes cavernous. Long fingers clawed and scabrous. The mottled scar around his neck looked fresh. As if the chains that had once bound it existed once more. Above his head, the Grayling hung in the air above his perch, his shrill chatter piercing. His fierce gold eyes wild with pain and fear. His magnificent wings a blur of panic.

"She's here! The woman!" Little Bird's shriek of terror echoed around the damp walls. "She's coming, Dominic. She'll take the Grayling's soul!"

Terrence lifted his left arm, extending it to the distant roof, where a faint scraping and the tremble of something heavy being dragged across the ceiling shook dust from on high. It floated in the pulsing light of Terrence's conjured circle. His uncle took no notice. His hand trembled. He appeared to be dragging more power from the very sky itself, and still his insistent chant wound on, blistering the ears, seizing Dominic's brain. Image after image of his previous life flickered through his mind, each a picture of dark despair. Struggling against them, he forced himself to his feet, straining every muscle to disobey Terrence's frightful control.

And then, he saw someone. A flicker at the corner of his vision. A flash of long, dark hair, a tall, slender form, cloaked in white. For an instant, he thought of Petronella, and his heart leaped at the thought she might be here, ready to step in. But the woman moved closer, and he saw it was not his beloved Queen. Avarice and malice lit this woman's gaze. No ancient, majestic diamond ring shone on her finger. Terrence took no notice of her. His whole attention was locked on the Grayling. A vortex of pulsing, ebony power was growing, its roots deep in the stone, buried in the heart of Epera. Dominic's eyes drifted to the ceiling, where an opening had appeared. His astonished gaze rode the vortex upward, to the endless night sky circling far above, framed by the broken temple roof. Still chanting, his uncle moved the cage with the Grayling, desperate to escape, bloodying his beak as he tried to bite his way through. Whimpering, Dominic fought just as hard to get free. If the Grayling was taken by this disgusting well of dark energy, it would be over. He knew it to the depths of his soul.

"I'm sorry, I'm sorry." He whispered it, his heart breaking. The Grayling was out of his reach. Going...going...

"No." Felicia's quiet voice dragged his attention away. His eyes jerked from the pulsing malevolence of the Shadow vortex and rounded with new terror as the girl sprinted grimly across the space, braids flying. For one, dizzying moment, their eyes locked. His heart jumped with startled pleasure at the sight of her swollen lips, free of the disfiguring stitches. Terrence whirled. His control dropped, just for a second, but it was all Dominic needed. He hurled his dagger. It hit his target with unerring accuracy, but Felicia was faster. Eyes narrowed, determination in every line of her, she gathered her skirts and leapt straight as an arrow into the swirling whirlwind of black energy.

CHAPTER THIRTY-FOUR

Felicia's scream as she entered the towering spiral of dark energy scraped the air and torched his nerves. With the hilt of Dominic's knife buried deep in his shoulder, Terrence staggered aside. His famed control slipped, and the Grayling's cage crashed abruptly to the altar. The falcon toppled with it and Dominic's heart lurched with dread at the sight of his motionless body at the bottom of the cage. The sudden silence after the incessant chant and the Grayling's crazed screeching was dizzying. Swaying where he stood, Dominic caught the merest flash of the expression on the ghostly woman's face. Speculative. Thoughtful. He squinted to see her clearly. It was impossible to determine whether she was really in the temple at all. The vortex swirled with maddened energy. Felicia's robes were a blur of grey as she rotated within it. He glimpsed her face, white and startled, and then the dark force dissipated like a spent tornado, sucked both underground and upwards into the stars. It left nothing behind but the clear night sky and clouds driven forward on an ever-rising gale. His heart pounded, and he gave his uncle a wide berth as he sidled across the space between them. Watching the man out of the corner of his eye, he grabbed the Grayling's cage and searched the surroundings, fully expecting to see the young girl broken and crumpled on the dusty floor.

Fear took hold of him, twining deep in his gut. There was nothing there.

Uncle and nephew stared at each other across the block of granite. Dominic's face hardened. Terrence's face as he recovered his senses was a study of age-old regret. The terrible blackness in his eyes vanished, his shoulders slumped, his face creased and white with fatigue. The dagger protruded nastily from his shoulder, a patch of blood staining his robe. He did not remove it. Spent, Dominic realised, suddenly. All that power. Gone. For good? For now? Struggling with shock, his mind worked absently on the problem. He blinked, clenching his fists, trying to gather his shattered wits. The damaged handle of the Grayling's cage dug deep and sharp into his palm.

"Where is Felicia?" His voice rang in the cavernous space under the Temple of the Mage, his demand bouncing off the stone walls and pillars. "What have you done to her?"

Terrence closed his eyes, one hand massaging the heavy frown lines crisscrossing his forehead. He shrugged, a gesture so steeped in help-lessness that Dominic's heart almost softened.

The action seemed to remind Terrence of his injury. He surveyed the dagger, and then looked at Dominic again, eyes sparking with a sudden new respect.

"You could have killed me," he said.

Almost unable to speak, such was the rage boiling inside him, Dominic inclined his head in a curt nod. "Where's Felicia?" he asked again.

His uncle didn't answer. Moving stiffly, he grasped the dagger and jerked it from his shoulder. Dominic winced at the sucking noise it made, and Terrence gasped at the sudden pain, clamping his free hand on the wound. He tossed the knife to the altar. The bloodied edge lay on the black stone, pointing at Dominic like an accusing finger. Almost in a daze, he picked it up.

Just in time.

"Dominic!" Little Bird's terrified scream ended in the beat of fast-approaching feet.

His gaze snapped to the stone stairway leading upwards to the temple. Arabella's companions edged downwards, their eyes darting nervous as sparrows at the black altar before narrowing on their targets.

Minus the soldiers left fighting on the street, her force was small but still dangerous. Dominic's heart sank as Guildford took the steep stairs two at a time. His grey eyes gleamed in the faint starlight. Pieter and Carl crowded close behind. One quick, the other massively strong. Rosa brought up the rear, a scowl locked onto her square, freckled face.

His own young companions erupted from their hidden position. Meridan headed the charge. Head up, eyes narrow slits of determination, she raced towards the enemy, Little Bird and Will right behind her.

"Where's my sister? What have you done with her?"

To Dominic's astonishment, Guildford wasn't shouting at him. The lad closed the distance between himself and Terrence, standing in front of the older man like an avenging angel. Ducking to miss a lump of stone aimed at his head, Dominic put down the cage. The recovery from his crouch earned a jab of agony through his injured legs and a hiss of pain through his clenched teeth. He threw a punch that collided with Pieter's narrow chest. The impact sent shock waves up his abused ribs. Pieter lurched back and surveyed him, panting, his yellowed teeth revealed by a sneer of hatred. His own knife appeared in his fist as if by magic. The other grimy hand beckoned.

"Come on then, Master Skinner," he growled. Dominic's eyes darted to the Grayling. The bird still lay motionless at the base of his cage, half hidden in the shadow cast by the altar. Impossible to tell if he was alive or not.

He risked a glance around the battleground. Arabella lingered halfway down the steps, a satisfied smile curving her thin lips as she observed the mayhem. Short sword in his fist, Guildford was still remonstrating with Terrence, questioning him about Felicia's whereabouts. Meridan and Will circled Carl like wary cats, blades out, waiting for their chance. The burly man glared at them from behind a black eye and swollen jaw, courtesy of Kismet's rear hind hoof. He turned slowly, trying to monitor both of them at once, his thick fists bunching and relaxing, waiting for his chance to reach and squeeze.

Dominic's gaze snared on Rosa. Darting from the shadows, she launched herself on Little Bird. The younger girl screeched like a banshee. Curls flying, she rolled under Rosa's heavier form and twisted to one side. Her navy eyes lit her face like lamps. It was almost a signal to let the battle begin.

Pieter danced forward, agile, weight balanced on the balls of his feet. His blade slashed forward. Dominic jumped back, sucking in his stomach, trying to ignore the aches in his abused body that slowed him down.

"Can't you even take me?" Pieter taunted, pulling back for another parry.

Dominic didn't wait for him to finish his sentence. He lunged forward, his blade tangling with Pieter's, and swept his legs out from under him with a well-timed kick. Pieter crashed to the floor. Dominic rammed a foot into his knife hand, forcing it down. His teeth clenched in distaste as he ground his opponent's wrist against the chill stone flags, moving his feet to avoid Pieter's thrashing legs as the lad tried to free himself. He increased the pressure, putting all his weight on the joint.

Pieter yelped, his face contorting. He let go of his blade. Dominic winced as he felt a bone snap under his foot. His breath pounded from his lungs. Nausea rolled somewhere deep in his stomach. He stood back. Pieter rolled on the floor, clutching his arm, his thin, feral face contorted in a whimper. "Bastard, you bastard, I'll teach you," he hissed.

Dominic didn't hear him. Guildford's shout of surprise echoed in the chamber, overriding the pants of effort issuing from Rosa and Little Bird as they fought their way across the floor trading kicks and punches. He looked up in time to see Guildford blasted backwards off his feet. The boy hit his head hard against the wall. Terrence glared at him, and then stalked into the depths of one of the endless tunnels, his robes trailing behind him. Dazed, wiping a trickle of blood from his temple, Guildford stumbled upright, but he let the older man go. Swaying slightly, he glanced at his mother, looking for direction. She raised her eyebrows, her arms crossed in front of her, and nodded at the battered cage. Her grey eyes blazed, their message clear. Dominic didn't need mind talk to read her silent direction.

Intent on guarding the precious bird, he limped to the altar. Little Bird's scream of pain halted him. It shrilled through his ears. He whirled. Rosa had caught her in a heavy arm lock, forcing her arm up her back. Both Will and Meridan jumped at the shout. They left Carl to sprint across the space, Meridan's lips were drawn back in a snarl of pure rage. Will's face was an agony of indecision. Meridan snatched at a fallen plank as she ran and she didn't stop as she reached her sister. Face red with fury, she swung it hard against Rosa's skull. The younger girl crashed to the floor. Will howled, an animal sound, and Dominic grabbed the cage, limping fast across the space to join them.

Meridan's arms closed around her little sister. Little Bird buried her face against her chest, shoulders heaving. At the sound of heavy footfall, Dominic turned to face the horrible sight of Carl, striding towards him like a colossus, grinding his fists into his palm.

He backed up, drawing Carl away from the children, and held his blade out in front of him.

"Ah yes. The chatty one," Carl said. His grin exposed a hole where a tooth used to be. Dominic's mouth tightened into a stubborn line. He held the cage behind his back and moved further away. Out of the corner of his eye, he could see Arabella conferring urgently with her son.

Guildford was unsteady on his feet. Arabella waved a dismissive hand to where Dominic guarded the falcon from the looming approach of the stocky giant and then gestured upwards. With nary a glance back, the two ascended the stairs, Guildford supporting his weight against the wall as he climbed. Dominic's heart sank. Sure of Carl's success, they were abandoning the falcon and heading upwards. He groaned inwardly. The signal fire. Of course. The tallest place in Blade. The unfinished towers of the Temple of the Mage. Easily seen by someone watching at the distant castle. His eyes flicked to Carl, judging the distance between them.

"Not talking today, no?" Carl pressed, stalking him in a slow circle.

Not to be drawn, Dominic paced slowly back towards the altar. Will was leaning over his sister, pressing a piece of his torn shirt against her scalp. Meridan watched Dominic over Little Bird's head, her eyes dark with shadows in the starlit night. Brought up short, Dominic halted, the weight of the granite block hard against his back. Carl loomed over him, heavy fist raised. Dominic didn't wait for the blow to descend. He struck with all his weight behind it. The dagger landed true, but Carl just laughed. Dominic cursed as the blade bounced off the heavy leather garment the heavy man wore under his everyday tunic.

"Too bad, good try." Carl gave him a mock sympathetic smile as he swung. Dominic lurched to one side, and Carl swore as his punch met solid granite. Heart in his mouth, Dominic shuffled away, edging towards the stairs. He had to get to the top of the tower before the Wessendeans lit their blasted fire.

Carl followed him, the light of battle in his eyes. Dominic gained the stairs and had taken two limping treads upwards when Will's shout of warning slashed through the air.

His eyes snapped around in time to see Pieter's looming shadow and the deadly gleam of the knife he held in his left hand rising behind the huddled shapes of the two girls. Will was too late to save Meridan.

Pieter punched his blade into her back as she leaned over her sister. Meridan screamed, her body arching like a bow, eyes wide with shock. Little Bird tumbled from her embrace, her face a mask of horror, her rising shriek of anguish as chilling as the wail of ghosts. Will scrambled to his feet, the plank that had felled his sister held fast in his stubby hands, the light of murder in his eyes. Pieter fell under the onslaught that Will launched. The smaller boy had not reached his full growth, but what he lacked in size, he made up for in pure, concentrated fury. He hounded the taller boy. The plank descended with lightning speed. Once, twice, thrice. Pieter's sharp features distorted under the relentless battering. Flattened and bloodied. The thud of plank on sticky flesh thundered in Dominic's ears. Sickened, he averted his eyes. Carl glanced back at Meridan's slumped figure, and Will's berserker fury, his own small eyes alive with malice.

"See lad, if you fought like that, you'd win," he said.

CHAPTER THIRTY-FIVE

D ominic took advantage of Carl's moment of distraction to move further up the stairs. Removing himself from the pitiful sight of Meridan and Little Bird made no difference. Little Bird's pitiful cries followed him. Meridan's body, shocked and rigid at the moment of death, replayed across his mental vision. The copper tang of spilled blood clogged his nostrils. Heart aching with guilt and misery, Dominic left Will staring at the misshapen lump of flesh that had once been his fellow thief. Sure of his eventual success, Carl followed him. A small smear of saliva edged the corner of his bearded mouth. The man swiped at it as he climbed, his expression alive with menace.

The short stairwell ended in the gloomy, star-filled, windy magnificence of the ruined temple. Despite himself, Dominic's eyes flicked around, noting the dusty white marble statues erected to the Mage. The altar itself had been pressed back into service. Incense twisted wildly from the alabaster bowls, crowding its smooth surface, an offering skyward to the home of the Eperan God. The delicate scent tickled his senses. Newly carved blocks of fresh, pale stone cluttered the floor, ready to be lifted to dizzying heights. Dust swirled in the air. Above him, the twin towers were a mess of scaffolding, ropes, and platforms. A narrow walkway stretched between them, swaying in the gale. Terror struck him anew at the realisation that he did not know which of them contained the signal fire.

Carl kept close in front of him as he retreated, stalking him across the cluttered floor. Dominic kept the Grayling's cage carefully behind his back. He felt it shake just a little in his grip and he breathed an inward prayer of thanks. The falcon had regained his senses. The plunge to the altar had not killed him. Swallowing, his mouth dry, he cast his gaze upwards. Carl grinned.

"Thinking you'll get there in time, aren't ye?" he said, "but which one is it? That's the thing. And, of course, you still have to get past me." He stooped and picked up a length of solid lead piping, smacking it experimentally against the nearest statue. The resulting noise clanged like a dull bell and echoed around the enormous expanse. Heart racing, Dominic edged to the base of the nearest tower, preparing to run. The enormous man moved forward. But his grin dropped from his mouth as Dominic's face lifted in a feral smile.

"Oh, I think I'll get past you," Dominic said. He took a couple more steps towards the low door set in the base of the closest tower as another figure advanced out of the wind wild night. Someone tall, blood-smeared, and dishevelled, ready humour sparking in his eyes despite his clear exhaustion.

"Well met, Dominic Skinner," Thomas Buttledon said, raising a standard-issue blade in salute. His smile was pure fox. "I'll get this, shall I?"

Carl jerked around with a grunt of surprise, and Thomas closed, his blade a threatening wall of impending doom. Dominic took to his heels, shoving his blade into his belt, and scurried onward with all the strength left in his battered body.

"Did you see the prince?" he yelled as he went.

"Already on the road," Thomas said, over the ring of battle. "There was fighting. I believe the prince is winning."

"But will he get back in time?"

Thomas grunted. There was a crash as something heavy smashed to the floor.

"That, I do not know. Be swift lad, stay true."

The clang of steel on lead followed him as he ascended, one hand pressed against the clammy wall, the other holding the Grayling's cage. His neck cricked as he looked upward, trying to make out where he was in the confined, corkscrewing space. The ancient stone stairs were steep and treacherous, worn smooth with the constant tread of many feet. Already injured, Dominic's legs burned with the strain of climbing. Heart pounding, chest heaving, he clawed his way upwards. A patch of grey in the dark and a gust of wind from his right denoted the opening to the narrow walkway stretching across the space between the two towers. He paused there, staring across it, hardly daring to look down. The scaffolding looked flimsy. A bird's nest of twigs and rope against the massive sturdiness of the opposite tower. Crawling with ladders, the broken dome of the temple roof stretched beneath it. Glancing up, he couldn't see the top of the opposite tower. He still couldn't tell which contained the signal fire. Clenching his free fist, he pounded his frustration into the ancient stone and turned his gaze back to the dark stairwell. He had to check. It was the only way. Gathering more breath, mouth stretched in a grim line, he resumed his climb. The Grayling's quiet chatter as he found his voice sent a flood of relief through him. His eyes squeezed shut, sending out a prayer of gratitude to the Mage that the bird was well enough to speak. Dashing tears from his eyes, he gasped air into his lungs and carried on. The climb seemed endless. Each turn of the corkscrew led to another, and then another. Exhausted, all he could do was to continue in the dark, feeling his way forward, and pray he did not slip.

Reaching the top of the tower, he gasped with relief at the chance to stop. The workmen were yet to attend here. Wind sliced through gaps in the waist-high masonry, carrying with it the scent of moss and decay. The ferocity of the gale tore his hood from his head, and he grabbed the stone arch leading to the roof. He peered out, heart sinking. Empty. No fire, no Wessendeans. Terrified by the height, his gaze skidded across the sight of Blade's streets, dotted with lanterns winding far below. He caught a spare glimpse of the mighty Cryfell, a silver-grey ribbon reaching back to the black, jagged mountains. The castle hunched across the northern pass like a dragon guarding its lair. In the east, the sun had yet to start a new day. Stars wheeled above him. He scrubbed a dirty hand across his dry mouth and leaned cautiously against the archway to squint across the gap to the further tower. He groaned. People over there, their movements visible over the newly laid parapet. And was that a puff of smoke, snatched by the gale?

Cursing, he whirled, moving as fast as he dared, feet sliding on the damp stone, sweat bursting from every pore. The Grayling chirruped an alarm as his cage knocked against the wall.

"Sorry, sorry," Dominic gasped. He ground to a halt at the narrow walkway and looked across, his heart in his mouth. It swayed with the wind, a flimsy construction of planks and ropes stretching across the chasm to the opening on the far side. His mouth dried. A nightmare vision of his brother's shocked face flashed across his brain. The sickening thud of bone on stone. He glanced longingly down the stairs. He could go down. Get Thomas.

But there was no time.

Hands trembling, he lowered the Grayling's cage. The bird chirruped at him, his golden eyes alert as Dominic squatted next to him. He slid his hand into his satchel and pulled out a hunk of dry cheese.

"Here," Dominic whispered. "I don't know if you can fly." He opened the cage, his fingers fumbling with the catch. The Grayling regarded him with his head on one side. Dominic could make out blood on his sharp beak, some of his flight feathers bent. He held out his hand, and the falcon stepped onto his wrist, his talons sharp on Dominic's unprotected skin. He stretched to take the cheese Dominic offered him.

"At least you can eat."

He watched for a moment more as the Grayling devoured the meal, and then lowered him to the ground. The heavy wind swirled around them, and the falcon raised his head, scenting the air. He stretched his wings and then bent his head to them, trying to reorder his damaged feathers. Watching his efforts, Dominic's mouth twisted. "By the Gods, I hope you can fly," he muttered.

All his muscles protesting, he stood and ordered his fingers to loosen their claw-like grip on the gritty stone. The distance from his perch to the hard ground made his head spin. The Grayling stopped grooming and raised his head, watching him.

"I have to leave you," Dominic said, his heart wrenching in his chest. "If I fall, I'll be damned if you go with me. And I won't risk Arabella getting hold of you. You're on your own. Free." The Grayling chattered at him, his eyes focusing northwards to the mountains and the distant castle.

"Yes. There. Go there. You'll be safe. May the Gods go with you."

Scraping his hair back from his face, he reached for the support of the rope. He locked his gaze on the opposite wall. Not daring to look down, hardly daring to breathe, he put one shaking foot on the first plank.

It shuddered beneath him, and he snatched his foot back, soles tingling with panic, hands sweaty, heart racing. Gavin's face loomed in front of his vision again. Receding. Falling. Dying.

"By the Gods," he muttered. "I wish I were a bird."

The Grayling cackled from his perch by the cheese. Dominic could feel the wild yellow eyes boring into his back.

"Alright." He dragged his hands back and wiped them once more down his breeches. The wind slapped at his cheeks, stiffer than the sting of Felicia's wet kerchief. Her solemn grey eyes lingered at the centre of his brain, along with her voice, soft as wings. "If you run, the falcon will die."

Facing forward, clenching his teeth, he took a huge breath and locked his gaze once more on the distant opening. Every instinct in his body screaming at him, he stepped out.

"

Chapter Thirty-Six

The wind was a fist. Dominic shuffled into the void with the slow, shrinking steps of a man forty years his senior. Vertigo attacked him. His head swam. Only feet away from the building, the wind snatched at his cloak, filling its folds with air like the sails on a ship. The chill blasted through the stiff fustian of his tunic to raise goosebumps across his frozen skin. His hands slid on the rope, releasing minutely with every limping footstep to clutch once more for support. Wider in his terror than actuality, the gaps between the planks gaped beneath his feet like open mouths. The drop loomed beneath him. At the mercy of the gale, the entire structure tilted, dancing to the mournful tune of the wind as it whistled through the taut rope. Every cautious step felt like a lifetime. More than halfway across, panting for breath, he slipped. Bowels twisting, he gasped, bracing his feet at the juncture of plank and rope. Beneath him, the wood writhed like a dying snake as the storm strengthened. Hair whipped across his face, half blinding him. He dared not lift a hand to push it back. Another step, another slip. He fell to one knee on the damp wood as the platform lurched. His free leg waved madly in midair, his body sliding across the slippery surface. He scrambled an arm around the nearest support, whimpering with panic, and clung like an insect, cheek pressed hard against the planks. Infinitely aware of death. A mocking laugh drifted to his ears, almost unheard over the frantic pulse of blood at his temples.

Raising his chin, he squinted across the remaining space, eyes streaming. Arabella waited for him on the far side, her oval face a mere blur, her fine flaxen hair loose and rippling like pale satin ribbon. She leaned out towards him, reaching a hand forward, apparently not at all worried by the daunting drop below.

"Scared, are we?" she called. "What are you worried about? I'm here to catch you!" Her maddened laugh added another layer of chill to his already frayed nerves. His neck juddered as he raised his chin higher, casting his eyes to the top of the tower. A slim plume of smoke rose, snatched away immediately, and hard to see in the dark night, but no flame yet. He grabbed at the ropes with renewed purpose, dragging himself forward, not daring to stand. Instead, he inched forward like a centipede, face screwed into a mask of determination, using the ropes to pull himself along, his shoulder muscles protesting every movement.

"Come to me, little worm, I'm waiting," Arabella mocked from her position. He did his best to tune her out. Focused instead on nothing but the whine of the wind and the smell of the damp wood under his chin. The rhythmic catch of the planks against his belt, the press of his dagger against his bruised stomach.

A mere six feet away from her, he wobbled to his feet. One hand held fast to the rope, the other locked on his dagger. Arabella's slim form blocked his way to safety. Her grey robe made a stylish contrast with the dark charcoal of the soot-stained tower, the silken skirt flapping like a triumphal flag.

Her mad eyes screwed tight as they focused on his hands. "The bird," she hissed. "Where is the bird?"

Dominic didn't blink. "Dead," he said, with grim finality.

"Oh, really?" She looked at him, one eyebrow raised in disbelief, and stretched an arm out to one side, out of his line of vision. She yanked it back, and Dominic almost lost his grip on the rope.

"Aldric!"

A grimace of apology twisted Aldric's face as she wrenched him forward, but not an ounce of fear. Instead, trusting and confident, his dark eyes searched the pre-dawn sky. Arabella wound her arm around his scrawny neck, dragged him close to the edge, and removed a long needle from her bodice. Dominic shuddered as she pressed it almost lovingly against Aldric's thin cheek. Grim-faced, Aldric's dark eyes bored into his and then lifted again to the sky behind him. Pursing his lips. He mimed something, an action that was not immediately apparent. Dominic frowned.

"Care to think again?" Arabella asked, tightening her grip as Aldric wriggled in her grasp. "We found this skulking around up here. I think it belongs to you." Setting her jaw, she drove the needle deep into the boy's skin. Aldric hissed the pain out through his clenched teeth and pursed his lips again, a horrible sight with the bitter metal protruding from his cheek. Arabella twisted the needle once more and withdrew it. Blood welled from the puncture wound and trickled down the boy's face. Undeterred, he lifted his eyes and mimed again. And this time, Dominic understood. His heart raced. He whistled. A piercing cry that flew on the wind with wild hope. He did it again, and once more, for good luck.

Arabella's face twisted with rage. "Stop that and answer me. I'll take his eyes next time. Where is the falcon?" she demanded. "Tell me, or I'll let go of him."

"Why, Arabella, he's right here," Dominic said as the Grayling flashed overhead. Swaying with the bridge, he let go of the rope. Gritting his teeth, hatred flooding him, he swept his arm towards Arabella's face.

Following the command, talons outstretched, the falcon struck and arched away, his furious cry lost in the wind. Arabella shrieked, flinging herself backwards. She let go of Aldric, and Dominic barrelled forward, only just in time to block his fall.

Aldric stumbled to the hard tower stairs. Almost tripping on him, Dominic's momentum carried him on to the far wall. Hand still outstretched, his shove smacked Arabella hard against the opposite wall. Her head hit the unforgiving stone with a sickening thud. She slumped to the stairs, her gown a graceful river of silk flowing over the worn steps. Mouth slashed open by the Grayling's brutal strike, ruby blood flooded her face and stained her bared teeth.

Breath harsh, ribs aching, Dominic held out a hand to Aldric. The boy scrambled to his feet, one hand hard against his cheek.

"Are you alright?" Dominic asked, already starting the climb to the roof.

"Aye," Aldric said. "You'd better hurry. I was trying to make the wood wetter, but they caught me. Went up the wrong God's damned tower."

Open-mouthed, Dominic stared at him. "You've a quick wit, Aldric Haligon," he said.

Aldric shrugged. "Can't fight," he said. "Raced back the way we came and went in the front. Where're the others?"

Dominic shook his head. "Not good. Go below. Do what you can. I've got to see to the rest."

He left Aldric and scurried up the tower. His legs ached at every step, his sore ankle threatening to give way. Fresh blood from the arrow wound seeped from Meridan's earlier bandaging. His heart clenched at the thought of her, and he fingered his dagger, determined not to lose it this time. Guildford. Only Guildford stood between disaster and triumph. Rounding bend after bend, the familiar smell of smouldering wood drifted to him from above. He forced himself onwards, heart pounding like a piston.

Nearing the top, he paused and listened as the howling wind tugged at his hair. Guildford was swearing. Heartened by the sound, his lips curved in a grim smile. The earlier rain had helped him, and perhaps

Aldric had been somewhat successful. And what did nobles really know about lighting fires, anyway? That was a servant's work.

Hugging the shadows, he crept forward and took his bearings. The stone masons had been busy up here over the last few days. Freshly laid blocks lined the top of the old parapet, mortar yet to dry, although the wind would do a fine job of that. Several buckets lay stacked against one wall. A coarse sack of lime, a pile of sand. Guildford hissed his satisfaction as he hunched at the base of the massive mound of branches rising high over his shoulders. A patch of dried blood matted the back of his head. Dominic's lips thinned as the boy risked a small step away, allowing a breath of the undying gale to touch more life to the budding blaze. The dryer twigs at its heart crackled to life. Dominic glanced at the faraway castle, where he thought he could see a distant light waving from the battlements.

Waiting. They're still waiting for a signal, he thought, looking to the eastern range, where the first glimmer of pre-dawn edged delicate fingers over the jagged peaks. Had Joran made it back to the castle? Judging by the words of Thomas Buttledon, perhaps not. Weak from childbirth, without her powers, Petronella was still vulnerable to attack from whatever traitorous forces lurked there.

"Guildford," he yelled over the whine of the wind.

The young noble's head turned, his features flattening into a snarl. He reached for his sword. "You, again. Do you never give up?" he demanded. "Where's my mother?"

"Did you leave her there to guard you?" Dominic asked, limping forward. He swiped his dagger through the air. A negating action. "Didn't work. I hope she's still alive. She hit her head hard."

His eyes raised to clash with Guildford's. The boy darted his eyes to the bonfire, where a growing heat crept forward from its heart. The crackle and pop of blistering wood sounded ominous. Flames licked upward. Dominic inched forward. Guildford crouched, guarding the fire with his broad body, and Dominic wasted no more time.

He lunged. Guildford leapt, but he was much slower than usual, and Dominic had more space on the roof. He twisted to one side, skipping painfully away, narrowly avoiding the slash of his opponent's blade. Guildford followed him, his sword weaving a deadly path. The fire glowed red behind his back, outlining him with a ruby halo, growing in strength.

Dominic feinted and ran for the blaze, kicking out at it, trying to scatter the branches. Hampered by his injury, he made little impact. Guildford snatched at his flying cloak and wrenched him away. Dominic twisted painfully on his ankle as Guildford turned him and gave him a shove, followed up by a hard kick. He stumbled across the rain-slicked flags. Only slightly protected by the thick wool of his bunched hood, Dominic's head cracked painfully on the parapet wall. His dagger skidded across the roof. Much more unsteady on his feet than usual, Guildford staggered. Seeing stars, Dominic blinked, wondering if he'd imagined this unaccustomed weakness. With dawning horror, he realised some stars were genuine sparks. Aided by the wind, the fire was growing. It was a matter of minutes before the castle rebels saw the flames. Panic shot through him. Guildford smiled, his lips taunting. He approached, drawing back a hefty foot to kick. Eyes closed, Dominic ducked, pressing himself to the cold stone, and braced for impact.

It never came.

His head shot up at Guildford's shout of surprise and the terrifying grate of stone on stone. Dazed by his earlier injury, the lad had missed his kick by only an inch, but the mortar of the new wall was fresh. Yet to set. Guildford's momentum sent him staggering to the edge, and Dominic's heart leapt in his chest as the boy clawed desperately for purchase before the wind pushed him over.

Dominic lunged for the flailing hand automatically, sliding with it to the very edge of the precipitous drop. Guildford's weight dragged at his arm, his legs beating, scrabbling to gain a hold on the moss-clad wall. Dominic braced himself as best he could against the older stone, praying it wouldn't give way beneath their combined bodies. His eyes locked on Guildford's. The crystal gaze, so like Felicia's, was wide with panic. Supplication.

"Please," the boy muttered, "please…"

Heart pounding, Dominic heaved, but his strength was no match for the inexorable drag of gravity. Guildford's fingers slipped in his grasp. Desperately, he tightened his grip, every muscle burning, praying as he never had before, Gavin's beloved face fixed in his mental vision.

"Not again. Please let me help him!" He shrieked it into the teeth of the wind, holding on with every ounce of strength as Guilford's own weight tugged him down. The black drop yawned beneath the boy. The growing flames shed strange, incongruous warmth into Dominic's screaming muscles. Guildford's gaze was less hopeful, more terrified by the second. His sweating fingers slipped.

At the last possible second, he felt it. The warmth of telekinesis prickling through his palms, the clamour of telepathy buzzing at the back of his head. "By the Gods, thank you, thank you," he whispered, focusing his attention on the weight of the boy beneath him. Lifting, lifting again. Guildford's panicked face loomed close enough he could claw his own way to safety. The young noble's hand flew out, knuckles bloody, to latch onto the edge of the balustrade. Leaving him to it, panting with reaction, Dominic rolled over and stretched an arm toward the fire. He pushed the pyre towards the pile of sand in the corner. Rolled it over, buried it with sand like a bird in a dust bath. Dying sparks flew. He tasted their bitter ash on his tongue.

Overhead, his ears caught the soft chatter of the Grayling's hunting cry. The bird swooped around the tower, wings spread, playing with the wind. Wild, majestic. Dominic's gaze followed him upwards, into the rising sun as it blessed the sky with a new day.

Watching the falcon, allowing his guard to relax, he nearly missed the swift shuffle of approaching footsteps from the stairwell. He jerked around, hands up, in time to see Arabella speeding towards him. Her face was a mask of blood, her lips brutally torn, her hair matted. Dominic bit down on his newly found power and scrambled for his dagger, remembering too late he didn't have it. Guildford raised his head from his hands, his eyes bleary. An acrid pool of vomit stained the floor in front of him.

"Mother," he croaked.

Every feature contorted, she flashed him a bare glance and continued onwards, screaming. "My face! What has that bird done to my face?" Dominic dodged her, circling warily. Thin steel glinted at her fingertips. Her needles. "I'll kill you. I swear I will kill you!"

Howling like a soul in torment, hatred pouring from her, she rushed him. Dominic caught her arms as she raised them to strike, shocked at her maddened power. The air around her seemed almost black to his newly returned blessed senses. He fought her away, twisting his face from the lethal points, swearing as one narrowly missed his eye. Guildford's pleading was a distant, useless reproach. The lad could do nothing to prevent the attack.

The screech of the Grayling's approach warned him to step away. He dropped. The bird fell from the sky with the speed of a shooting star, his talons tangling in her hair. Arabella shrieked, batting him away. The Grayling dropped her matted locks and soared away, only to return time and again, twisting to avoid her clawing hands. Wheeling and circling. Ferocious and deadly. Arabella stumbled under the onslaught, driven back and back to the gaping, deadly edge.

The Grayling swooped in for one more pass. Arabella ducked and fell. Her shocked, dying scream echoed around the tower, and this time, Dominic made no move to save her. He stood, chest heaving, fists closed, his power held in tight control. He held out his arm. The Grayling circled and swooped to rest on his wrist. Dominic welcomed his slight weight and endured the pointed clutch of his talons. He looked at Guildford, only just gathering himself to stand. White under his freckles, the younger boy's face was a mask of shock. His lips trembled. "You could have...why didn't you....?" the question died on his lips.

Dominic drew himself up, one hand smoothing the Grayling's soft feathers, and stared hard at the northern horizon. Far in the distance, the mountains painted jagged angles on the sombre, paling sky, Grey. Like her eyes.

"That was for Felicia," he said.

EPILOGUE
Epera, Castle of Air 1607

Epera, Castle of Air 1607

T he sleeping castle slumbered in the light of pre-dawn. High on its battlements, handpicked from the ranks of the devout, a set of stern-faced soldiers patrolled the ramparts. They exchanged greetings as they passed each other, rubbing fingers grown chill in the night air.

High in his tower chamber, caught in the depths of a familiar nightmare, eighteen-year-old Dominic moaned in his sleep. The few objects he treasured rotated around him, drifting like leaves on a breeze. A new feathered cap. His enchanted blade, as yet unused. His old dagger and a new sword, gifted to him by Joran two years ago with an admonition to learn how to use it.

Trapped once more in the dim crypt under the temple, the swirling black energy of the Shadow Mage rotated in front of his dreaming eyes. Unable to move, he could only watch as it claimed Felicia and then Terrence, Meridan, and Little Bird. Will, Thomas, even Rosa. Petronella and Joran. Their children. Everyone he knew. All those he trusted. All those already dead, fighting for the Mage.

Deep within its malicious force, he felt the woman's eyes watching him. Waiting. She laughed, the sound cold and hard in his ears, and somewhere, hushed as the wing of a falcon, he heard Felicia.

"Dominic, where are you? Dominic, I need you. Please come, please..." Strangely, in the manner of dreams, her distant, fading voice seemed trapped behind the low wooden door to the Restricted section.

The cockerel blasted him awake from its usual station far below his window. Bleary with sleep, he propped himself up, dazed with the memory of her grey eyes, cursing the fact that he could never hear her familiar, withering voice when he was awake. She was gone. Lost. Somewhere. His mind refused to accept the possibility of her death.

Naked, he levered his body from the bed and took the couple of long strides across the room to his washstand. Constant training had bred hard muscle, quickened his reflexes, and concentrated his mind. He shrugged into a clean set of clothes and left the room in search of breakfast, snatching his weapons from the air and fastening them at his waist as he went.

"I will find you, Felicia," he muttered under his breath as he clattered down the winding stairs, taking them two at a time. "By the Gods, I swear I will."

The End

Afterword

I hope you enjoyed 'Page of Swords!'

If you did, please do Dominic a mighty big favour and leave a review so other people can discover him and share his adventures too!

Here are some country specific links to Page of Swords on Amazon – Choose the one that you normally use to shop in. You must be logged in to your account and have spent the equivalent of $50 us dollars in your Amazon store before you can leave a review!

US customers: https://www.amazon.com/review/create-review?&B0C9XDX76G

UK customers: https://www.amazon.co.uk/review/create-review?&B0C9XDX76G

Australia customers: https://www.amazon.au/review/create-review?&B0C9XDX76G

ALSO BY CHRISTINE CAZALY

Check out my other books available in ebook and paperback:

Seer of Epera

Queen of Swords

Knight of Swords (work in progress)

King of Swords (work in progress)

US and UK readers....

Did you know you can order paperback copies direct from my website at:

https://christinecazaly.com/shop

ABOUT THE AUTHOR

Growing up in England, Christine Cazaly spent her youth devouring as many books as she could get her hands on. She also harbours a fondness for tarot wisdom, and a good cup of tea.

When not writing fantasy fiction, she spends her time daydreaming, teaching people to ballroom dance, and striding the West Yorkshire woods in her wellies along with the mad poodle collie cross and long-suffering husband.

Long days at the keyboard are mitigated somewhat by regular incursions from three demanding cats, and fighting the urge to eat chocolate until her teeth fall out.

You can connect with her on:

website: https://christinecazaly.com

facebook: https://facebook.com/christinecazalyfantasyauthor

Amazon: https://www.amazon.com/author/christinecazaly

Bookbub: https://www.bookbub.com/profile/christine-cazaly

Goodreads: https://www.goodreads.com/author/show/22759981.Christine_Cazaly

Acknowledgements

As ever, massive thanks to my wonderful editor, Natasha Rajendram and the wonderful team at Scott Editorial. I'm blessed to have you looking after me! As ever, love and thanks to my sister Joy and BFF Aly for your ongoing enthusiasm. To my wonderful husband, Jim, and our menagerie, my undying love – couldn't do it without you! A shout out also to my Advance Reader team. Thanks for your reviews and support. As a new author, it means so much to know you enjoy your adventures in Tales from the Tarot! And last, but not least – everyone who follows my monthly newsletter – thank you for being there. Sometimes the life of an author can get lonely. It's great to have you alongside – get in touch with me. I'll always answer!

CC xx

Printed in Great Britain
by Amazon

34452176R00155